Against The Flow of MISSISSIPPI

By:
Anthony Oksenholt

Table of Contents

Preface	Page 4
About the Author	Page 5
Foreword	Page 7
Prologue	Page 11
Chapter 1: THE CAMPAIGN	Page 16
Chapter 2: THE SETUP	Page 49
Chapter 3: ROY GOES TO REHAB	Page 80
Chapter 4: THE DEAD SENATOR	Page 94
Chapter 5: JUSTICE IN DIXIE	Page 124
Chapter 6: JUDAS REARS HIS UGLY HEAD	Page 145
Chapter 7: PRESIDENTIAL ENDORSEMENT	Page 175
Chapter 8: ROY'S REHAB	Page 190
Chapter 9: JUDAS GETS CAUGHT	Page 201
Chapter 10: CHRISTINE STACY DEBATE	Page 210
Chapter 11: THE PRIMARY ELECTION	Page 226
Chapter 12: JIM BATES THE DEMOCRAT	Page 240
Chapter 13: GOVERNOR AND AGENT FORD	Page 254
Chapter 14: FIRST DEBATE	Page 265
Chapter 15: ASSASINATION PLOT	Page 273
Chapter 16: THE INVESTIGATION	Page 285
Chapter 17: THE SECOND DEBATE	Page 298
Chapter 18: THE SHOOTER	Page 306
Chapter 19: SNATCHED	Page 313

Table of Contents Continued

Chapter 20: CLOSING IN	Page 326
Chapter 21: EXPLOSIVE SITUATION	Page 331
Chapter 22: GOVERNOR'S FOLLY	Page 340
Chapter 23: OCTOBER SURPRISE	Page 344
Chapter 24: AN HONEST SENATOR	Page 354
Chapter 25: THE HEARING	Page 359
Chapter 26: SENATE DEBATE	Page 385
Chapter 27: THE REPORTER	Page 394
Chapter 28: BUSINESS AS USUAL	Page 416
Chapter 29: THE INDICTMENTS	Page 429
Chapter 30: LAST DAYS IN JACKSON	Page 444
Chapter 31: ROY'S REDEMPTION	Page 449
Chapter 32: THE GOVERNOR ON TRIAL	Page 453

Preface:

Against the Flow of Mississippi

Written by Anthony Oksenholt

This book is dedicated to the memory of all who lost their lives during Hurricane Katrina on August 29, 2005.

Hurricane Katrina made direct landfall on the Mississippi Gulf Coast as an intense Category three hurricane. Hurricane Katrina killed over 1200 people spanning from The Bahamas to the Mississippi and Louisiana Gulf Coast and forever changing the face of many the places mentioned in this book.

About the author:

Anthony Oksenholt is a native of Biloxi, Mississippi where he was born, September 4, 1984. His grandfather was a very corrupt public official in the 1960s, 1970s, and 1980s. Anthony despises the corruption and the misdeeds of those in office. He is very politically involved in the Libertarian movement, and he understands the injustice being committed on this country by the media and SuperPACs. Multi-million-dollar war chests given by donors who can't support the candidates with their votes and poor, honest candidates who don't get exposure from the media because either they can't pay for it, or their message isn't popular with the ones in charge.

He authored this book to show how easy the public can beat the corrupt political superpowers if they are informed and thoroughly research the candidates they consider giving their vote.

Copyright 2022
Against the Flow of Mississippi
Øksenholt-Biloxi Publishing LLC

Foreword

I first thought of the idea for this book during the 2018 midterm elections. I saw that candidates who would make excellent representatives and lawmakers serve our great country that were refused good press by either the good ol boy system or the media. If all of the prospective candidates who were running for office were given a chance to fill the office they sought, they might have significantly contributed to the freedom and liberties that we enjoy and take for granted in this country.

I have helped several third-party candidates by attempting to spread their word on social media or my podcast. I think the public is missing an excellent opportunity to move forward and progress by judging solely on party lines or voting for the lesser of two evils. If you vote for the lesser of two evils, evil still wins. I saw this during the 2016 and 2020 elections on both sides of the aisle. The media nearly silenced third-party candidates while the talking heads forced their agenda down our throats.

I feel we as a nation should rise and stand tall, especially with the beautiful invention of the internet at our disposal, to stand by our principles and vote our conscience. I further feel it is the obligation and duty of every voter to thoroughly research every candidate on the ballot to ensure the best candidate is elected. In 2016 and 2020, we have had more than two parties on every ballot in all fifty states for President. A third-party candidate, with those chances, is electable, with ballot access in every state.

I also feel that people get comfortable with the Devil you know. The devil you know does not have your best interest at heart. That is, in fact, why he or she is a devil. Uneducated or undereducated voters have set this example for years in my home state of Mississippi. We have had Senators in the same seat for over forty years. From 1943 until 2018, we had two Senators fill one seat. James Eastland was a Senator from 1943 until

1978 and Thad Cochran from 1978 until 2018. I feel this needs to stop.

Dick Nolan, a columnist for The San Francisco Examiner, is quoted in 1966 as saying, "Seasoned politics watchers can only remind the gloomies that a more or less regular turnover is good for the Republic. In a sound democracy, our rulers ought to be changed routinely, like diapers for the same reason." I agree wholeheartedly.

If politicians fear nothing but election time, we will forever have a problem that we cannot fix. We must hold our elected officials to a much higher standard and remind them that their campaign is a job interview. Re-election is not a popularity contest, yet an actual review of the job they are doing as our employees.

If a candidate promises, it is then our job to ensure that the candidate upholds that promise. An example would be if a mayoral candidate promised to mow the grass in front of city hall every week. It is always a good policy to ensure that said candidate upholds it. If a candidate doesn't follow through, it is our job to fire them with our ballots. We should never be afraid of telling our employees of our opinions regarding the job they are doing for us, good or bad. It is my hope, as the author of this book, that we will remember the power that we hold over our elected employees and that we may remind them that they will do what we want them to do or we will not give them their job back, meaning we will not vote for them in the next election. I believe that this is not only our right but our patriotic duty.

Prologue

Jake Fayard was an honorable man, well versed in the Constitution, entirely in love with the ideas of Liberty, the ones that the Founding Fathers George Washington, Thomas Jefferson, John Adams, Patrick Henry, and Thomas Paine stood for. He felt that community service was the purpose of every politician. He also felt that politicians who were for sale should be in prison for life.

Jake served in the United States Marine Corps as both an enlisted man and an officer. He graduated from the Naval Academy at Annapolis, Maryland. He served as a fighter for justice in the courtroom and on the battlefield. Jake didn't relish the idea of politics until he started paying attention and seeing the public corruption. He was tired of seeing the very fabric that made this country so great torn apart at the seams. During his stint in the Marine Corps, Jake was A-political. He refused to debate or discuss any current events. He was a man that simply did his job.

When the terrorist attacks on September 11, 2001, happened in New York City, Washington, D.C., and Shanksville, Pennsylvania, Jake was assigned as a special counsel on several intelligence commissions regarding the War on Terror in Afghanistan and Iraq. He saw the lies perpetrated on the citizens of the United States. He was ordered under the Classified nature not to report on what he heard or saw. It disturbed him greatly to see a government body manipulating the very people it was supposed to be protecting.

Jake was never a great fan of the Republican Party. He also distrusted the Democratic Party. He had a definite distrust of all politicians and the media. His Masonic Blue Lodge brother and best friend, Coby Barhonovich, convinced him that running for office was a tangible way to serve his country. It took Coby almost a year to convince him to put his name on the ballot.

Coby already had served two years as the Attorney General for the State of Mississippi by the time Jake decided to run for office. Jake was introduced to the leaders of the Mississippi Republican Party by Coby and wasn't impressed with the political machine that had a foothold on the state for decades.

On January 21, 1970, Jake Fayard was born and raised in a modest home in East Biloxi. His father was a small business owner who thrived in Biloxi's fishing heritage. His family had no political ambition, except for an uncle on his father's side, an attorney who ran for Circuit Court Judge and lost by five hundred votes.

The votes in that election came from constituents above and below ground. Many people resurrected themselves from the dead to cast their ballot for one candidate or the other. There were no safeguards in place to stop the departed from voting. This was the norm of the day.

Campaigning in the cemeteries was commonplace. Candidates had to be sure that the dead didn't vote twice so the candidates were careful of which cemeteries they took their prospective names from. Usually, candidates would pull the names of the recently departed from the families of close friends or other relatives. Obituaries of the recently departed were also a major source of information. These dead voters were not purged from the voter rolls and with the faces of so many obtaining a ballot to vote, keeping up with those who voted twice was almost impossible, especially in different precincts.

After the close loss of the election, public office would never again be sought after by a member of the Fayard family until the 21st Century. That is when Jake decided a run for Senate was in order. The race for Senate would be a personally trying and a very great struggle for Jake, who reminded himself to keep his temper in check. The trials would see his son arrested, his life threatened, and his world almost wholly ripped apart.

The trials would prove to be for a noble cause, though. Jake shows that he is a leader and a force to be reckoned with. He keeps his promises and overcomes the adversary with dignity and respect. He sets the example that men and women in office should follow.

Chapter One

The Campaign

The sign read Jake for Senate. Jake Fayard was a native of Biloxi, Mississippi, where he lived until his nineteenth birthday. He enlisted in the United States Marine Corps and was shipped to boot camp in Parris Island, South Carolina. He had served two tours in Iraq before being appointed to the Naval Academy in Annapolis, Maryland. He graduated with honors near the top of his class. He was commissioned a Second Lieutenant and had served another tour in Bosnia and finished his career in Afghanistan.

Jake was wounded in combat during his career as an infantryman. He was hit by shrapnel from a firefight in Kuwait. The details of his injury caused him to win the Navy Cross by saving three fellow Marines from a roadside ambush during the First Gulf War. After he recovered in a hospital in Germany, Jake applied for an appointment to the Naval Academy in Annapolis. Being already combat wounded and having won the Navy Cross for his heroism in combat, Congressman Al Greene of the Fifth District of Mississippi awarded him the request. Jake graduated summa cum laude from the US Naval Academy. In 1996 Jake was promoted to the rank of Second Lieutenant.

Once he was promoted to the rank of Captain, Jake asked his friend and commanding officer, Rear Admiral Thomas Bohn, to remain at Belle Chasse Naval Air Station in New Orleans. The Admiral approved Jake's request, and he began Law School at Tulane.

During his time at Tulane, he was often involved in harsh debates. Debates over the war, gun control, the military allowing gays, you name it. Most of the Law School students were ultra-Liberal. Many of them despised Jake and his best friend Coby Barhonovich for being Marines and being enrolled in class. Jake pulled Coby, the hot-headed of the two, out of many fights and very honestly probably kept Coby from being expelled on more than one occasion.

Jake was a giant of a man when he walked into the room of his peers, standing six feet four inches tall and weighing 230 pounds. His athletic build and low body fat were probably due to his workout regimen. He enjoyed running three miles every morning on the beach in solitude, just before sunrise. His hair was just turning slightly grey around the sideburns, but overall, Jake aged well. The Marine Corps had taught him how to be tough. He still sported a clean-shaven look and still carried his military bearing when he walked into his campaign headquarters on Pass Road in Biloxi.

Everybody in Biloxi knew Jake well. After his combat tours, he attended Tulane Law School on his G.I. Bill and became a JAG officer. He had helped prosecute a few terrorists for war crimes and served on various intelligence commissions and military tribunals. He was promoted fast and, now at age 45, retired from the Marine Corps as a Full Bird Colonel.

Jake had a small law office in Downtown Biloxi on Howard Avenue in the Vieux Marche Mall. The mall was a walking mall with a concrete one-lane road. The bars and restaurants that the City of Biloxi envisioned calling the place home were slow in arriving. A couple of nightclubs, one hardware store, a medical office, located one block from Biloxi Regional Medical Center, and a small po boy restaurant called Shuckers, which Jake frequented.

Jake's Masonic Lodge, Magnolia Lodge number 120, was also located two blocks from his office, on the corner of Howard Avenue and Main Street, where he would attend lodge meetings and fellowship with his brethren on Thursday nights. It was at the lodge that Jake formally announced his campaign intentions. His brethren applauded his efforts. Jake served as a Past Master of the lodge with distinction.

Jake had no vices, an oddity coming from a town with such a checkered past and was once known as the "Playground of the South." He spoke with a thick East Biloxi accent made up of a southern drawl with a New Orleans swagger. Point Cadet, or simply The Point, was East Biloxi's rougher side. It was known back in the old days of the late 1890s to the 1960s as producing some of the most uncivilized people alive. Those descendants of Slavic, Croatian, Cajun, and later Vietnamese families who were natural pull themselves up from the bootstraps kind of people are now the ones running the city. Jake Fayard was of French descent, being one of the oldest names in Biloxi. It was something he prided himself on.

Jake's family arrived in Biloxi in the early 1720s. Biloxi, at the time, was a French possession. His seventh great grandfather Jacques Fayard was a French settler convinced by the infamously fraudulent John Law to move to the Louisiana Colony. John Law was a notable con artist who swindled multiple people into moving to the area with claims of lush green farmland and prey that practically posed before the hunter.

When the settlers arrived, they saw rough conditions and an unwelcome climate of high humidity and hurricanes. Jacques flourished and his descendants, Jake being one of them, still call Biloxi home.

Jacques Fayard was a carpenter, serving on a French Ship of the Line, which docked in Brest, France. Jacques left Brest in 1719 and made his voyage across the Atlantic and arrived in Biloxi in 1720. There he became a settler and became a soldier defending the Capitol of New France.

In 1723 the Capitol moved to New Orleans. Jacques Fayard resigned his appointment and stayed in Biloxi. With a French land grant, he owned land on the north side of the bay, in what is presently called d'Iberville, named for a founder of the City of Biloxi. The Fayard family has remained in Biloxi since the ship landed over three hundred years ago.

Jake was a proud member of several societies and organizations. Such as Phi Kappa Phi, which he joined as a Midshipman at the Naval Academy in Annapolis, Third Degree Freemason, Thirty-second Degree Scottish Rite, a

Shriner, Sons of the American Revolution, General Society of the War of 1812, Sons of Confederate Veterans, Military Order of the Stars and Bars, American Legion, and the Veterans of Foreign Wars.

Jake loved history, and he knew it well. He was known for his community service not just for taking on "pro-bono" legal work for indigent clients but also for his community service as a ham radio operator. He was also an Auxiliary Police Officer for the Biloxi Police Department. He helped and directed traffic for Mardi Gras Parades and special events where the Biloxi Police Department needed a few extra officers. Auxiliary cops didn't get paid, but they still had arrest powers and were sworn law enforcement officers. He didn't do this very often due to his time constraints with his law firm, but he was always in the mood to help.

Jake prided himself on being one of the foremost self-proclaimed historians on the Biloxi Rifles, Third Mississippi Infantry, Confederate States Army, which he descended. He was a real child of Biloxi. He loved his heritage and held it with a badge of honor.

In his office was a picture of his third great grandfather in uniform. The grandfather was a Captain in the Biloxi Rifles. His second great-grandfather had fought under Theodore Roosevelt in the Spanish-American war. His great grandfather served in the US Army during World War 1, his grandfather served in the US Navy during World War 2 and his father served in the Marine Corps during the Vietnam War. Jake followed the tradition of military service and was proud to enlist to serve in the Gulf War. Jake loved the military so much that he made a career out of it.

Biloxi was once known as a boomtown full of illegal gambling establishments, strip clubs, prostitution, and vibrant drug trade. Biloxi, founded in 1699 by the French when they needed a base close to the Mississippi River, was almost entirely lawless until recent history. The Biloxi Strip, as it was known, was located between Beauvoir, the last home of Confederate President Jefferson Davis, and Rodenburg Avenue has since been cleaned up.

Biloxi hadn't had a gangland-style shooting or killing in the last few decades. The last time such an occurrence happened was in 1967 when Harry Bennett was murdered on the strip. The last majorly publicized crime in Biloxi was a Circuit Court Judge, and his wife, a Mayoral candidate, was murdered in the 1980s. That was the end of the corruption from the Coast's central organized criminal element. When the judge and his wife were murdered the end result was all of the previously illegal vices in Biloxi became legal, legitimate, licensed businesses.

All that was left now were the usual regular street thugs that ran the ghettos and the low rent apartment complexes in the City of Biloxi. It did not exclude the possibility that one may occur, though. Biloxi still possessed a noticeably quiet underworld.

The old strip clubs are gone, either wiped away by the tides of the various hurricanes, or the bulldozer to make way for legitimate businesses, and the gambling that is conducted is legal. The near dockside casinos are mostly run by Las Vegas corporations and pay taxes. The old underworld was a very vivid memory to some but was fading fast to others.

Other than an occasional fifty dollars played at the craps table, on a rare occasion, none of the vices of Biloxi had caught Jake. He didn't smoke at all; he would drink very rarely, hardly gambled, didn't run around with a bunch of women, or anything of the sort. He was a very devout Catholic and attended mass at Our Lady of Fatima, one of the prominent Catholic churches that dotted the Mississippi Gulf Coast.

Jake was a widower, losing his wife to cancer just four years after they married, and had dated some but had never remarried. His last date was almost eight years previous, and he was contented living his life in solitude. His son Roy was three years old when his mother died, and Jake did his best to juggle home life, the military, college, and being a father. His maternal grandmother raised Roy for most of his youth. He was known for running with a rough crowd.

Jake's mother was still alive and lived in their old family home on Hoxie Street. His father had died five years earlier at the age of seventy. He left Jake a large inheritance that allowed Jake to buy a house in West Biloxi, on Travia Avenue, and open his law firm.

Jake's home in West Biloxi was modest enough. A small 1500 square foot, three-bedroom house located in the center of the street was innocuous enough that Jake could lead a quiet life. No high walls or fences were surrounding the yellow brick structure, a carport, a 40-foot ham radio tower, containing a medium size Cushcraft Yagi antenna for high frequency communications, and a small tool shed, just merely a short chain-link fence. There were no security measures either, as this too was unnecessary. The house could have fit in on any block in any medium-sized city in America.

Jake's father, Jake Senior, was a shrimp boat captain and had a run of good luck trading on Wall Street. He left Jake an extensive portfolio of Blue-Chip Stocks for him to fall back on. Jake Senior smartly bought Apple and Microsoft stock in the 1980's and Google stock in the late 1990's. This also made it possible for Jake to fund most of his campaign on his own. Jake maintained ownership of the shrimp boat, but he had no formal business dealings with it. He allowed a friend of the family who was in the seafood industry named Slick Desporte to manage the boat and distribute to Jake his share. It brought a mild income but not much more. Jake used the shrimp boat as a tax deduction for business expenses.

Anna's mother and father were both still alive. They were in their seventies and lived in a retirement community in Ocean Springs. The old house that Roy grew up in was demolished during Hurricane Katrina when the water covered East Biloxi.

The house was a beautiful white single-story structure.

The walls were of tongue and groove construction. The house was built in the 1920s, presumably by some Croatian immigrants who wanted their home to last for years. The house stayed through several hurricanes until the water from Katrina moved the structure off its foundation and deposited the house into the middle of Howard Avenue. As a result, the house was demolished to reopen the infrastructure in East Biloxi.

Jake Fayard was an honorable man; everybody could vouch for his loyalty and integrity. As he informed his standing-room-only crowd at the Biloxi White House Hotel, his reasons for running were to defeat the old corruption running rampant and unchecked for years. He started thinking about running a year ago when he read an article online calling Mississippi the most corrupt state in America.

Jake hated the image that other people had of his state being a bunch of backward rednecks. He was a proud Mississippian and wished that people would see Mississippi for its excellent culture. He was tired of the reputation that Mississippi was full of poor, bigoted, racist, uneducated, unkempt, and shut out white people who refused the times' change.

Jake swore to limit the size, scope, and role of government and bring more jobs to Mississippi. He pledged to bring about term limits. "Nobody should be a Senator for more than two terms," he loudly proclaimed. He also swore that he would be a two-term Senator and would not seek re-election. "I am committed to standing by my principles, and for that, I am not an exception to my own rule," he promised the crowd. He also spoke about crony capitalism which he disproved.

Jake also swore to do his damnedest to repeal Obamacare, which was a disaster from the start. "Socialism will drag down this country by the backs of the working class." He was, in fact, against all social entitlements such as Welfare, food stamps, Medicaid, Medicare, and Social Security. He kept those opinions to himself because he understood the beliefs could be political suicide.

Privately though, Jake thought them all a burden on the working people who barely lived hand to mouth. He was also against taxes and vowed no new taxes. He also promised to make the government live within its means and never to raise the debt ceiling. His biggest question was if an agency can operate for a specified budget this year, why did they need more the next?

He had a Political Action Committee created to fund his campaign and the issues called MSPAC. "MSPAC puts Mississippi and her interests first," he swore. He would only take donations from people living in Mississippi and would not accept any volunteers from out of state. "If they can't vote for me, I don't want their money."

At first, the establishment was dismissive of his campaign until the

Clarion-Ledger, a Jackson newspaper, put an online poll showing Jake was gaining a lot of steam. This was significant because the Jackson elite didn't respect people from the Mississippi Coast. The coast was mainly bastardized from the rest of the state, and it often joked that Biloxi was the Devil's Playground in the Bible Belt.

This stemmed back to the old days when Mississippi tried its hand at "The Noble Experiment." Jackson and the rest of the state tried to keep their anti-vice principles, and the Coast decided to live freely in their sinful ways. However, the rest of the state did enjoy the benefit of the Coast and its gambling revenue.

Mississippi was primarily protestant. Baptists and Methodists ran the northern and central parts of the state. At the same time, the coast remained Catholic true to its French roots going back to the French exploration period and later Spanish colonization.

The incumbent Senator, Robert Wallace, was a very connected Democrat when he was first elected in the early 1970s when most of the old South was Democrat, and in the 1990's he followed the change of the south and became a Reagan Republican. He was a "yes man" to the Governor and anybody else who was connected to the immense political machine of the Mississippi Establishment. He took his orders and did what he was told without question. forty-six years in the Senate, and all he ever did was learn to take orders and be a worm for the establishment.

Anybody who dared to challenge him was usually swallowed up whole and spit out on the wrong end of a dead political career. Most people wouldn't dare try to come after the frail seventy-four-year-old man, who, even though he looked like a strong breeze could blow him in half, was the most dangerous person in the Senate Chamber. He had served his second year as the President Pro-Tempore, which means he was the most senior of the Senators in the majority party.

Senator Wallace used this position to rally Mississippi voters behind him for fear that they would lose the privilege. This status also made him the third in line of succession to the Presidency, should anything happen to the President and the Vice President was unable to serve.

Jake knew that running this campaign was sure to be an uphill battle. The Governor, Bill Creel, who was in his second term, owed his career to the Mississippi political machine. Bill Creel was a prominent Jackson attorney before being elected Governor of the State of Mississippi. He was fifty-five years old, stood about five feet six inches tall, weighed about 275 pounds, and smoked illegal Cuban cigars imported into Miami, Florida, by a business acquaintance of his. He had short, grey hair and a bushy gray goatee. He was a round, pompous ass, and he boasted himself as a trial lawyer, but he hadn't seen the inside of a courtroom personally in about fifteen years.

Governor Creel was known to be a warm, almost grandfatherly speaker, in front of the camera, with the ability to connect with most voters. It probably helped him as a trial lawyer to connect him with most juries. He won a few significant lawsuits and had collected hefty multi-million-dollar fees with his law firm in Jackson. He was also a lobbyist, which garnered him most of the clout that he possessed in the Republican Party. He once represented a family killed in an airplane crash by suing a large airline and suing the manufacturer of the jumbo jet. The family won seventy-five million dollars, and Bill Creel raked off a cool one-third of the settlement.

It was rumored that Senator John Kennard, a hardcore right-wing Republican from Central Mississippi, and his Judiciary Committee had investigated his Senior Senator Wallace and Governor Bill Creel for corruption and bribery. The investigation turned up nothing, but some of the allegations stemmed back to the 1980s and continuing to this day. The alleged crimes included bribery, racketeering, public corruption, misappropriation of public funds, and he also suspected, but could not prove, murder for hire. "I'll not rest until I see y'all in jail or Hell," Senator Kennard once said.

Senator Kennard was a former Mayor of the small town of Mendenhall, Mississippi. Before he was elected mayor, he spent eight years as a field agent for the Federal Bureau of Investigation. He was trained at Quantico but was medically retired from the job after a bullet found its way into his left kneecap, a friendly fire accident while executing a warrant on a known Cyberterrorist in Des Moines. He returned to his native Mendenhall, Mississippi, and joined the Simpson County Sheriff's Office before being turned on by politics. He served three terms as Mayor of Mendenhall before running against an old guard Senator and winning handily. He was in his second term as Senator. An average-size man of five feet nine inches tall and about 175 pounds, he was a giant when he spoke. His judicial committee had thus far investigated all sorts of corruption and netted twelve indictments.

Jake was sitting at his meticulously organized desk. Nothing was out of place about it. A few pictures were casually arranged on the top. His beloved Anna, twenty years after her death, and he was still in love with her. He knew she watched over him. He stared at the picture with her long flowing blond hair under her veil. It was a picture of her that her mother took on the day before they were married. She had tried on the old wedding dress, and her mother decided she looked too beautiful not to capture the image. It was Jake's favorite portrait of her.

Jake thought of the day they met. They were so young and innocent. He was ten years old, and she was nine. They played together, and the two children's parents saw a spark. The day they met was so fresh and vivid in his mind that he could see it in high definition.

The two were so innocent. They played on the swing at Miramar Park, a small playground located at the foot of Miramar and Acacia Avenue, right along the beachfront. The two were playing on the toy ship that was there. The park still exists; however, the ship was removed after Hurricane Katrina.

The friendship grew into a lasting relationship that spanned their teens. It survived Junior High, at Michelle Middle School, High School, at Mercy Cross Catholic High School for Jake, and Biloxi High School for Anna. They rarely had a cross word. They were nearly inseparable. Even the usual high school drama couldn't pull the two apart, even though some of their friends objected to the union.

"He's going to marry that girl," Jake's father often said. The two graduated from High School one year apart and were married one year after crossing the old stage. He was deeply in love with her to this day.

The other pictures on the desk were one of the entire family taken nearly twenty-one years ago, shortly after the cancer diagnosis that would claim his wife's life. A towering handsome Jake in his Marine Corps dress blue uniform, a lovely blond lady nearly a foot shorter than him, at five feet five inches tall she was a giant in his life, and their two-year-old son Roy, dressed in a shirt that said: "I'd rather be Smashing Pumpkins." He wondered what his life would be like if she had survived. The other pictures on his desk were of one in Iraq with Coby Barhonovich, the current Attorney General for Mississippi.

They were best friends. They met in kindergarten and have been closer than brothers ever since. They were the same age, enjoyed the same hobbies, and both had similar backgrounds.

Coby was of Slavic descent. His family arrived in Biloxi at the turn of the century to work in the canneries that dotted the coast. His father ran for Constable in the 1980s in Harrison County and had lost by seven votes. It was rumored that the race was won by the number of dead voters that returned from the grave and cast their ballots from the great beyond. Both had known each other from growing up in the same neighborhood on the Point. Both graduated from Mercy Cross High

School and served in Iraq together in the 1990s and had graduated from Tulane Law School together in 1999. Coby didn't stay in the Marine Corps after his initial enlistment though instead opting to use his G.I. Bill to attend Mississippi State University and eventually Tulane University School of Law in New Orleans.

The other picture on the desk was when both Coby and Jake were raised as Master Mason's in the Magnolia Lodge number 120 in Biloxi. It was a proud day for both of them.

Jake's rented campaign office was a three-room storefront that used to be an old bicycle store located on Pass Road near Popps Ferry Road. It was a red brick structure with large windows in the front of the building. The large red, white, and blue, four-foot letters on the windows read proudly "JAKE FAYARD FOR SENATE." The building was well kept, and for $500 per month, was a bargain.

Jake had his own office at the rear of the suite. The office had white, sheetrock walls, a fake marble tile floor, and three chairs for visitors to sit while in Jake's office, it also contained an old desk.

In Jake's office, the old mahogany desk, a hand-me-down from his great uncle, another lawyer in the family, was fifty years old and held sentimental value to Jake. It was the desk that his father was sitting behind when Jake informed him that he would be joining the Marine Corps. It was the same desk that Jake filled out his college admission forms on; it was the same desk that his father's last will had been written, it was the same desk that he grew up playing on when he was a child. That desk gave the feeling of generations of the Fayard family sitting in the office.

The main room, where guests were received, had large windows and a large glass table in the center. Plush couches were rented for the office, and the floor had red carpet, aged from the use of its previous tenants but still in reasonably decent shape. The large room also had four desks where staff members would do their work and answer the telephone. They were busy fielding calls from reporters all over the state, and once Jake announced his candidacy, the phones seemed never to stop ringing.

Jake's uncle was still alive but had retired from law practice years earlier. He had a small law firm called Fayard, and Fayard, of which he was the only attorney. He sued Big Tobacco in the 1990s and won major lawsuits while working in partnership with other Coast attorneys. Unfortunately, the lawyer, Uncle Cal, as Jake lovingly called him, had found the casino very tempting.

Cal Fayard won a fortune almost overnight, had the reputation of being a shark in the courtroom, showed Jake a lot of skill that he possessed, and lost it all on the craps table. It also instilled in Jake to stay away from the vices of problematic gambling, which Jake did.

After the fortune was lost, Cal had left the coast, and Jake hadn't heard from him in years. The last Jake knew, Cal had met some rich widow and was living in Huntington Beach,

California. He used to call, but he hadn't in years.

"Good morning, Jake" a polite greeting from his campaign manager Joe Holloway. "Nice day to have a crawfish boil, doncha think?"

Joe was talking about the crawfish boil, a staple in any political campaign and the way to any South Mississippian's heart.

"Yes, such a beautiful day. I hope people turn out in droves." Jake replied.

Free crawfish was indeed a way to turn people out in droves. The event was scheduled for the afternoon of April twenty-fourth on a beautiful sunny spring day. The event was to be held at the old Broadwater Marina, formerly a grand hotel built during the 1920s, was once the site of illegal gambling and frequented by Chicago mob figure Al Capone before his arrest. The hotel and the marina were destroyed during Hurricane Katrina and had now turned into a hang-out for fisherman and partygoers alike.

Jake drove his 2005 Ford F-150 XLT from his office to the Broadwater Marina. At one point, the Broadwater Marina was one of the most beautiful marinas on the Gulf Coast from Texas to Florida before Hurricane Katrina leveled the hotel and laid waste to the marina.

The marina belonged to a grand hotel called the Broadwater. Before Katrina, the property was renamed "The President Casino Resort." It was one of the original legal casinos that dotted the Mississippi Gulf Coast and provided a place for families to make memories for decades.

The dirt road that used to be a concrete paved road with some of the biggest yachts on the coast was slapping and beating his truck hard. "I have got to fix this suspension," he thought as he hit another pothole. His truck was not a new truck, but the old 4.6-liter Ford V8 still cranked up and ran very well. Jake wasn't the one to buy a new vehicle unless he needed to. His magnetic signs on the doors read JAKE FOR SENATE and on the rear of the red Ford were likewise magnetic signs. His Masonic Square and Compass of the Blue Lodge were there as well as his Shriner's emblem. His greatest joy in the world was taking kids who could not afford to get medical treatment to the Shriner's Hospital in Shreveport, Louisiana. The amateur radio antennas on Jake's truck shook and smacked each other with every bump and made a twanging noise above his head which nearly gave him a headache.

Jake arrived early, at about nine o'clock. He helped set up the tents and the podium. A few volunteers offered to set up the crawfish pots. The flags were waving in the strong southernly breeze coming off of the Mississippi Sound and the weather was perfect. It was a nice sunny 80-degree day with a good breeze and not a cloud in the sky.

The crawfish boil started about eleven o'clock that morning. People poured in so tight that the Biloxi Police Department had to usher in people for parking. About 1500 attendees showed up for the rally. It was a masterpiece, more than had shown up in a while. Jake was unsure if it was the free crawfish or the curiosity of a Biloxian taking on the corruption that brought people out.

A big podium was set up, and loudspeakers were rented so that the speech was clear. Jake was standing behind the stage to shake the hands of his supporters and potential constituents.

Once it was clear that everybody had enjoyed their fill of free crawfish and Barq's root beer, a Coast favorite, and was settled down in their folding chairs, Jake gave an excellent speech. Jake advanced to the podium and commanded the crowd with his presence. All eyes shot forward to this giant of a man standing in front of the bank of microphones.

His speech was well-rehearsed and came with the booming baritone of a battlefield commander. His demeanor kept the audience engaged and dazzled with his impression. Jake loudly proclaimed from the podium "I am Jake Fayard. I am running to be your next

Senator. I hope y'all enjoyed the crawfish and fellowship that this event has offered y'all. I appreciate all of y'all for coming out. I stand on limited government, low taxes, and no gun control. I also offer integrity and a mission statement of service and ethics. Ethics is severely missing from politics in this state, and we desperately need our voice to be heard in Washington. I have offered Senator Wallace the chance to debate me, and he ignores me."

"BOOOO" the cries came from the crowd in unison. "WALLACE HAS GOT TO GO!"

Jake continued "He thinks he isn't accountable to us. He doesn't care about you; all he cares about is his Georgetown house and his political cronies. I am of you; I am a veteran. I am tired of grand designs turning into Grand Juries." A hush fell over the crowd as people couldn't believe the boldness of the young candidate. "My record of public service speaks for itself, and just as I served y'all in Iraq, I will again in Washington. I believe in small government, personal responsibility, public accountability, and the United States Constitution. I vow not to raise any taxes and to make the government live within its means. Do y'all have any questions?"

Just then, a voice stepped up from the back and asked, "Mr. Fayard, what do you say to the accusation that your son is a drug addict?" A hush fell over the crowd as Jake got red-faced. "My friends, this is what I expected from my political foes. They can't attack me, so they attack my family. I refuse to dignify that question with a response, sir."

The campaign party concluded, and Jake went back to his office. "Those god damned sons of bitches have fucked with me for the last time," Jake said as he walked into his office. "Calm down, man," Joe said.

Jake returned from his event, entered his office, and set down a large plastic bin full of crawfish. He sat at his computer and began to type press releases to be released for the next day. Jake knew he would work tirelessly for most of the night, then go home and get about four hours of sleep and begin his assault on the day.

Jake researched legislation and the voting record of Senator Wallace in case he finally got his wish for a debate. He found that Senator Wallace had voted against legislation that would have sanctioned Iran, developing nuclear weapons, and who Jake saw as a potential threat. Jake may have been against war, but he did believe in National Security. He also knew how radical Iran was, and the fact that they were developing nuclear weapons worried him. He didn't want his brothers and sisters serving to fight a regime with those kinds of weapons.

Jake researched the voting record back to the 1970s and saw the flip flop. During the midterm election, he saw a momentous change in 1982 when Wallace transformed from the party of a Dixiecrat to a Reagan Conservative Republican. He saw it for what it was, a political move, nothing more, nothing less. Senator Wallace was anything but a 'Reagan Republican.'

Chapter Two

The Setup

At the same time as the campaign party in Biloxi, a blue Ford Fusion was driving down Gregory Street in Pensacola, Florida. The Ford was driving at 35 miles per hour, not swerving, and the driver was wearing a seatbelt. No red lights or stop signs were ignored.

The Ford pulled into a parking lot behind a double decker bus and noticed the flashing lights on a brand-new black on black Dodge Charger behind him. Roy Fayard pulled into a parking spot, rolled down the driver's side window, turned off the ignition, placed his keys on the dashboard, and placed his hands on the steering wheel.

A clean-cut officer in black tactical gear stood behind the driver's door of the unmarked Dodge with his weapon trained on Roy.

"Driver, with your left hand, open the door and exit the vehicle!" a voice cried over the megaphone. Roy complied.

"Driver, place your hands over the top of your head and get down on your knees!" The voice ordered once more. Roy complied all too willingly.

Another officer retrieved his staged handcuffs and with a pistol grip technique firmly in his right hand, grabbed jakes wrists with his left, and swiftly cuffed Roy. The officer then escorted Roy to the front bumper of his unmarked patrol car and introduced himself as Lieutenant Suarez of the Pensacola Police Department. Lieutenant Suarez then asked Roy what he was doing in Pensacola today.

"Nothing officer." Roy pathetically and helplessly replied.

"Do you mind if I search your car?" The Lieutenant asked firmly. He knew he was going to search it anyway as a probable cause warrant was being issued as they spoke.

"No sir, go right ahead." Roy replied.

Roy's wallet was located, and the contents inventoried. Roy's cellular phone was also recovered but it was locked so it couldn't be investigated. Four more squad cars including a K9 entered the parking lot with flashing blue lights.

The K9 was deployed and hit on the trunk alerting to the possibility of the presence of narcotics. Roy's keys were retrieved from the dashboard and upon opening the trunk several kilograms of cocaine was discovered. Roy was read his Miranda rights and placed under arrest. Under the driver's seat was a loaded .22 Caliber semi-automatic pistol.

"That's not mine!" Roy screamed and pleaded with the officers.

"Haha yeah sure we've never heard that before. Oh, I know it was the cocaine fairy that paid you a visit." One of the Officers laughed.

Roy was taken to the Escambia County Jail and booked on charges of Possession of a controlled substance with intent to sell and possession of a firearm by a convicted felon. He was allowed one phone call, which was to Coby Barhonovich, his dad's best friend.

When Jake returned to his campaign headquarters on Pass Road, a voicemail was on Jake's phone from his best friend and college roommate, Coby Barhonovich. Coby was a very honest and tireless Attorney General who had defeated a four-term incumbent and then had him indicted for conspiracy shortly after being elected. The message played, "Mr. Fayard, I order you to call the Attorney General immediately, or you will be arrested within thirty minutes!"

The two were always playing practical jokes on each other. Jake looked at the time of the call. "Hmm… ten-thirty… I'll call him back at eleven oh one and see what he does." He called back at the precise time of 11:01, and on cue, he responded: "Thirty-one minutes, and I'm not in handcuffs, you lying son of a bitch!" The tone of the Attorney General wasn't playful; in fact, it was severe and genuinely concerned.

"Hey Bro, they got your son Roy down in Florida. They busted him with five kilos of coke in Pensacola." Coby said.

"Shit, I'm gonna kill him…. Does he have a bond yet?" Jake replied angrily.

"No, he won't be eligible for bond because they also got him for being a felon in possession of a firearm," Coby replied sadly. Jake hung up the phone and cursed his son.

Jake took the day off from campaigning to talk to the State's Attorney in Pensacola. He got in his truck, started his engine, turned on a local talk radio station, and made the 120-mile drive from Biloxi to Pensacola.

He crossed the Pascagoula River bridge on Interstate 10 and took note of its beauty. The barge that was traveling under calmed him down a bit. Traffic in Mobile, Alabama was slow going, being Lunch Hour Rush, but he made it through quickly and entered the George Wallace Tunnel.

Once on the other side of the Bayway, a long bridge that crosses the Mobile Bay, he received a phone call from Joe Holloway.

"Hey, Jake?" Joe asked.

"Yeah, Joe, what can I do for you?" Jake replied.

"You left in a hurry. Are you ok, bud?" Joe asked, sounding sincerely concerned.

"Yeah, my son got arrested in Florida, and I am on my way to take care of it," Jake responded.

"Ok, buddy, be careful. Let me know if I can help you." Joe said, and the phone went dead.

After the phone call, Joe excused himself from the office and left another clerk in charge. He told the clerk he was going to pick up more campaign signs and would be back later.

Joe sat in his truck, an old Dodge Ram, pulled away from his parking spot and called George Walter, an investigator with the Mississippi Highway Patrol.

"Hey, George?" Joe said.

"Yeah, what's up?" George asked.

"Little Junior has been a bad boy. Did you hear he got arrested?" Joe said almost with a smirk.

"Yeah, I do recall hearing something about that. A little birdie told me he was playing with guns and something about nose candy. Didn't anybody ever teach that boy to just say no to drugs?" George said with a laugh.

"Yeah, well, maybe that will teach Colonel Fayard that he shouldn't play with people who are out of his league," Joe replied, and the phone went dead.

Jake arrived in the State's Attorney's office to discuss young Roy's case. The drive had somewhat calmed him down a bit. If Jake Fayard had one flaw, it was his famous temper. The Marine Corps had slightly made him a bit more mellow, but after all, he was a father, and his son's flaws were enough to try the patience of Job.

"I'm sorry, I can't let him go on this one. I can arrange for you to speak with him if you agree to represent him, though." Jake being a licensed attorney in Mississippi, Louisiana, Alabama, Florida, and Washington D.C., decided to take his son's case until he can find a local attorney who wasn't so pissed off to defend him.

"I'll take the case for now," Jake said with a sigh.

"Ok, well, you can go speak to him. I'll call the jail and make all of the arrangements that way; you won't have to make two trips." The Prosecutor said.

Jake thanked the State's Attorney for his candor and waited for the phone call authorizing the conference. He then went to the Escambia County Jail.

"Do you have any firearms, knives, alcoholic beverages, cell phones, cash over twenty dollars, recording devices, USB Flash drives, cameras, PDAs, or p38 can openers?" a Deputy Sheriff in a dark green uniform asked. "No sir," Jake respectfully replied. He was then directed through a metal detector.

Jake couldn't clear the metal detector because of a metal plate in his leg, a wound he sustained in Iraq so many years ago. He was made to lift his pants leg and remove his shoes. A handheld metal detector was waved over the offending limb. He was cleared to enter after his briefcase was inventoried, then was directed into a room labeled "ATTORNEYS" by another Deputy Sheriff.

After waiting about forty-five minutes, Roy Fayard was permitted to enter. He was handcuffed, shackled, adorned with a waist chain with a black box and a padlock holding the chain and his handcuffs around his waist. A large corrections deputy removed the waist chain, hand restraints, and black box and then Roy was placed in a chair on the opposite side of a Plexiglas window with a telephone receiver.

"Ok, boy, what the hell did you do now?" Jake angrily said in a shallow tone through clenched teeth.

"This is a bullshit bust, dad," Roy said with all sincerity he could muster. He was sober and had been for some time. "They set me up. I don't even do coke anymore." If nothing else, Roy was honest with his disproving father about what drugs he had been on and what his life was like regularly.

"What do you mean you don't do coke *anymore*?" Jake said, puzzled.

"Dad, I came down to Florida to go into rehab. I have been clean for two weeks, but I know to stay clean, I have to get away from Biloxi and get into a facility." Roy replied earnestly.

"Ok, boy, I'll look into it, but you'll have to sit here awhile until we figure this out," Jake said before he left.

On the two-hour drive back to Biloxi, Jake received a phone call from none other than the Honorable Bill Creel, Governor of the State of Mississippi, and a very vocal political foe of his. "I heard your boy is locked up again, Jake," the voice said with almost a laugh "Man, y'all sure do know how to party down on the beach." Jake slung the phone across his truck and began to think about what his son meant when he said he didn't do coke anymore. "Was this a setup?" he thought.

Jake began to think of other cases which he called "bum rap" cases. Cases to which officers planted drugs or other contraband on suspects to get rid of them. Rumors had circulated of other political foes of the Governor and his cronies of being bum rapped by corrupt members of the Mississippi Highway Patrol, but they are often hard to prove as possession is nine-tenths of the law. Exculpatory evidence was frequently lost, and the victim was sent to prison for long sentences. "How the hell am I gonna fix this?" Jake thought to himself.

By the time he arrived home and turned on the news, he finally got hit with it. "Senate Candidate's son arrested in Florida for possession of drugs, full story at six." The voice screamed from the television. He cursed himself for putting his career above raising his son.

Jake researched search and seizure laws in Florida. He typed a motion for discovery, printed it out, and prepared it for the State's Attorney. He also researched other cases to determine what kind of deal could be made with the prosecutor. He couldn't sleep because he thought of his son and the impending prison sentence, which Jake knew could be lengthy.

The next day, Roy Fayard was arraigned, and bail was set at $50,000. A bail bondsman from A-One Beach Bail Bonds, named Martin Stamper, answered the phone. He wasn't thrilled at the idea of writing such a high bond for an out-of-state client, but Jake assured him that he would appear in court. Martin asked Jake to meet him in the office.

The office was located on L Street near the jail, known as "bail bond row." About ten bail bond offices with neon signs that read "Open 24 Hours" dotted this strip of land. Jake walked into the dingy office and saw Martin or "Marty" as he preferred, smoking a cigarette and talking on the phone to someone about surrendering himself. "Look, man, if you don't come turn yourself in, I will take your mother's house and throw her on the street!" Marty said in a thundering voice.

The office was cluttered with pictures of fugitives who had jumped bail. There were all sorts of tactical gear strewn around the office in a situation of unorganized chaos. It showed that neatness and cleanliness wasn't high on Marty's priorities.

Jake stood in front of the desk, weary of the chair that was provided for him, and when Marty had secured a time that the client would turn himself in, he hung the phone up.

"What can I do for you?" Marty asked Jake.

Jake looked at the man in a black T-Shirt with white lettering that simply said SURETY AGENT and thought that he was the one that should be helped. Marty was about six feet two inches tall and 320 pounds. He looked like he could use some time at the gym. His stomach protruded from under his shirt and covered his belt buckle. He had on a pair of black tactical boots and black BDU pants. Jake noted that this "Marty" seemed to watch too much television on what a bounty hunter should look like.

"I am the one that called about Roy Fayard, the man from Mississippi," Jake said, unsure if he should do business with the man on the other side of the cluttered desk.

"Ok, first I need you to fill this out," Marty said as he slid the bail application over to him.

Jake filled out the application thoroughly, and when he was done, he slid it back across the desk. Marty read the application, made a copy of Jake's identification and other credentials, and called the Clerk of Court.

"Ok, Mr. Fayard." Marty finally said. "For a bond of $50,000. The cost of the bail bond will be a premium of $5,000. I will not set up any payment arrangement because the client lives out of state. If he doesn't show up for court and I cannot find him or revoke his bond, you are responsible for the entire $50,000. I will also need ten percent for collateral. If he shows up and I have no problem finding him, you will get back this amount."

"Ok, so you want $10,000 to get him out of jail?" Jake asked, a bit concerned.

"Yes, sir. Normally I don't write out-of-state clients, but in your case, because I have researched you, and you are an attorney, I will make the exception but only on those conditions." Marty said.

Jake said that would be fine and asked if Marty could make drug rehabilitation a condition of his bond. Marty said that was fine and added this clause to the bail bond contract. Once the bail contract was read and agreed to, Jake drove to his bank. Luckily, Pensacola had a branch to withdraw the money promptly and pay the bondsman without the need to make a return trip to Biloxi.

When Jake returned with the money, Marty called the jail and set the bond up. "It'll take a couple of hours," Marty said, and Jake decided to wait. Roy was released from the Escambia County Jail two and a half hours later.

When Jake and Roy were on their way back to Biloxi, Jake decided to find out exactly what happened.

"Tell me what happened, son," Jake said.

"Dad, I shit you not. I was driving along Gregory Street and looking to meet up with this girl I met on the net. I was clean, had no drugs on me or in my system; you can drug test me right now…." Roy said as he was shaking.

"Son... stop… I believe you…. Just tell me what happened…" Jake said calmly.

"Ok, so I was driving and went to meet this girl at McGuire's Irish Pub. One last date before I go to rehab. I pulled into the parking lot behind it, and five cop cars surrounded me." Roy said.

"Wait, they didn't pull you over on the road?" Jake said, very confused.

"No, Dad, I swear they were waiting for my ass, man it was crazy! They blue lighted me in the parking lot right as I pulled in." Roy replied.

"Had you spoken to this girl on the phone or met this girl in person?" Jake asked.

"No, dad I didn't." Roy replied.

"So, you were going to see this girl and you didn't even know if she was real?" Jake asked, annoyed.

"Yeah, dad but her picture looked real. She kinda looked like your average girl next door, no drugs didn't smoke you would have liked her." Roy said enthusiastically.

"God damn it, they set you up," Jake said with his teeth clenched, and fist bawled. "Don't you think it's interesting that while you have no alibi you find yourself meeting some whore online to get your dick wet and all of a sudden you get busted for cocaine? Where is your brain son? Were you not thinking?"

"Dad, I swear I never thought about it. She seemed like a really nice girl. It never occurred to me that she could be a catfish." Roy said in a low tone.

"You need to be smart. I raised you to think and you should be street smart. This stunt that you pulled could cost you about 20 years of your life. You are too God damn smart to throw your life away over a piece of ass." Jake snapped.

They continued to drive home, and the phone rang. It was Joe calling to tell him that reporters from all over the state had been trying to reach him for comments. "They pulled out all the stops now," he said. Joe always could be counted on to say the wrong things at the wrong time to Jake. That Marine gung-ho mentality, along with his southern temper, didn't help much either.

Jake pulled into the driveway and gave specific instructions to Roy. "Ok, listen, boy, this is what you're going to do. You will speak to nobody; you will visit nobody; you will not leave this house without me. I am your shadow and for god's sake, leave them whores alone online! You thinking with the wrong head put you and me in this fucked up mess." Roy agreed and thanked his dad. So far, other than a week once, Roy had avoided severe jail time. The felony charge for possession he got convicted of netted him two years' probation, which he completed. "Dad, I am sorry I fucked things up, man, but I swear I didn't have anything on me."

Jake knew that Florida was a very unforgiving state for drugs and would surely send him to prison for several years. Governor Creel was also friends with Governor John Brooks in Florida, and the Florida Governor owed him his seat as Chairman of the Republican Governor's Convention. He knew that political favors would be exchanged, and his son could quite possibly be sentenced to Florida State Prison in Raiford, which was known for its horrors as one of the cruelest prisons in the country.

The chain gang and convict leasing had long since been stopped nearly a century ago in Florida. They didn't work inmates to death as they do in Parchman Prison in Mississippi, where an inmate would spend years picking cotton, tomatoes, and soybeans, but conditions were still just as rough, and the guards were just as mean. Jake had a client once sentenced to Florida State Prison for getting caught in Orlando on vacation for having two pounds of pot.

Jake once toured the prison with a friend and fellow Marine who later became a State Representative of Florida.

Jake saw the infamous Q Wing, where they house the most violent offenders. Q wing was at the end of the large compound and contained cells known as "max management," a cell within a cell within a cell. He saw the inner workings of Florida State Prison and shuttered to think what was housed there. It takes two officers to open one door, and they are very well trained.

As Jake traversed the winding road back toward the interstate known as Florida State Road 16 and eventually Florida State Highway 121, he realized that Raiford was a prison community with not one but three prisons side by side. Florida State Prison, New River Correctional Institution, and Union Correctional Institution, which used to be home to "The Rock," known for its large block wall and escape-proof structure much like its California cousin. Union Correctional Institute used to be the old Florida State Prison before the new one was built in 1968.

Convict leasing had begun in Florida in 1868 to perpetuate the foul institution of slavery, and in 1913, the farm at Raiford was open to house prisoners who were too sick to be leased out. Convict leasing was phased out in 1923 in favor of road prisons.

Jake thought about all of this and got a bit worried. He knew that Florida was a prison state boasting the third largest correctional system in the country. He knew they would stop at nothing to get him to play ball. His Marine mentality of never quit and surrender is not in our creed was heavily conflicting with his duties as a father. He loved his son as any man would, and since his son was all that he had left in this world as far as family goes, he would do anything to protect him. He decided to act.

Jake woke up the following day and started driving to Pensacola. He wanted to depose the officers who arrested his son. He arranged it with the State's Attorney to meet with all eight officers. As they sat down, Jake asked to speak with them one by one. The first one was the officer in charge of Narcotics for the Pensacola Police Department, an imposing man in his thirties named Lieutenant Miguel Suarez.

Lieutenant Suarez was annoyed, having been pulled away from a major case to answer questions. He hated lawyers, and he did not attempt to hide his contempt for Jake. He knew that lawyers could always find a way to let the guilty go free, and because he was working a case that caused the deaths of twenty-eight people, who overdosed on Fentanyl, he was in no mood for a lawyer. He was a professional, though, and knew this was part of his job description.

"Lieutenant Suarez I am Jake Fayard. I am an attorney for Roy Fayard, the man from Biloxi y'all arrested the other day. I will need to ask you some questions, and for this, I am going to have to swear you in. Please raise your right hand." Jake said firmly.

The Lieutenant complied.

"Do you solemnly swear, under penalty of perjury, that the statement or testimony you are about to give is the truth to the best of your knowledge, so help you, God?" Jake asked.

"Yes, I do," The Lieutenant replied.

"Okay, sir, please state your name, official position, and place of employment for the record, please," Jake said politely.

"Okay, first off, I know that I arrested your son, I know who you are, I know your lawyer tricks, and I don't give a flying fuck that you're some big shot Senator from Mississippi. Don't try any of your bullshit with me, or I will walk out that God damn door, job be damned." Lieutenant Suarez said with all of the contempt he could muster.

"No problem, sir, now please answer my questions," Jake replied pleasantly.

"Lieutenant Miguel Suarez, Narcotics Interdiction Team, Pensacola Police Department, Pensacola, Florida." The cop replied.

"Lieutenant Suarez, why did y'all stop my client?" Jake asked.

"We stopped your son because we got an anonymous tip that he would be at this location to make a drug deal." Lieutenant Suarez answered.

"Where did this anonymous tip originate?" Jake asked as he wrote down the information he was given.

"I am not sure. It was passed on to me that your son would be selling a large quantity of cocaine to somebody. Upon identifying your son by his vehicle license plate number and description, we dispatched a Police K9 to walk around the car; the dog hit on the trunk. Upon that probable cause, we located what appeared to be five kilograms of cocaine under the mat of the trunk." The Lieutenant replied.

"So, sir, you are telling me that the tip was so well described that it not only gave you my client's car, license plate, description of the person, and location of the drugs, and you didn't find it odd. Have you ever had a tip with that much detail before?" Jake asked, surprised.

"Yes and no, I can't recall getting a tip with that much detail in the past, but it sure would be nice if it happened regularly." Lieutenant Suarez said confidently.

"What about the firearm that was found in the car?" Jake asked.

"What about it? It was a Ruger 9mm semi-automatic that was loaded with fifteen rounds of 115-grain full metal jackets and found under the driver's seat." Lieutenant Suarez answered as he looked at the notes in the police report.

"Did any fingerprints come back on either the cocaine packaging or the weapon?" Jake asked.

"I am not sure we're still waiting on the crime lab to determine that." Lieutenant Suarez said.

"What, if anything, did my client say to you when you arrested him?" Jake asked.

"Mr. Fayard indicated that the drugs were not his and he was in the city to meet up with a female that he allegedly met online. He could not positively identify this female, her address, her last name, or provide a phone number to corroborate his story." Lieutenant Suarez said.

"Did you search his cell phone?" Jake asked.

"No, we were unable to unlock his iPhone. We also didn't have a warrant and didn't need one because it was not germane to our investigation. We had him, his car, his gun, and his drugs in the car. Why would we need to look at his cell phone?" Lieutenant Suarez said smugly.

The depositions of the other seven officers sounded pretty much like that of Lieutenant Suarez's. Jake thanked them all for their time and left. Once he was in the parking lot, he decided to grab some lunch. A lunch truck was located near the courthouse, and Jake bought a BBQ burger.

Jake then walked into the courthouse and asked again to speak to the State's Attorney. He was told that the State's Attorney was in a meeting and instructed to wait outside.

An hour later, a junior secretary informed Jake that he would be received and directed him in. When jake entered the State Attorney's office, he asked, "What are you offering?"

"Well," the State's Attorney said, "I believe if he pleads guilty, I can give him four years. If you go to trial, I am going to push for twenty. Florida is an eighty-five percent State, which means that he could get out in forty-one months."

"I'll think about it. I just want to look at all of the evidence first." Jake replied.

"Well, don't take too long. We are securing an indictment as we speak and should have one within a month. If we get one, the offer of four years is off the table." The Prosecutor said arrogantly.

"Dude don't try to fast track me. My son will get all the Due Process the Constitution allows him." Jake snarled.

"Mr. Fayard, I wasn't trying to rush you for my benefit. It's your campaign that's on the hook." The Prosecutor said cautiously.

Jake rudely left the office and drove back to Biloxi. "That son of a bitch is pulling out everything," he said to himself.

On the two-hour drive back to Biloxi, right about when he was coming out of the tunnel at Mobile, Alabama, his phone rang. A retired Biloxi Police Officer named Richard Marks that Jake went to high school with, offering to investigate the charges. "I'll let you know as soon as I figure out what I am doing," Jake replied.

Chapter Three

Roy goes to Rehab

Jake Fayard had to humble himself and place calls to get his son into rehab. He had been in several designer drug facilities all up and down the coast where sometimes he made it, and most times he failed. Jake knew that some of the lower quality ones would grant interviews to the press and break their oaths of confidentiality.

Jake visited several and wasn't impressed at the relaxed security of most of them. He knew that he had $50,000 on the line if Roy escaped and wanted one of the highest qualities he could afford. He also knew that he should avoid rehabilitation centers on the coast for fear that Jake would find friends to sneak him contraband.

One facility that Jake visited was located on the grounds of a mental hospital in Mobile, Alabama. Still, when he saw some of the street characters hanging around outside, this was vetoed. "This is a cesspool." Jake thought.

Jake visited three more, one in Hattiesburg, Mississippi, had a violent mental patient attack, three orderlies, with a butcher knife stolen from the kitchen while Jake was there. He promptly thanked them for their time and left. The next one was in Jackson but was quickly vetoed before he even pulled into the parking lot. He knew that Jackson was no place for Roy and that the Governor and his do-boy, Highway Patrolman George Walter, could grab him at any time or cause other harm.

Jake's last stop was New Orleans. He had been driving all day and visiting more drug treatment facilities than he had ever cared to see and had grown tired of it. He scheduled a meeting with The Charter House and found this to look somewhat acceptable on its appearance. After meeting with an orderly, Jake was sure he had located a suitable place for Roy.

Jake went back to Biloxi and informed Roy of his decision. When he arrived at his house in Biloxi, he heard a loud commotion in Roy's bedroom and smelled the stench of marijuana. An old girlfriend of Roy heard he was back in town and stopped by for a quick session. Jake kicked the door open, saw the two naked bodies on top of the bed, and interrupted the sex in progress. The girl, who was about twenty-five years old but looked like she was forty, was one that Jake had seen before.

The smell of sex and marijuana angered Jake. He yanked Roy off of the girl and ordered the naked female out of the house.

"What the fuck did I tell you about those whores?" Jake shouted as the young female got dressed.

"Dad, I'm sorry, I was just trying to blow off some steam before going to rehab," Roy yelled back to his fuming father.

"Boy, I am about two seconds from calling your bail bondsman and taking you back to jail right now," Jake yelled.

The interrupted sex had caught the wind of the neighbors who called the police. Two uniformed officers, who Jake knew well, showed up at the door and demanded to know what was going on. Jake explained the situation, and the young girl was arrested on an outstanding warrant for possession of narcotics.

Jake searched Roy's room and found a marijuana cigarette half-smoked sitting in the ashtray.

"What the fuck is this boy? Are you doing drugs in my house now?' Jake screamed.

"No, dad, that was hers. She wanted to get high before we did anything." Roy replied.

"Oh, so you let somebody else do drugs in my house?" Jake yelled. "Y'all wanna smoke that shit then do it back in jail."

Jake confiscated Roy's cell phone, flushed the contraband cigarette down the toilet, and locked his doors. Roy protested the removal of his cell phone and Jake ignored him. Jake went to bed and left Roy to spend the night in his room watching a movie.

The next day at the precise time of five o'clock in the morning, Jake woke Roy up. The two went for a three-mile beach run and then went home to cook breakfast. Roy was exhausted by the time he had finished his grits, eggs, toast, two pop tarts, and a glass of orange juice, but Jake made him pack his bags anyway.

The two set out for the hour and a half drive to New Orleans. By the time the pair turned onto Interstate 10 Roy was snoring. Once they got past the daily traffic jam on the High Rise, they exited Interstate 10 onto Claiborne Avenue Roy was awaken again by his father. When they made their turn into the parking lot of the rehab center on Magazine Street, Jake said to Roy, "Alright boy, this is to help you. I will not be checking you out, and you can't leave. You are here to get rid of that habit. Also, if you run from this place or miss court, I am out fifty grand for your bond. Don't fuck this up, son. I love you."

The Charter House in New Orleans was a reputable establishment where they would lock Roy down and keep him away from the internet and reporters. The only way he could be released before completion of his drug treatment was by a court order or by Jake signing his son out.

They pulled up to the building, an old renovated antebellum bed and breakfast condemned by the city after Hurricane Katrina, remodeled and rebuilt to near historical look. It had a gate outside made of wrought iron and operated via remote pin pad or by a switch inside operated by a security guard. The building was surrounded by similar-looking buildings on Magazine Street, which was known for its art decor.

The facility was an all-male, all upper-class clientele and was heavily guarded. It housed twenty or so patients and played a host to about fifty outpatient group meetings for Narcotics and Alcoholics Anonymous. The inpatients and outpatients were kept segregated so that contraband could not be introduced. Security was a solemn part of treatment here.

A security guard with a police-issued forty caliber Glock 22 on his hip walked to the car, no smiles, no warm handshakes or greetings, no welcoming qualities about him at all. Just a simple "ID please." and they were escorted inside once the appointment had been verified via the radio on his hip.

"This place looks like fun," Roy said.

"Shut the fuck up, boy. It's either this, or I'll take your ass back to Pensacola and watch them lock you up." Jake said

"Yes, sir," Roy replied. He knew his father was in no mood for his antics.

They were searched, and Jake was instructed to return to his vehicle with his concealed carry weapon. Roy was strip-searched, the potential client, and separated from his father while a counselor evaluated him.

Jake sat in a waiting room with a receptionist desk and a painting of the Mississippi River on the wall. The other paintings were from Jazz Fest and were dated years earlier. He sat in the room for about ninety minutes until he was led into a room that used to be a bedroom of the old bed and breakfast.

It was a large room with big windows, a vaulted ceiling, and rolled molding that met the walls and ceiling consistent with its age. A man that identified himself as Doctor Meaut walked in with Roy in tow. Doctor Meaut had a long ponytail and a three-day beard that was white with a hint of red in it. He was of average height with a slim build in his fifties with the hard-knowing eyes of a drinker.

"Alright, Mr. Fayard," he said with a drawl. "Here's the deal. You will be admitted to this facility. You are on a bail bond, am I correct?" Doctor Meaut asked.

"Yes, sir," Roy replied.

"Ok," the doctor continued, "First thing is I have spoken with your bail bondsman. All these rules are now a condition of your bond. Violation of these rules will require me to pick up the phone and have you transported back to Florida in handcuffs."

"Yes, sir," Roy said

"You will not leave this facility for any reason. This is a lockdown facility, and it is guarded by off-duty officers with the New Orleans Police Department. Our orderlies are also on contract from the Orleans Parish Prison. They have seen it all, and nothing impresses them. They do not care about your father running for Senate. I DO NOT care about your father running for Senate as he will have some obligations of this facility. You will not leave this campus without permission. You will not engage in any fornication while you are here. You will not possess any drugs, tobacco, cigarette lighters, matches, cell phone, tablets, laptops, currency, credit cards; nothing but your State-issued ID will be acceptable for you to possess. You will go to therapy three times a day. You will take all medications you are prescribed. If you can't handle these conditions, just say the word, and without wasting one more second of my time, you will be locked back up. Do you agree?" Doctor Meaut asked.

"Uhm, I guess....?" Roy replied.

Just then, the doctor pulled out a pair of handcuffs from a desk drawer. "You guess?" he said as he stood up and moved into a position behind Roy.

"YES, SIR, I UNDERSTAND PERFECTLY," Roy shouted as he felt the handcuffs touch his skin.

Doctor Meaut put the cuffs back down and said, "Ok now for you, Mr.

Fayard." looking at Jake, "You will meet these conditions. Failure to do so will violate your son. I understand you have a campaign to run, but treatment is more important than some job you are trying to get in Washington."

Obviously, Doctor Meaut cared nothing about politics or politicians, making his stock with Jake go up quite a bit. "You will be here once a week for therapy. You will attend a family counseling session once a month. If you would like, we can do one right now and get it over with, but next week you will be here for therapy with your son." Doctor Meaut said.

"Yeah, sure, just let me know when," Jake said.

"Except for the therapy sessions, there is going to be no visitation for at least three months," the Doctor said. "The fewer visits we have, the less chance of contraband entering into our facility. You will be searched before entering and after leaving this facility." Doctor Meaut ordered.

"I agree," said Jake.

"Roy, you will be able to place one phone call a week to your father only, and it will be monitored by one of our security staff." Doctor Meaut said.

"What if I want to call my girlfriend," Roy asked.

"What girlfriend? The one that got hauled away from the house in handcuffs?" Jake asked.

"Maybe I didn't make myself clear, Mr. Fayard." Doctor Meaut said. "You will call no one except your father. Just let me know if my rules are too tough, and you can go back to jail. My rules are not flexible, the rules of this facility are not flexible, and I am not flexible."

"Yea, I agree," Roy replied almost to himself.

"What was that? I know I heard a 'sir' in there somewhere!" Jake said with authority.

"Yes, sir, Doctor Meaut, I understand, and I will comply with your rules," Roy said a little louder.

"Ok good deal. I'm not trying to be difficult, but I find that many people enter these doors with a sense of entitlement. I am telling you that you are entitled to nothing except treatment and care. We remove the temptation and outside influences so that we can best manage your care. We don't do this for fun." Doctor Meaut explained.

After the session, Jake drove back to Biloxi. He knew that his son's arrest was enough to kill any chance of him being elected. Mississippi is a very conservative and unforgiving state. The consensus would be, "If you can't raise your son, can you do the job representing Mississippi?" He also knew that his son's arrest was a setup by the Honorable Governor, who hated him.

Jake was hopeful that getting his son treatment would assist him in stopping the drugs, though. Win or lose, as far as the election was concerned; Jake was still a father. He still had obligations to his son and would support him, even if he disapproved of his life decisions, regardless. Roy was a pain in the ass, but at least he did have a good heart. When Roy was sober, he would go out of his way to help anybody he encountered.

Chapter Four

The Dead Senator

Just as you would expect, the honorable Senator Robert Wallace challenged Jake to a debate. "He has been begging for some attention for his failing campaign, and I will oblige him." Senator Wallace said. It wasn't enough to hurt the man's family. He wanted to destroy the reputation of the man personally.

The two candidates danced around a bit on several different news outlets about the impending debate. The debate time and date changed so much over the next two weeks that nobody could keep track. The moderators were selected, and then for one reason or another, usually because of the Wallace camp would be changed. It was a mess.

Jake grew tired of the game. He wanted his message to be heard. He didn't care who the moderator was, what location it was, who was allowed to attend. His only requirement was that the debate be public, and Senator Wallace show up.

Jake accepted the debate, which was to be held at the Mississippi Fairgrounds and Convention Center in Jackson, Senator Wallace's turf. When Jake arrived, he saw a sea of red and white yard signs saying, "RE-ELECT ROBERT WALLACE FOR SENATE" and hearing chants of "SPANK YOUR KID SPANK YOUR KID."

Jake parked his truck near the service entrance and was joined by his friend Coby Barhonovich. The two quickly were surrounded by reporters from several newspapers and TV stations in and around the state. Jake had arrived two hours early with hopes to avoid the ambush but found this to be futile.

Jake was dressed in his best designer suit with an American Flag on his left lapel and the Eagle Globe and Anchor on the right. He heard a few people shout Semper Fi as he took the stage, but the chants and heckles showed him, he was not on his own ground. Senator Robert Wallace was born in Canton, Mississippi, about thirty miles north of Jackson, and he knew his home crowd. He was the son of large plantation owners, and growing up in Madison County, Mississippi, was generally regarded for his old "family money." Unlike most of the south that used the term "family money" loosely, the Wallace family was rich and powerful.

Wallace's great grandfather was a Governor before the Civil War, and his grandfather was one of the original architects of the 1890 Mississippi Constitution.

The moderator was Clayton Burke, a wiry little man with a bowtie, undoubtedly handpicked by the Wallace campaign.

"Good evening, y'all welcome to the Mississippi Fairgrounds for the first debate between our own Senator Robert Wallace and candidate Jake Fayard. Here are the rules of the debate. Everybody will be respectful. I will ask a question, give each candidate two minutes to answer, and thirty seconds to rebut. I have all of the questions that will be asked, and this will be done in an orderly fashion. At the end of the questions that I have asked, I will allow the candidates to ask each other some questions. I will limit this to five minutes. I will also permit a one-minute introduction before the question-and-answer debate forum begins." Burke said with a smile. Jake wanted to slap that bowtie off of him.

Jake researched the moderator before arriving at the debate. He found that the Wallace camp indeed picked the moderator. As it turned out, Burke was the brother-in-law of one of Wallace's cousins. The good ol' boy system in Mississippi was hard at work,

Jake and Wallace introduced themselves to the crowd. While Jake was making his introduction, he was mocked by an attendee, who called Jake a deadbeat father, and a security guard was slow in removing the patron. This irritated Jake as he thought of the gentlemanly pursuit of politics was losing its charm.

The first question was to Wallace. "Mr. Wallace, how long have you been in the Senate?" "Forty-six Long, proud years that I have proudly served with distinction," he responded.

Jake's first question had to do with his stance on foreign relations. Jake answered truthfully that he felt America should take care of our own first and was heckled.

The softball questions to Mr. Wallace were very annoying to Jake as he sat back like a sniper waiting to strike. He finally got his chance when Mr. Wallace was asked about term limits by a Fayard supporter.

"Well, if we have a man that is doing so much for the State, why would you replace him?" he responded.

Jake nailed him with a question. "If absolute power corrupts absolutely, then why would we keep somebody in Washington for so long that they forget where they came from?"

Mr. Wallace went from the warm, grandfatherly figure to a red face bull looking for a brawl.

"How can you say such a thing to me! I have been in office long enough to prove my merit!" Wallace answered.

"Why are you under investigation by Attorney General Coby Barhonovich?" Jake asked with as much contempt as he could muster.

"Isn't that your old college buddy?" Senator Wallace asked.

"Yes, but that's beside the point, sir. He's still the Attorney General, and he is investigating you for corruption and bribery. Is that not true?" Jake asked.

"Have I ever been indicted?" Senator Wallace asked in rebuttal.

"No, sir, you haven't, but you also don't deny that you and the Governor have been under investigation by the

Attorney General, and the Governor, who endorsed you, is under investigation by the Justice Department," Jake said with anger and frustration.

A hush fell over the crowd as the Washington paper pusher and the combat veteran duked it out in a boxing match of words.

"Didn't your son recently get arrested in Florida for possession of cocaine?" Senator Wallace asked sarcastically.

"YOU, SIR, ARE OUT OF LINE!" Jake screamed.

"Alright, y'all, that's enough," the moderator said in a half-laughing voice.

"No, I would like an answer," Mr. Wallace said, "Did your son get arrested recently in Florida for possession of cocaine?"

"Yes, he did, and I am representing him. I do not agree with his choices, and I do not agree with what his life has become, but he is my son, and I do love him. Any man would take care of his family, wouldn't you?" Jake said with sincerity.

Jake was disappointed that he couldn't ask Senator Wallace about the issues. He wanted to make him accountable for his voting record. He tried to hold him responsible for his corruption allegations. He tried to put the political machine on trial for the entire State of Mississippi and the world to see. He wasn't surprised when he didn't get the chance, but he was irritated, nonetheless.

The debate was a disaster which is precisely what the Wallace Camp wanted. They knew he would not win many constituents here with the scandal. Jake was squeaky clean himself, but his son's arrest was hanging over him.

Online opinion polls started shifting rapidly to the Incumbent Senator's favor. Before the debate, Jake had a solid seventy to thirty percent lead.

Two days later, the polls were dwindling to fifty-five to forty-five. By the end of the week, the Incumbent Senator had a fifty-one to forty-nine percent lead. Jake came out of nowhere, completely unexpected, except for a few of his closest friends when he announced his candidacy in February and had a strong campaign.

Jake was a small government, Libertarian-leaning, Conservative Republican that followed the teachings of Former Texas Representative Doctor Ron Paul. He touted his phrase of "Audit the Fed" and wanted the government to live within its means instead of writing a blank check and raising the debt ceiling. He opposed any new taxes and wanted to stop wasteful military spending. This was sort of bittersweet being from a town with one of the largest Air Force Bases in the country and who gave the city most of its economy for decades.

His opposite candidate never saw a spending bill he didn't like. He favored growing the military budget, social entitlements, and everything he could spend the government's money on.

He had opposed the balanced budget amendment passed in the House of Representatives several years ago. He mainly stuck to the party lines of the Democrats but occasionally voted with the Republicans on some Conservative legislation that would fit his plan of being re-elected.

Two weeks after the debate, as he picked up the newspaper on his way to his campaign office, Jake saw the news. Big, bold, black letters, larger than life that read SENATOR WALLACE FOUND DEAD. The headline was shocking to all. Forty-six years a Senator, a loving husband to his third wife, four children, seven grandchildren, a great man had perished. The cause of death was a heart attack caused by a life of drinking too much and smoking too many cigars.

Mourners from all over the country descended upon Jackson. Senatorial colleagues, members of the United States House of Representatives, current and former Governors of various states from as far away as Alaska all showed up for the viewing.

According to most accounts, the former Senator Wallace was a beloved man, but many of the attendees were curious about who the Governor would appoint. Several speculations were rumored to have been heard, but nobody knew for sure. Senator Wallace's body hadn't had time to get cold yet, and people were gunning for his job from all over the State of Mississippi.

The self-serving "stuff shirt" convention, as Coby Barhonovich called it, was something neither he nor Jake wanted any part of. Jake made a brief appearance to show some form of respect, but he was not well received. He heard a few people whisper and wonder why he was there, to begin with. He heard some aids of the dead Senator mention something about Jake salivating over the death. Jake simply ignored the innuendos and accusations.

"What the hell are you doing here?" The Governor snapped as he caught a glimpse of the man in the grey suit.

"Paying my respects. Good morning Governor." Jake responded plainly, almost with no emotion.

"You're not worthy of being here. Why don't you go back to the coast and take that little bastard sorry excuse of a dope head son of yours back to jail where he belongs and get the hell out of here." The Governor snapped.

Jake didn't respond. He knew the Governor was baiting him, and a reporter with a camera was close by. Jake saw the setup and wisely decided not to react. The party broke up, and Jake returned to Biloxi.

This untimely passing of Senator Wallace upset the old guard of Mississippi, and the Governor went into panic mode. "Who will I appoint?" Governor Creel asked his closest confidant, a highway patrol investigator named George Walter, who cleaned up messes for the governor and was rumored to be a major part of the bum rap.

George Walter was one of the meanest, nastiest, most corrupt people in the State of Mississippi. He was an older man, about sixty years old, with a fat stomach from spending little time at the gym. He had a military crew cut that was grey and a pencil-thin mustache that had turned white. He may have looked the part of a fit officer of the law thirty years ago, but the excellent shape he may have once been in to pass the elite Mississippi Highway Patrol academy had since faded gravely.

It was once said that he shot a suspect and claimed self-defense stating he came at him with a knife. The alleged suspect owed a gambling debt to a loan shark that used him as a collector.

Investigator Walter may have held the title of Sergeant Major of the Mississippi Highway Patrol, Troop C, but was seldom seen in uniform lately or at the office. He had an unmarked dark blue Ford Crown Victoria with license plate MHP C03. He used this car primarily for personal reasons and to clean up the Governor's mess.

"It's got to be somebody strong enough to beat that son of a bitch on the coast," the Governor said. "I have ten days to defeat this asshole, and I want a man that will take orders!"

"Do you have anybody in mind?" Walter asked

"Yes, I have somebody in mind, but he may take some convincing," Governor Creel said.

"Who is it?" Walter asked.

"The Attorney General. He can't investigate us if he owes his career to us, and if he doesn't take orders well, you will just have to off him." The Governor said with a laugh.

"Seems a little risky, but what the hell you are the one in office," Walter responded skeptically.

"I think I'll call him into my office today and see what he thinks. George, thanks for passing by. The next time we meet will be at the mansion. Bring your wife and kids, and I'll have the cook make some of the finest baby backs you have ever had." The Governor said.

"See you later, Billy," Walter replied.

George Walter was the only man who could call the governor "Billy" to his face. The two shared so much dirt over the years that the informality was almost overlooked. There was no other law enforcement officer, even the Commissioner of the Mississippi Department of Public Safety, which had so much access to the Governor. No one man could speak to the Honorable William Creel in the manner that George Walter could.

At precisely on cue at nine o'clock in the morning, the Governor called the Honorable Coby Barhonovich esquire on his cell phone. Coby had just returned from a meeting at his Alma Mater, Mississippi State University in Starkville. The previous night, he was giving a speech to a group of Political Science students.

"What the hell do you want?" Coby answered rudely.

"That's no way to talk to a man who is giving you a job," The Governor said.

"What job? Investigating the death of your buddy? Who do you want to pin it on?" Coby said with sarcasm.

"No, no, it's nothing like that. I want to talk to you about something else. Can you come by the Mansion?" Governor Creel asked.

"Why the fuck would I want to do that?" Coby responded with no respect for the Governor at all.

"Just come by for lunch. I have a proposition for you." The Governor said.

"Should I bring my gun?" Coby asked sarcastically.

"No, no man, let's be gentlemen about this. Just come by, and let's talk." The Governor said pleasantly.

"Fine, I'll drop by to talk, but I'll be damned if I break bread with you," Coby responded.

"Alright, Coby, see you at noon." The Governor said.

Coby hung up without saying goodbye. "What does that mother fucker want with me?" he thought.

Coby walked into his office, opened a drawer in his old roll-top desk, an heirloom that was passed down by his grandfather, who was the first attorney in his family and pulled out a .40 caliber Smith and Wesson M&P Shield, put it into his conceal carry holster and went back to his secretary's desk.

"Cancel all my appointments and call a bail bondsman. I have a meeting with the Governor, and if I'm not back by two, call the jail." She laughed and said, "I'm sure you'll be alright, but if you shoot him, just be nice and don't shoot him in his pretty face."

"Fuck his face." Coby said as he slammed the door.

Coby walked downstairs, exited the building onto High Street, walked to his brand new Z71 Chevy Truck, and drove to the Rankin County Courthouse in Brandon. He had to discuss something with a prosecutor about a case they were trying. When he arrived and handled the business at hand, he told the prosecutor, "Man, you ain't gonna believe this shit. The governor wants to meet with me the day after that pig-headed bastard died. Ain't this a crazy world?"

The prosecutor replied, "Well, maybe he wants to appoint you as his replacement. "And then laughed.

"Yeah, that'll be the fuckin day," Coby said.

Coby arrived at the Governor's Mansion a little afternoon. He wanted to show the Governor that his contempt was ever-present. A protest about the Governor ignoring a recent medical marijuana ballot initiative was taking place on the sidewalk outside the Governor's Mansion, and Coby was immediately accosted. He smiled at the twenty something year old college kid who was holding a sign and shouting in the general direction of the mansion.

"Hey kid come here." Coby said to the kid.

"Yeah what do you want?" The kid snapped.

"I'll give you a hundred bucks if you move to the rear of the building and use your bullhorn loudly. If anybody says anything to you tell them you have permission from the Attorney General. Here's my card." Coby replied as he handed the kid the business card and two fifty-dollar bills. The kid readily complied.

Coby walked into the large house on Capitol Street with large white columns and reminiscent of something from the antebellum age when slavery and cotton was king in Mississippi. Shortly after Coby laid eyes on the Governor, he heard the bullhorn. The Governor sent three of his security officers outside to deal with the noise and then greeted Coby.

"Welcome, my friend; come on in and welcome to my home!" the Governor greeted Coby warmly.

"Oh, we're friends now?" Coby said as he thought about the pistol in his waist. The marble floor would be too expensive to clean the blood from for the taxpayers to handle, he decided.

"Yes, we're friends. We are both public servants, and both should behave like gentlemen." the Governor replied.

"Sounds like you have quite a party outside. Your fans love you." Coby said smugly.

"Oh, I suspect it'll quiet down soon" The Governor replied.

Yeah that's typical. We all know you don't like anybody who dares to speak against your sorry ass. Anyway, what the fuck do you want, Governor? Are you here to waste my time as usual?" Coby said with no regard for the man who had summoned him.

"Ok, well, can't we at least be cordial?" The Governor asked, very guarded, and stepped back from Coby.

"Ok fine. Cordially, what the fuck do you want?" Coby said.

"Ok, as I'm sure you know, Senator Wallace died yesterday morning." The Governor said with a sense of sadness.

"Yeah, so.....?" Coby said without emotion.

"So, would you like to be his replacement?" The Governor asked.

Coby looked at the Governor with as much confusion and contempt as he could muster.

"Are you fucking kidding me? You would appoint me... somebody who is going to piss on your grave... as your bitch boy's replacement?" Coby said with resentment.

"Yes, if you accept. I need the voters to know that we in Mississippi want new blood. We want the world to know that we are changing. The sixties are over, and the politicians from that era will reign no more. Are you up to the job?" The Governor asked.

"Let me think about it, Governor," Coby said.

"Keep it under your hat Senator Barhonovich," the Governor said, smiling.

The two parted without shaking hands, and Coby returned to his office.

Upon returning to his truck, Coby immediately called Jake. "Man, you ain't gonna believe this shit..... That son of a bitch in the Governor's Mansion has flipped his fuckin lid."

"What do you mean, man?" Asked Jake

"He wants me to replace Wallace. Can you believe that shit?" Coby said.

"Uh... Seriously dude? Does he not realize you target shoot with pictures of him?" Jake asked, confused.

"I almost shot him today, but he ain't worth my bullets," Coby said.

They both laughed, and Jake finally said, "Dude, if you take it, that will pit us against each other. They would love that, but I can't figure out any other angle."

"I'm not going to take it and run against you, bro. We were roommates at Tulane, served together in Iraq, and you are my brother. I am my brother's keeper, and we keep it on the level." Coby promised.

"Let's keep them on the Square," Jake replied.

Coby realized that he had a chance to toy with the big wigs in Jackson and upset the old guard, but he would never run against his friend.

Later that evening, a dark blue Ford Crown Victoria bearing the license plate MHP C03 was spotted in Biloxi. It was parked across the street from the campaign office of Jake Fayard. A security officer was pulled away from his post by a homeless man digging in a dumpster, and that's when Investigator George Walter made his move. He placed some illegal wiretaps in the telephones of the campaign headquarters and a key logger on all the computers and bugs in the walls. There was nothing about this campaign that the Governor wasn't going to know about. He completed his work in under one hour then returned to Jackson.

The next day Jake Fayard entered his office and began his attack. He started calling everybody he knew that he could trust that was close to the Governor to determine who he would nominate. Mississippi Law says that the Governor has ten days to appoint a new Senator upon the vacation of office by the predecessor. By lunch, he hadn't heard anything, but a few names were floating around.

Clayton Harlan, a big-time supporter of the Governor and the Mayor of Hattiesburg,

Trent Allen, the Mayor of Biloxi, but this was unlikely as he and Jake were close friends,

Christine Stacy, The Mayor of Grenada and a longtime ally of the Governor,

Terri Lamar, the Lieutenant Governor, but this too was unlikely because she had gone against the Governor on gay rights legislation,

Finally, was Jake's old friend Coby Barhonovich, the Attorney General, who hated the Governor.

None of these choices made much sense as the Governor wanted a "Yes man." None of these people save for Clayton Harlan of Hattiesburg would fit that bill, but he was seventy years old and was in poor health himself. The old guard was dying out rapidly. "Who's it gonna be?" Jake thought.

Joe Holloway was on one of his many sign runs while Jake did his research. Along the way, he received a phone call from George Walter and relayed Jake's day's movements.

 "He's trying to figure out who the Governor will get to replace Wallace," Joe said.

"Let him keep guessing. He will never see this coming." George said with a hint of pride.

"Well, I hope it's a good one. Little Dope head is in New Orleans, and that seems to be weighing on his mind. He seems to be a little out of focus." Joe replied.

George liked that Jake was out of focus. The news of this was relayed to the Governor with a smile, and the two conspirators shared a drink over the thought. Politics in Mississippi was played by keeping someone down and kicking them while they were there. It was a game that the Governor and his political machine knew well. The last person who ran against him fell victim and had to leave the state. The Governor relished this and hoped that Jake would do the same.

Jake was deep in research. It was nearing eight o'clock in the evening when he finally ordered something to eat. He had been going since five-thirty that morning, and his only fuel had been coffee. He ordered a pizza, ate it, and went back to work. By the time he left the suite, it was almost midnight.

Jake returned to his campaign headquarters at five o'clock the following day with the carefully compiled information. None of his staff was at the suite yet, and Jake turned on his radio. The Jazz CD he bought was Kermit Ruffins, and the sounds of New Orleans comforted him. Jake enjoyed the leftover cold pizza for breakfast and then took a break from the computer to tidy up the small office.

He moved a large stack of signs from the main part of the suite and into a closet in his office. When he was carrying the last pile, he bumped his telephone off of his desk. The handset fell from the cradle and came crashing to the floor with a thud. The handset was destroyed. Small pieces of plastic, wire and electronic circuit board covered the floor. One of the tiny devices that George Walter placed in the telephone was mixed in with the debris. Jake was too tired to notice and put most of it in the trash.

Jake took a two-hour nap on one of the sofas in the main part of the suite. When he awoke, Joe Holloway was entering the office. The two startled each other, and Joe decided to make coffee.

Jake returned to his office to find a curious-looking piece of debris on the floor and picked it up. It had a long cylindrical part with what looked like a speaker assembly. Jake wasn't sure what this was, but it looked curious enough that he kept the piece and placed it in a drawer in his desk. He would have it examined later and decided it would be best to keep his guard up.

Jake recalled a State Senator from the Pine Belt region of Mississippi who went against the grain several years ago that was all but destroyed when he beat Senator Wallace in the Primary Election but lost in the Runoff for not having fifty percent plus one vote. The State Senator from Laurel was called out by the Republican Party, who used Mississippi's open primaries to garner Democrat's votes and beat the politicians that were not handpicked by the Republican big wigs.

The candidate only narrowly beat Wallace in the Primary election, which was split three ways. There was all manner of smearing and underhanded deals involved, and the whole state knew it. Court battles lasted for months, and the young State Senator was decimated. Going against the grain is a dangerous thing in Mississippi. He knew the Governor would stop at nothing to attempt to discredit him, and with everything that happened, Jake was on high alert.

Chapter Five

Justice in Dixie

Jake decided to work on the campaign strategy a little more. He was in the process of planning his campaign tour of the Mississippi Delta. He made plans to stop in Greenwood, Greenville, Indianola, Grenada, Clarksdale, Tunica, Batesville, Senatobia, and even smaller towns like Rolling Fork, Belzoni, and other cities that were usually not on the whistle-stop of Republican candidates. The Delta was mainly poor black farmers. The education level was deficient, and nobody seemed to care about it.

The Mississippi Delta is one of the poorest places in the entire United States and has been riveted with racism, and the ruling elite in Jackson had forgotten. Jake knew if he could win the Delta, he could win the election.

Historically the Delta was impoverished, black, and democrat-voting. The Republican party had long since forgotten the area, which made up about one-third of the state.

Just then, the phone rang. "Hello?" Jake answered.

"Are you Jake Fayard?" the voice asked.

"Yes, sir, how may I help you?" Jake said, confused.

"This is Senator John Kennard. I heard about your problems with your son, and I have also heard other things. Can you meet me at my office in Jackson this afternoon?" The voice replied.

"Yes, sir, I sure can. I can be there in three hours if you would like." Jake said.

"Ok, meet me here at 650 High Street in Jackson as soon as you can. I'll wait on you." Senator Kennard said.

"Ok, sir, I am leaving now," Jake said.

"Oh, one more thing. Tell nobody that we are meeting up. As far as the world knows, I am in Washington, and I don't want anybody to know I am in the State." Senator Kennard said.

"Yes, sir, I will. I'm on my way. Thank you. Goodbye." Jake replied.

Jake did what he was told. He made the long drive-up Highway 49 to Jackson. It was such a relaxing drive through the piney woods and the small towns. He stopped at an old BBQ joint just south of Hattiesburg and got some lunch to go. Mississippi was known for its great food and Southern Hospitality. He took the bypass around Hattiesburg to save time, and unbeknownst to him; he was being followed by a dark blue Ford Crown Victoria driven by George Walter. He kept to the speed limit and drove as carefully as possible.

About the time he reached Magee, a mere forty miles from Jackson, his cell phone rang.

"Hello?" Jake answered.

"Hey, brother, where the hell are you?" the voice belonging to the Attorney General demanded.

"I'm on my way up to Jackson. Do me a favor and meet me when I get done with my rat killin." Jake said.

"Alright, man, just watch your ass. I got a bad feeling about some things." Coby warned.

"I'll see ya tonight," Jake said.

He hung up and made it to the Senators office.

Jake Fayard had never met Senator Kennard in person. This was an honor as he had always admired the man. He was greeted with a violent handshake by a man in his late fifties that could have passed for a youth in his twenties. His perfect smile and tailored suit told the story of success on Capitol Hill. A few moments later, a bald headed middle aged Black man appeared in a black off the rack suit and produced a badge.

"U.S. Department of Justice, huh"? Jake exclaimed.

"Oh, don't worry, I'm not after you." The agent replied. "Agent Albert Ford at your service, sir."

Agent Albert Ford was a striking man, six foot five inches tall and about 275 pounds with almost no body fat. He was a serious gym rat and wanted people to know it. He was in his late fifties but looked like he was in his mid-30's. Agent Ford had been with the Department of Justice for twenty years and worked organized crime. Him and Senator Kennard knew each other when Kennard was an agent with the Federal Bureau of Investigation and the two had long remained close friends.

"Jake Fayard, nice to meet you, sir. Welcome to Mississippi." Jake replied pleasantly.

"Mr. Fayard, I have heard about your son. A federal crime was committed when he allegedly crossed state lines with the drugs...." Agent Ford said.

"... NOW WAIT ONE GOD DAMN MINUTE........" Jake exclaimed with pure rage

"Mr. Fayard, relax, sir. I am not here to investigate or arrest your son. I want the man that planted the drugs on him. The Florida Department of Law Enforcement investigated at their crime lab in Pensacola at the direction of the Justice Department. Other than the drugs being in your son's car, his fingerprints were nowhere to be found on the dope itself. We have no way other than them being in his car to link him to the cocaine." Agent Ford explained.

"So, what are you saying, Agent Ford?" Jake asked, almost in a panic.

"What I am saying is I know it was a setup. I can't prove it beyond a reasonable doubt enough to take to court, but if you allow us to make this a federal case, we can do what needs to be done in the interest of justice."

Just then, another agent, a younger white man with a high and tight haircut named Jones walked in and asked, "Mr. Fayard do you know any reason the Mississippi Highway Patrol would have followed you?"

"No, I obeyed the speed limit and didn't run any red lights," Jake replied.

"Well, an investigator is taking an awfully hard look at your truck. Here's a picture. Do you recognize this man?" Jones said.

The agent produced a picture of George Walter.

"No, sir, I don't know who that is," Jake said.

The agent continued, "That is George Walter. We have had him under investigation for a long time, but we can't get anything to stick that would be considered a federal crime. He is a Sergeant Major with the Mississippi Highway Patrol and is the dirtiest bastard I have ever seen in my sixteen years with the Department. He's so crooked that when he dies, we'll have to screw him into the ground." Agent Jones said.

"Ok, so why is he following me?" Jake asked.

Agent Ford stepped up and said, "We think he planted the drugs on your son. He may have been the source of the anonymous call. His job with the Highway Patrol as an investigator is all for show. His real job is cleaning up after Governor Creel. I would watch your back around him if I were you. He doesn't mind getting his hands dirty."

"So, what do you want me to do," Jake asked.

"Well, if you help us, we can help you. We want to sweep your office and see if anything has been planted there. We swept Senator Kennard's office and found all manner of bugs and devices. That's why we have surveillance set up while the office is unoccupied." Agent Ford said.

"What the fuck is this, the Italian Mob?" Jake exclaimed, "They think they can pull this secret police bullshit on citizens of this State?"

"Jake, they have been using tactics of the former Mississippi Sovereignty Commission. The only difference is instead of using this against Black people and civil rights; they are using this against anybody they feel threatened by. They also, instead of using the private citizens who were rabid racists like they did in the old days, they use extra-legal means, and when that fails, they use your friend outside." Senator Kennard said.

The Mississippi Sovereignty Commission was a fascist state agency created in 1956 and disbanded in 1977 that used violence and coercion to combat civil rights. It was highly effective in the 1960s employing the terrorist group known as the Ku Klux Klan and the White Citizens Council to kill brave men like Vernon Dahmer, Medgar Evers, and the three civil rights workers, James Cheney, Micky Schwerner, and Andrew Goodman. They used the State to sanction surveillance against private citizens who dared to challenge the State's anti-civil rights stances. If the Governor was employing their methods, somebody's life could be in danger, and Jake knew it.

"Oh my god, y'all are serious!" Jake exclaimed, "Three fucking wars, twenty years in the Marine Corps, and I come home to Mississippi to deal with this bullshit... lovely... just lovely."

Jake reached in his jacket and retrieved a Glock 21 .45 Caliber pistol from a shoulder holster. "I'll tell you what. Let that mother fucker come near me again, and I'll drop him like a dirty shirt badge or no badge."

"Put the weapon down, Jake," Agent Ford ordered. "It's not worth it. Let us do our job, and we'll nail this asshole to the cross."

"Alright, fine," Jake said as he holstered the weapon. "You better do it soon because this is the wrong Marine to fuck with today."

"Can we sweep your office in the morning?" Agent Ford asked cautiously and watching Jake's hands.

Jake thought about the device he found only this morning and got nervous. Jake had a basic understanding of electronics being a ham radio operator. Still, he was very much out of date with technology as many things had changed in the years since he last built anything.

"Yes, and I have an idea. If you find anything, act like you didn't. Leave em right where they are, identify them to me only, and leave em alone. I got a ploy for this dude that will drive him bat shit crazy." Jake said.

"I can do that, Jake. What's the plan?" Agent Ford asked.

"I'll call you tomorrow. I am going to include one other person in this, and he would make the perfect dance partner." Jake said.

"Jake, I'm not supposed to be here," Senator Kennard said, "Nobody can know I am here."

"I trust this man with my life, and I did several times over the last years in multiple countries. I can damn sure trust him in my own backyard." Jake said.

"You mean your friend the Attorney General? You know Creel wants him to take Wallace's spot, right?' Ford said

"No, I mean my brother, the Attorney General. Me and you might be friends. Coby Barhonovich is my brother." Jake replied.

The company parted ways, and Jake called Coby to ask where they were meeting up.

"Meet me at my office in thirty minutes." Coby demanded, "Some shit is fixing to go down."

When the two met up, there were no warm smiles or handshakes. It was all business, and raw emotion, almost panic, from the both of them as Jake explained what had just happened.

"Kennard and two DOJ Agents met with you and told you to watch your ass? What do you have in mind?" Coby asked in a panic.

"Well," Jake said, "I want you to toy with the Governor about his proposal."

"Do you mean to tell that son of a bitch I want to run against my brother?" Coby gasped

"Yes, I want you to butter him up like a biscuit and pump him for information. Make him think your friendship with me can be bought with a Senatorial appointment. Play the Judas he wants you to be. When he's all done, we can feed him his ass. Make this look good though we have eight days to do it," Jake said.

"Man, I don't know. Do you think he's that stupid?" Coby asked.

"No, but I'm working on other things as well," Jake said.

"Alright, man, let's do it. I just hope this doesn't come back to bite you in the ass." Coby said.

Later that night, Jake drove back to Biloxi. He had informed Agent Ford when he could sweep the office this weekend. Until then, he would tell his campaign volunteers privately and quietly to watch what they say around the office without going into too much detail. He had no idea how he would explain why they had to keep a hushed tone, but he would try to reassure them that everything was ok.

While Jake was on his way to the coast, another meeting took place between two unlikely allies. Joe Holloway, the faithful and trusted campaign manager for Jake Fayard for Senate, had called his old friend George Walter. The two had met up in a motel room on the Biloxi beachfront to exchange information about the events of the week.

"Does he know anything?" Investigator George Walter asked

"Hell no, he's worried about little Junior Dope head," Joe responded

"Aww, well, just keep watching him. Here put this in your pocket." and Joe was handed a wad of folded over money. "Governor Creel sends his warmest regards."

"Well, you tell the Governor I surely appreciate this very much," Joe said.

"Just call me if anything suspicious happens. Here's the key to the office back. I won't be needing it again." Walter said.

"Did you plant the wires already?" Joe asked.

"Yeah, man, I planted them wires the other night. Nice rent a cop, by the way." Walter said with a smile.

"I handpicked him—a real Barney Fife. I told him his job was to run off anybody trying to break in the back, so he keeps a hard watch on the rear of the building. You could set off a bomb in the front, and he would still be looking the other way." Joe laughed.

"Well then," the investigator laughed, "Sounds like my kinda night watchman."

The next day went by without incident. Jake ran his office as usual, and Joe acted like the friend Jake believed him to be. Just your typical Friday of answering phone calls and scheduling press conferences. A reporter from the local TV station interviewed Jake and asked what he thought about local issues such as the Mississippi State Flag, and he gave his thoughts. "We voted to keep the Confederate symbol on the flag in 2001 by a two to one margin. I respect the voter's opinion and think we should move on." Jake said.

The Mississippi State Flag had long since been under fire. The Confederate emblem in the canton had been there since 1894 but, starting in the 1990s, had come under fire for Mississippi's racist past. Originally it was a unity flag used to heal the wounds of Reconstruction and unite Mississippi under the Union again. Still, that meaning had been lost by people who needed something to complain about. The citizenry generally had strong feelings one way or the other on the issue.

Once, at a City Council meeting Jake had attended for an unrelated topic, a fistfight broke out between two people who were on opposite sides of the debate. "So much for common civility," Jake thought as the two were whisked away in handcuffs. Overall, it was a non-issue to Jake because a US Senator had almost no control over a State Flag. "Just another reporter with an agenda" was the usual thought when such questions were asked.

The following day Jake was met at the office door by Agent Ford and several other DOJ Agents. Their names escaped him as the introductions were brief, but Jake let them in to do their jobs. He served them coffee and doughnuts from the best bakery in Biloxi. The Back Bay Bakery had been operated in Biloxi since 1954 and had a wide selection of almost anything you ever wanted. "I'm gonna get fat," Agent Ford said as he ate his third cherry triangle. "Do y'all ever do anything but eat down here?" Jake replied with "Yea, try to frame people for felonies they didn't commit."

Jake went to his desk to retrieve the electronic device that he found a couple of days before. He showed it to the agents, and they closely examined it.

"This is what we call a micro-interceptor. The FBI used these in the early 1990s, but nobody has used them in the last couple of decades. Where did you find it?" The agent asked Jake.

"I knocked my phone off my desk when I was moving some things, and the receiver was smashed to bits," Jake replied. "That was in the debris."

"That thing is a relic." Agent Ford said. "I wonder where they even found one."

"Well, whoever had it, must have some ties to law enforcement." The other agent responded. "We're the only ones to have that kind."

After the morning of bug detection and digital scanners with frequency readers and all sorts of other things that Jake didn't even want to think about, he left with Agent Ford and another agent named Cates to a hotel suite at one of the large casinos that dotted the coast. There they discussed what they had found and where.

"Man, whoever put those bugs in your phone was good," Cates said. "They were done with such precision I almost didn't catch them."

"What do you mean?" Jake asked

"Well, they were dropped in and connected to a small power wire. It was hard-wired to the phone so that the listener could hear both sides of the call and any other conversation near the phone. It was then transmitted to a small receiver hooked to a computer placed in the ceiling. The computer is hooked to the internet using your Wi-Fi complete with your Wi-Fi password and then accessed from an outside source." Cates said, nearly impressed with the work of George Walter.

"Oh, that's lovely," Jake said, "How did they get my password?"

"You have a leak," Ford said

"The only people who know anything about my Wi-Fi password are me and Joe Holloway, my campaign manager," Jake said.

"Well, there ya go. I think you found the source of your problems." Agent Ford replied.

"That son of a bitch knows everything." Jake said, "I didn't tell him about this, but he hired that stupid rent a cop that couldn't find tits on Bourbon Street during Mardi Gras, and I bet that's why." Jake said.

"Don't let the cat out of the bag yet," Ford said. "Just act normal and don't fire him. We need this to be kept low for now."

"Fire my ass. I wanna beat the hell out of the little son of a bitch." Jake snapped back.

Chapter Six

Judas rears his ugly head

Monday morning at the bright and early time of five-thirty, Jake took off on his morning run. The beach was quiet with a slight breeze off of the Gulf. The weather was already humid, though, almost 100 percent. The temperature was about seventy-five degrees, a warm, muggy morning, which Biloxi was known for in the late Spring.

Jake ran three miles a day just to keep in shape. His Parris Island habits had not ceased, and his daily workout regimen included a three-mile beach run, fifty push-ups, fifty sit-ups, and a cool off walk of at least one mile. He liked running at these times. The beach was quiet, with only an occasional car passing by. The tide was low, so he chose to run on the hard-packed sand. On the way home, he walked across the boardwalk that sat on top of the old seawall.

Biloxi beach was an artificial beach twenty-six miles long and followed the coastline down US Highway 90 in Harrison County. Highway 90 at points would veer off from the sand beach to allow a parking area, and at other times the East Bound lanes would only be a few feet away. Occasionally US 90 would break contact with the beach to allow for a hotel or casino on the south side of the road. Once off the boardwalk and on the seawall, he would be very near the highway.

Not long after he hit the seawall, around St. George Street, a car pulled close to him. "Jake, get in the car!" a voice ordered. Jake recognized the voice as his campaign manager Joe Holloway. He did as he was told and asked, "Man, just what in the hell is going on?"

"Your good buddy Coby? He is going to accept an appointment from the Governor. To make matters worse, he is investigating you for campaign fund fraud."

Jake smiled at this and thought, "Yup, I got him, I finally got him."

"What the hell is he going to investigate me for?' Jake asked, "I haven't done anything wrong, and I have submitted my finance records early every time."

"He might find an error I made when I submitted my last quarterly report. We were so pressed for time with the deadline YOU set that I forgot to include MSPAC contributions from the previous three weeks."

"Oh well, it's an honest mistake, and that can be easily corrected." Jake said, "How do you know this stuff anyway?"

"I have friends in low places. That's why you hired me." Joe replied

"Yeah, well, so did Garth Brooks, but what's your point." Jake thought, mentally strangling this little worm he had been annoyed by before he had a chance to have his morning cup of coffee.

"Everything is under control. I'll put out a press statement later this morning. Now, in the meantime, may I pretty please finish my run?"

"Yeah, sure, man, go ahead. See you at the office in a couple of hours." Joe answered, not realizing that he had seriously upset the balance of the day.

Jake got out of the car, and as soon as Joe was out of sight, he called the Attorney General. "Coby, I see you have taken the appointment." Jake said, "Congrats on it, Senator. The investigation into my finance was a nice touch."

"How did you hear about that already? I just initiated the paperwork last night." Coby shot back.

"A little worm interrupted my morning run to annoy me with this information," Jake replied.

"Oh well, tell Captain Dumbass I said hello when you see him at the office today," Coby said.

"I'll be sure to do that. When do you meet with his majesty again?" Jake asked.

"He wants me for lunch at the Mansion. He's having his chef make some baby-backs. I'd rather a shrimp po boy, but they don't cook like that up here in Jackson." Coby answered.

"Well, play nice. I want him on ice until we nail him." Jake reminded.

"You're asking a lot, my friend," Coby said.

"Play nice with the Governor, and I'll have someone deliver you a po boy for supper. Deal?" Jake laughed.

"Deal. Now go get a shower. I can smell you all the way up here." Coby laughed.

"Later, brother, let's nail his ass," Jake said.

He hung up the phone and continued his morning ritual uninterrupted. When Jake arrived at the campaign office, Joe was already there.

"Listen, Chuckle fuck" Jake yelled at Joe. "Don't you EVER interrupt my morning again with that bullshit. Do you understand me? I don't think of the campaign while I'm running. All I think about is running." Jake was standing over him with a clenched fist.

"My bad, dude, I'm sorry it won't happen again. I just wanted you to know what was up with your friend, is all," Joe replied, almost ducking from the inevitable punch that wouldn't be thrown.

The rest of the day, Joe avoided Jake like the plague. He spent most of the day placing signs all over the coast in prime locations.

A camera crew showed up at the campaign office to cut a commercial. Jake had a room cleaned, and a Green Board installed. He changed his suit to a pair of jeans and a polo shirt. A microphone was seated on his shirt, and a shotgun microphone was used as well. "I am Jake Fayard. I stand on the principles of freedom, liberty, and small government. I will never pass any new taxes while I am in office. I will reduce the size, scope, and role of government; I will never pass any gun control legislation. I was a Marine Colonel, and I fought for you in three wars, and I will fight for you in Washington."

He didn't want any fancy TV special effects or images of him swinging a hammer. He vetoed the use of the Eagle Globe and Anchor on the commercial. He wanted people to vote based solely on his merits. He fired a former associate for even suggesting things like a smear campaign or robocalls. He also didn't want out-of-state help. "If they don't live in Mississippi, then I don't want them on the campaign trail." He got a check from a significant contributor from out of state, and he ordered his secretary to send it back with a proper and polite "no thank you" letter. He wanted the people of the Great State of Mississippi and only the people of Mississippi on his team.

He cut one more commercial, and it was a fifteen-second recording. Jake was standing in front of the Mississippi flag superimposed over the US Capitol Building. "I love Mississippi; she is the land of my birth; she has so much to offer this great country of ours from new ships to rockets. I am Jake Fayard, and I want Mississippi to be as great as she can."

At six o'clock that evening, he dismissed everybody and called Coby from his truck. "Hey, brother, how goes it with the Governor?"

"He said he's looking at other people. I guess he wants me to find something with my 'investigation' into you." Coby answered.

"Find it. Chuckle Fuck said he forgot some kind of donation in my campaign finance report." Jake remarked.

"Joe Holloway would forget his head if it wasn't so far up his ass," Coby said.

"Yeah, that's kinda my thoughts too." Jake agreed.

"I have a meeting at the Mansion for lunch tomorrow. Allegedly he had something urgent come up and had to reschedule his appointments. Let's see what happens." Coby said.

"Alright, watch your six. I don't trust him," Jake said.

The phone went dead, and Jake retired for the evening.

At noon precisely as requested, Coby parked his truck at the Governor's Mansion. He walked up the stairs and admired the polished wood and marble. He was treated with a tonic the

Governor loved, a mixture of Bourbon and Sweet Tea. The baby backs were on a large stainless steel propane grill in the backyard, and baked beans were in the kitchen. The Governor and George Walter were already discussing something when Coby walked up.

"Coby, this is George Walter." the Governor said. "He's going to be in on this conversation. We go back to when his hair was brown, and mine was red."

Coby already knew precisely who Investigator George Walter was, up to and including the size of his boots, but he pleasantly introduced himself anyway in an attempt to act cordial and sincere.

"Alright, you got me curious." Coby finally said, "Why do you want me to replace Wallace?"

"I want you because I want somebody honest. Somebody who can be trusted to do what's right. Somebody who will protect Mississippi's interests as well as takes care of those who got him where he is." The Governor said with a plastic smile.

"So, in other words, you want me to be your bitch" Coby blurted out, his temper getting the best of him

"No, if I wanted a 'bitch' as you say, I would pick a man that knows how to take orders." The Governor said

"I haven't taken orders since I hung up my uniform." Coby said, "In fact, I don't even take them from my wife."

"Let's get something to eat," The Governor said

"I told you I refuse to share a meal with you," Coby replied. "The thought of watching you stuff your mouth the same way that you are trying to stuff my ears with your bullshit is completely unappealing to me. Say what you asked me here to tell me so that I can get back to work. I have a lot of lawsuits to deal with stemming from your mis-leadership."

Coby was mentally dreaming of his boot meeting the governor's throat. He would indict the distinguished George Walter if it weren't for the eventual pardon that the pompous ass in the grey suit two feet from him would grant. He knew of at least four dead bodies he could pin on this George guy in the Highway Patrol uniform, but he knew he would never see the inside of a jail over it.

"Will you consider my offer?" The Governor asked

"Only if you give me a good reason, and I better be satisfied with the answer," Coby replied

"I told you. I want a man with balls to sit that Senate seat." The Governor said.

"Oh, balls, I have plenty of, but what I don't have is patience for bullshit. Make your point, or I'm leaving and the next time I return here it will be with half a dozen Federal Agents with arrest warrants." Coby hissed.

"Just think about it, please. I want you for this job." The Governor said with an attempt to be sincere.

Coby's face was the color of a beet. He was so red-faced and full of rage that he could have killed them both right then and there. He felt his blood almost boiling and decided to take his leave.

"I'll see the two of you sons of bitches in hell," Coby said as he walked out. "Oh, and by the way, quit fucking with my God-son."

Coby got in his truck, squealing his tires as he drove off, and got angrier by the second. "God, how I would love to keel haul both of them behind my boat," he thought.

He called Jake, who was in the middle of cutting a radio commercial. "Hey bro, I'll call you back in a few hours. I'm a little busy," he said and hung the phone up before Coby could get a word out.

Coby decided to skip out on the rest of his afternoon. He drove to the coast and met up with Jake in person. Three hours later, he was sitting outside of Jake's house, and he noticed something out of the corner of his eye, a dark blue Ford Crown Victoria with a face he vividly recognized.

Coby pulled his truck pistol, a shiny Smith and Wesson Model 629 with three speed loaders, from his glovebox and walked up to the car, then stuck the barrel up to the window. "Why the fuck are you following me?" he demanded.

"Woah, relax, put the pistol down. I just came to talk face to face." George Walter said, his voice trembling.

"Mother fucker, I will pop your head like a champagne cork. You ever had a .44 Magnum suppository?" Coby shouted, "Why the fuck are you following me? Do you have a death wish?"

"No, I don't have a death wish, but I just wanted to talk." The Investigator said, shaking.

"Alright, if you want to talk, I wanna see your fuckin hands. Here's what I want you to do. You will step the fuck out of the car using your left hand to open the door and keeping your right hand on the steering wheel. If you do anything other than my orders, I will blow your mother fucking scalp off." Coby shouted.

George Walter complied all too eagerly, and when he was adequately searched for weapons, Coby still had a gun trained on him. He knew the rumors. He knew what the man standing in front of him was capable of. "Cuff yourself," Coby ordered. George started to cuff himself in the front and Coby yelled again. "MOTHER FUCKER I MEANT CUFF YOURSELF IN THE BACK!" Coby screamed. George complied and said, "This is getting a bit silly, doncha think?" Coby didn't reply. He just kept that weapon trained on him.

"Ok, now that we got this shit out of the way," Coby said. I'm going to zip tie you to the door of your car." Coby wasn't taking any chances and produced two large thick black zip ties from his toolbox in the bed of his truck. "Open your fuckin door," he said, and George complied. "Walk to the door backward with your arms extended behind you as far as you can." Coby said as he rolled down the driver's side window.

George complied with Coby's orders, and you could hear the bones and joints in the investigator's arms pop as he was cable tied to the door. The zip ties went between the cuffs and over the chain. Coby tightened the grip on the zip tie as tightly as he could, nearly breaking the zip tie.

"Now that I feel safe." Coby said, "Just what in the actual blue fuck did you think you were doing following me all the god damn way down here from Jackson?" Coby snapped.

The highway patrolman knew he didn't have an adequate answer that wouldn't cost him his life, so he said nothing. It was pretty clear that Coby was almost hell-bent on actually shooting this little piss ant standing in front of him. Just at that point, Jake turned into his driveway and got out of his truck.

When Jake saw the two and took note of the condition of the highway patrolman, bound to his car, Jake drew his Glock. Furious at the sight of George Walter and remembering the conversation in Senator Kennard's office, Jake walked over to the pair, gun in hand.

"What the hell are you two doing here at my house?" Jake demanded.

"This mother fucker is about to commit suicide," Coby replied, "He followed me from Jackson, and I think he wants to try me."

Jake demanded from the investigator, "Why the fuck are you at my house?"

It was the first time George Walter had ever been caught in the act of any nefarious activities, and he was visibly shaken to the core. The two friends decided to hold him for a while in Jake's garage.

Coby produced a knife and cut the cable ties from the door. They walked George into the garage backward, arm in arm, on his sides and placed him in a metal folding chair.

After they secured him in the garage, Jake immediately called the Governor.

"Hey, Governor?" Jake said almost politely, "We got your boy down here in Biloxi, and we're going to a beach party."

The Governor gasped as he hung up the phone. Jake slapped George hard in his mouth with an open right hand. Blood began dripping from George's bottom lip. A tooth was knocked loose with the next punch to the right side of George Walter's jaw.

Coby cable-tied George to the folding chair. Jake dragged an old folding table out from behind some boxes that were used for storage. The table was set up in front of the chair that George was restrained to. Coby went into the bathroom and retrieved a towel. Jake took an old garden hose and filled a five-gallon bucket full of water. The two were silent while they set up the scene.

"What the fuck are you doing?" George screamed. "Your assholes can't get away with this. I am a god damn officer of the law!"

Coby slapped George on the side of the head with an open hand He then produced the same knife that he used to free George from his car, stuck it to his throat, and said "Shut the fuck up, asshole or I will cut your fuckin tongue out and pull it through your fuckin' throat!" Coby said and slapped him in the face again.

The chair was turned with the back of the chair facing the floor. George found himself leaned backward. The back was propped up using an old sawhorse. Coby covered George's face with the towel. "You ready to talk now, mother fucker?" Jake asked.

"Yes! Please don't kill me!" George cried. His pants were wet. The sound of running water coming from George's crotch, hitting the floor, made the pair laugh.

"Aww, big man done pissed his pants like a baby," Coby said with a smirk.

This mother fucker isn't gonna talk, so I'm just gonna do what I do best." Jake said as he unscrewed the cap from a thirty-two-ounce bottle of water that was in his hand. He started slowly pouring the water over the towel, and George shrieked. Coby opened and emptied another bottle of water on George's head, and George gasped for air. The towel was removed, and George spit water from his mouth.

"Are you going to talk now, you son of a bitch?" Coby asked, holding the towel.

In a coughing fit, George cried "YES!" and spit more water from his mouth.

While they didn't waterboard him, they sure made it look like they were about to. Fifteen minutes after George Walter arrived at Jake's house, he began spilling the beans. He told them about his plan for Coby and his orders if Coby didn't play ball. He told about his role in Roy Fayard being framed; he told them about Joe Holloway and his betrayal of Jake. He told it all. He told the pair of his orders to bug Coby's home in Jackson as well as his office. He told Coby about the bug that was in his truck. Of course, all it was good for was intelligence as none of it could be used in a court of law because of the illegal activities of Coby and Jake for assault and kidnapping.

If they were to call Agent ford right now, the only crimes that would be seen were theirs for kidnapping and torture. They let the Highway Patrolman go, after Coby kicked him in his ass with the side of his foot, and Jake told him, "Mother fucker, you ever come around here again, and I'll fucking kill you." Coby added, "I'll fucking dig the hole to hide the body."

The investigator drove back to Jackson and reported the events to Governor Creel. Governor Creel wasn't upset at all, to the surprise of the investigator. "I knew that wouldn't work. Those two Jarheads are fucking inseparable."

"Do you want me to kill one of them?" George asked

"Oh no, no, no, that shouldn't be necessary unless they decide to get cute and go to the media." The Governor frowned.

"If they did," George replied, "I could go after em for kidnapping a law enforcement officer."

"Oh no, too many questions like what you were doing there and why you followed Coby and all that unpleasantness. Just let it go, for now, George." The Governor said cautiously.

"Well, who are you going to appoint?" George asked.

"Do you know Christine Stacy of Grenada?" The Governor asked.

"Yes, she's the mayor there. Good choice. Her appointment would rally the feminists against that son of a bitch. Nice pick, Billy." George said.

"Yeah, I'm going to call her down here tomorrow. I know she will play ball, and she will be tough to defeat." The Governor said,

"Good on ya' Billy. I like her, plus she's a damn fine-looking woman too." George said with a smile.

The two conspirators parted ways, and the Governor called the honorable Mayor Christine Stacy.

"Hey, sweet thing, you want a job?" the Governor said in a playful tone.

"Sure, you can appoint me as Senator," she shot back jokingly

"Done." The Governor responded quickly and casually.

"Excuse me? She said

"Done. Congratulations, Senator Stacy." The Governor said.

"Oh, um, what do I do about my job here in Grenada?" Stacy asked.

"Inform your City Manager and City Council members that you are going to accept your appointment in the morning here in Jackson." The Governor said.

"You're serious…" Stacy said almost silently.

"I am very serious, Senator Stacy." The Governor replied. "I am announcing tomorrow afternoon, and I need you to come to Jackson to assume your appointment."

"Ok, will do. See you in the morning." Stacy said with a smile.

The two hung up, and the newly appointed Senator Stacy made all the appropriate phone calls. The Governor ordered his press secretary to put out a statement announcing his appointment. Jake was awoken in the middle of the night by Coby calling him and screaming in his ear, "THAT SON OF A BITCH APPOINTED CHRISTINE STACY FROM GRENADA, GET READY FOR HER TO HILLARY CLINTON YOUR ASS."

"Huh?" Jake said, "Dude, it's two-thirty in the god damn morning, and you woke me up with this bullshit?" He slammed the phone down and went back to sleep.

When Jake arrived at his office, a television crew was already there. "Have you heard of the Governor's new appointment for Senate?" was the question they wanted to know. Jake wasted no time in telling them what he thought of the Governor and his appointment.

"Anybody that Governor Creel appoints to the Senate will be conducting business as usual as the Establishment wants and will only serve him instead of the citizens of the State of Mississippi."

"Will you debate her?" the Reporter, a bald round man with a bulging gut, asked

"Anytime, anyplace, any platform," Jake responded confidently.

The TV interview reached the governor's ears, and the newly appointed Senator almost as fast as Jake had said it.

"If he wants to get a debate, he will have to fight for it." The Governor decided. It was a popular tactic for the sitting Senator to duck and hide from a debate, although not a particularly good one for a newly appointed Senator.

The American Flag laden banners and banquet tables were lined along the Capitol building's walls and hall. A podium had been set up on the ground floor. The acoustics were so great that the sound system was almost not needed.

At one o'clock that afternoon, the Governor, the Lieutenant Governor, and all the cabinet members were surrounding the podium and the guest of honor. A bible was produced, and Christine Stacy was ordered to raise her right hand while placing her left hand on the Holy Bible.

A Chaplain handpicked by the Governor administered the oath. The Chaplain, a Baptist minister from The First Baptist Church of Clinton, was Clayton Briggs. He was about sixty, very tall and thin, and wore a blue suit. He was chosen because the church was where the Governor attended services and his friendship with the Governor.

"Repeat after me," the Chaplain said as he administered the Oath "I, Christine Stacy, do solemnly swear, that I will support and defend the Constitution of the United States against all enemies, foreign and domestic; that I will bear true faith and allegiance to the same; that I take this obligation freely, without any mental reservation or purpose of evasion; and that I will well and faithfully discharge the duties of the office on which I am about to enter: So help me God."

She repeated the phrase and was thus sworn into her new office.

"Congratulations Senator," the Governor said with a plastic smile. "Do us proud!"

Congratulations came from everybody there, and the press was hot for an interview with the attractive young Senator.

The newly appointed Senator Stacy was a stunning beauty, just a mere thirty-five years old, five feet seven inches tall, 125 pounds, with wavy long dark hair. She was the first female Senator as well as the youngest Senator from Mississippi. Reporters gathered around her, pushing ever so close to admire her beauty as well as gain an interview. She had come out of nowhere to get to this place. Very few people outside of Grenada, a small town of about 15,000 people, knew anything about her. She was a virtual stranger in Jackson. She had only been Mayor for almost two years and before then served four years on the City Council.

Her father owned a large cotton dispensary, and her family owned a large plantation in Grenada County for the last 170 years. Her family was well known for having "old money," which in Mississippi usually meant that the family was well off at some point, usually generations ago. The case with the Stacy family wasn't like that. Her family still owned the same land they started on and managed to keep it during The Great Depression when most rural families lost everything.

Her uncle was a banker in the small town, and because of her family contacts, she had been groomed for public office. She attended Ole Miss for four years and got her bachelor's degree in Business Management. She, like Jake, also had no vices. She had been married and divorced, but it wasn't a nasty divorce like most public officials experienced. The reason for the divorce was her husband, whom she met at Ole Miss, wanted her to move with him back to his home in Illinois. She vowed she would never leave Mississippi. The two divorced but remained friends and sometimes lovers.

Chapter Seven

Presidential Endorsement

With the Governor's Appointment of the new Senator, Jake had his work cut out for him. Senator Kennard wasted no time casting his endorsement on Jake, but he was a junior Senator himself, and he knew that somebody more known was needed. A Republican President had just been elected two years before, and this being a Mid-Term election, he would want a solid political ally.

Jason Finch was a staunch Conservative Republican. An Air Force Major, fighter pilot, and later a Governor of Arizona for two terms before running for President and defeating the Democrat Incumbent by twenty Electoral Votes. He was a war hawk which Jake didn't much care for, but he had fixed the economy and reversed the damage of the last five Presidential Administrations. He had vowed to renegotiate the foreign trade treaties that had been hurting private business for years. He was tough on crime, big on gun rights, a massive promoter of small business, and an all-around decent politician if there ever was one.

His friendship with Senator Kennard and his working relationship with him had put him at odds with some of the more corrupt politicians. It cost him some of the support he would have had otherwise with some of his policies. The late Senator Wallace was constantly at odds with the President, mainly at the behest of the Honorable Governor of the State of Mississippi, to which he took his orders.

The Governor didn't endorse the current President, and he has fought some of his most famous efforts, so there was no doubt that there would be no cooperation between the two. The Junior Senator, Mr. Kennard, had collaborated well with the President on some current legislation he was trying to pass and would meet with him later in the week.

The Governor had without a doubt cast his endorsement to the newly made Madam Senator Christine Stacy. He pledged his Political Action Campaigns and pledged to create a Super PAC to ensure her campaign was fully funded.

Jake supported most of what the President stood for, but he had an issue with some of his foreign policies. He didn't like that we were flirting with going to war with Yemen. Though not well known, his stance was if a sovereign nation wasn't a direct threat to us, then military action was not only not called for but Unconstitutional. He privately explained this to Senator Kennard when he suggested a Presidential endorsement.

"Jake, just keep your mouth shut and play the game." was the Senator's reply.

The Primary was to be held on the sixth of June, and it was only about three weeks away. Jake started ramping up his campaign ads, and so did the lovely Madam Senator with her Super PAC fund by the Governor and his political machine.

Jake was brainstorming about making a commercial when he suddenly remembered hearing about an excellent rifle range in the NASA Stennis Buffer Zone in Hancock County. He called the owner, Ted Keith, and requested to use the range for the commercial. "Come on down, Jake, we would love to have you." Was the reply from Ted and Jake scheduled the shoot for that afternoon.

Jake, Coby, and Agent Ford drove down Texas Flat Road, a two-lane road in a completely wooded area in rural Hancock County. There were no houses or buildings, but it was used as a back road, twelve miles long, to get from Picayune, Mississippi to Bay Saint Louis. The backwoods and bayous of Hancock County were very calming.

The NASA Stennis Buffer Zone is a 125,000-acre perimeter of the John C. Stennis NASA facility located in rural Hancock County, Mississippi, near the Louisiana border. While people are allowed to own land in the buffer zone, nobody is permitted to live there to protect from the gasses that may be expelled from rockets that were being built and tested there.

Once he followed the exact directions that Ted had given him and turned right onto Flat Top Road, Jake thought he was utterly lost until he heard the sound of gunfire. He saw three pickup trucks pulling out of the range and about a half dozen other vehicles parked. The trio walked up to a man sitting on the tailgate of a truck, wearing a red shirt that read "Range Safety Officer," and asked for Ted.

The man stepped off the tailgate and introduced himself as Ted, one of the co-owners of the range. Jake knew Ted's brother Ralph when he had an unsuccessful bid for office years ago, but this was his first encounter with the elder brother.

Ted was sitting next to several custom-built rifles of varying AR-15 and M4 design, some firing 5.56x45mm, some firing .300 Blackout, and some firing 7.62x39. All of the weapons were stamped with the custom logo of "Keith Firearms, Poplarville,

Mississippi." The guns were also for sale as Ted was the owner and operator of Keith Firearms.

Gulf Coast Free Fire Zone, which is what the range was called, had a dirt driveway. The ranges were dirt with a small table on one end. The other end had boards where one could nail their targets up. There was a large mound of earth, or a berm, at the far end of the range.

Jake bought one of Ted's rifles, loaded thirty rounds of .300 Blackout, fired the weapon, and instantly loved the quality and craftsmanship. The gun fit perfectly in his hands. Jake was impressed.

Coby and Agent Ford set up a camera and began shooting the footage. Jake loaded another thirty-round magazine, closed the bolt, and began firing. Every round made its mark perfectly. All thirty rounds exited near the center of the target as he was firing from fifty yards away. Jake prepared another weapon. The camera was still rolling.

"This is how I stand on your gun rights," he said as he pulled another fully automatic M4 from the bed of a truck. The weapon was black and had the emblem of Keith Firearms, Poplarville, Mississippi, stamped on the receiver. He opened fire, and each of the thirty rounds exiting the magazine hit their mark accurately. Coby was there and slightly chuckled. "Every Marine a rifleman," he said. Then after showing the footage, an endorsement from Mississippi Gun Lobby popped up on the screen.

Jake had long since refused anything to do with the National Rifle Association after they shunned the owner of Keith Firearm's son and endorsed the incumbent candidate who opposed Open Carry in a previous election.

The camera was still rolling as Jake pulled his Glock 21 from his shoulder holster. He fired from the three-yard, seven-yard, fifteen yards, and twenty-five-yard line into metal plates that danced back in forth with every round striking them. Jake was a perfect shot.

On May 28, Jake got a call from a voice he vividly recognized. He was almost stunned to hear the very crisp, unmistakable voice of none other than the President of the United States calling him. He actually pinched himself twice to make sure he wasn't dreaming.

"Mr. Fayard?" The President asked

"YYYY uh Yes SIR?" Jake replied meekly

"Do you know who this is?" The President asked.

"Yes, Sir Mr. President," Jake said and snapped to attention as he spoke

"I would like to invite you to come to Washington and have a meeting with me in the Oval Office. When can you be here?" The President asked.

"Uh, Sir, I can be there whenever you want me!" Jake said, nearly having a heart attack.

"Can you fly in tomorrow? I can send Air Force One to pick you up at the Mississippi Air National Guard base in Gulfport if you wish." The President asked.

"Uh... Air Force One?? Sure, Mr. President, that would be fine!" Jake said this with the excitement of a child getting to ride in a fire truck for the first time.

"Ok, Mr. Fayard, I'll arrange it with the post commander. Be there at three o'clock sharp tomorrow afternoon." The President said.

"Yes, sir, I will be there. Thank you, sir, and may God bless you." Jake replied.

The phone went dead, and Jake was still trying to pinch himself. Jake rushed his best designer pinstripe suit to the cleaners. The neon sign buzzing "Same day cleaning" was all that caught his eye. He polished his boots with a Marine Corps strip and shine so perfect that you could shave while looking in the toes and the heel. He laid out four of his best suits and pressed them to perfection.

The next afternoon at precisely three o'clock, Jake boarded the Boeing 747 with the Presidential staff. He expected to be greeted by a few workers and be a typical plane ride with the notable exception that it was Air Force One he was flying on.

He found a seat and was just about to buckle himself down when a fit man in a tailored suit with an earpiece in his ear said, "Follow me, sir."

"Where are we going?" Jake asked

"Follow me, sir, and I'll show you where you will sit," The man said.

Jake did what he was told, and two minutes later, he found himself standing in front of a large oak desk sitting opposite the President of the United States.

"Good afternoon Mr. President," Jake said as he snapped to attention like he was on a parade ground.

"Good afternoon Mr. Fayard," the President said, "or may I call you Jake?"

"You can call me Peggy Sue if you like," he thought. "Yes, sir, you may call me Jake if you wish," Jake said, almost stammering

"Jake, I have a problem. I need your help, and you are just the man for the job." The President said.

"Yes, sir," Jake whimpered

"I need Mississippi. I need a strong Senator with morals. I need a man who will command the respect of the people." The President said.

"Yes, sir, I can be that man," Jake said

"I have one reservation about you, sir. I have been talking with Senator Kennard, and we have worked well together for several years. I know the man to be truthful, and only an honest word comes from his mouth, but I hate a scandal." The President said cautiously.

"I think I know where this is going, Mr. President," Jake said

"Do you, Jake?" The President responded.

"Yes, sir, you are worried about my son Roy," Jake said almost silently.

"No, sir, I am not. I have asked the FBI to investigate since a federal crime had taken place. They have been keeping me informed, and they see that your son isn't connected to the cocaine. He was a soft target, and they used him to throw you off track. You are the attorney of record, so I'll let you check with the State's Attorney." The President said confidently.

"Well, sir, what are you worried about?" Jake asked, a little more confused

"Jake, allow me to be blunt. I better not hear about you kidnapping, waterboarding, and interrogating any more Highway Patrolmen again. You and Mr. Barhonovich can leave all that advanced interrogation tactics back in Iraq where y'all learned it." The President ordered

Jake didn't know whether to laugh or to be concerned as nobody outside of those three, as far as he knew, had a clue of the events that happened in his garage. Jake finally asked the question. "Mr. President, am I under surveillance?"

"Of course, I am not going to endorse somebody without doing comprehensive research on him; that would be stupid. Although the bastard deserved more than he got off the record, a U.S. Senator does not conduct himself in such a manner. Am I clear?" The President said sternly.

"Yes, sir, we concur," Jake replied.

"Then you have my endorsement. I'll announce it later this evening." The President said.

Jake was so star-struck that he was unaware that he never left Gulfport. He got back in his truck and watched as the plane took off, headed for the next stop on the President's itinerary. Jake had never had any connection to the power players in Washington before, and he couldn't keep a thought in his head on the drive home.

When The President arrived at his next stop, a military hospital in Florida, he announced his endorsement for Jake Fayard for Senator of Mississippi. He announced it not just as a casual endorsement but as an indictment of the Governor of Mississippi.

Reporters from WLBT News in Jackson immediately called the Governor's office for comment. The Governor responded by writing a memorandum to all of the media that he was friendly with.

"Outsiders have swayed the President's advisors in endorsing a disreputable man who can't even raise his son properly." The Governor wrote, "It is a shame that Washington wants to play politics with those who work solely for Mississippians and our interests."

The indictment by the Governor started a firestorm in Jake's campaign office. Phones rang almost non-stop from reporters locally and nationally regarding the Governor's contemptuous words in the press.

Jake responded by saying, "While I did not seek out the President's endorsement, I am humbled and honored to accept the honor. The Governor handpicked the current Senator and is attempting some form of damage control."

Chapter Eight

Roy's Rehab

Precisely at nine o'clock the following day, Jake called the state's Attorney in Pensacola. The Prosecutor informed Jake that he would be filing a Nolle Proseque, a relatively routine motion in which the prosecutor feels he doesn't have enough evidence to get a conviction.

Jake was puzzled by this based on the sheer volume of the physical evidence. The prosecutor explained, "Man, I was asked by a United States Attorney. I don't ask questions; I just take orders. Personally, I hoped that I nail his ass to the cross. I don't like drugs entering my community, but all of my evidence was snatched up under a federal subpoena."

"Who is pulling strings?" Jake silently wondered.

Jake called The Charter House in New Orleans. They had already been informed of Roy's situation. They also informed Jake that they did not tell Roy for fear that he would walk out and leave the rehab facility because they had no leverage on him.

Jake thanked them for this and requested an unscheduled visit. Doctor Meaut was put on the phone and said, "Generally, Mr. Fayard, I don't allow unscheduled visitations, but, in this case, I will make an exception on one condition."

"What's that, Doctor Meaut?" Jake asked.

"If I may sit in on the visit. We can call it this week's family session." Doctor Meaut said.

"Yes, sir, that would be fine." Jake said, "When can I visit?"

"How soon can you be here?" Doctor Meaut asked

"I can be there within three and a half hours traffic depending," Jake replied.

Jake made the drive to New Orleans. He crossed the Twin-span, the Interstate 10 bridge over Lake Pontchartrain in record time and entered New Orleans East. As he got to the Read Blvd exit, he saw blue lights behind him. A New Orleans Police Officer was in the left lane near the neutral ground on Interstate 10 and saw him driving erratically.

The officer walked up to his car and demanded his driver's license, registration, and proof of insurance. The officer recognized him as a man he had seen a few days before while working his off-duty post at The Charter House.

"Mr. Fayard, I am Officer Guidry of the New Orleans Police Department. Do you know why I stopped you?" the officer asked.

Jake was a lawyer and knew he didn't have to answer the questions, but the officer seemed reasonable enough, so he responded, "I have an idea, sir."

"I clocked you at 90 in a 60 mile per hour zone." Officer Guidry said, "What is your hurry, sir?"

"I am on my way to a meeting with Doctor Meaut at The Charter House," Jake responded.

"I'm going to let you off with a stern warning. Slow your ass down, and I'll call ahead to Doctor Meaut and let him know you are on your way." Officer Guidry said.

"Yes, sir, I will and thank you," Jake replied with a sigh of relief.

Jake continued to drive, and thirty minutes later, he arrived at The Charter House. "Senator Lead Foot, how nice to see you." Doctor Meaut joked. "Welcome back to the Big Easy."

Jake smiled and chuckled a little. "Thank God I got friends in low places with the NOPD," he said with a slight laugh.

"Where's that boy of mine?' Jake asked

"Well, there seems to be a problem, Mr. Fayard…." Doctor Meaut said hesitantly.

"Oh shit." Jake exclaimed, "What happened?"

"Well, I send an orderly to inform Roy that we had a meeting today, and his room was found empty with his window raised." Doctor Meaut said. "We notified the police, but we can't hold him because we have no court order, and he's no longer on a bail bond."

"Does he know that?" Jake asked

"No, sir, not at all." Doctor Meaut responded.

"I'm going to go looking for him," Jake said.

"Are you familiar with New Orleans at all?" Doctor Meaut asked.

"Yes, sir, I was stationed at Belle Chasse Naval Air Station, and I went to school at Tulane. I lived in Harahan." Jake responded.

"Ok, well, be careful. New Orleans can be a dangerous place." Doctor Meaut warned.

"No problem, I'm armed," Jake replied.

Jake left and started looking for Roy on Magazine Street. He found Jefferson Avenue and took a left to go to Claiborne Avenue. He took a right on Claiborne and headed toward Downtown. He searched the French Quarter and could not find him. He then took a turn on Elysian Fields Avenue and started heading toward Saint Claud Avenue. When he got to Chalmette, Jake turned around and headed back into the city.

Jake retraced his steps through the French Quarter and got on the Westbank

Expressway. He was getting desperate and worried that the next time he would see Roy would be on a slab in the coroner's office. He checked with the Jefferson Parish Sheriff's Department, and they knew nothing of the missing troubled youth.

Jake recrossed the Mississippi River on the Huey P. Long bridge and drove down Jefferson Highway toward the city. It was getting late, and he was even more worried. New Orleans was notoriously dangerous, especially in this area.

Jake was driving through Central City and saw a man sitting on the curb outside of a closed-down strip mall storefront in the 3400 block of Claiborne Avenue that he recognized, it was Roy sitting on a curb, crying and high as a kite.

"You mother fucking son of a bitch, I should beat your ass all over Central City," Jake screamed out in rage. "What the fuck were you thinking?"

"I don't wanna go to prison, dad." Roy cried, "I just wanna go home."

"What the fuck were you thinking? Dry your fucking eyes, boy. Man, the fuck up and stop that god damn boohooing and bullshit." Jake snapped

Jake was a hard-core gung-ho Marine who couldn't stand for a man to cry, especially when it was his own actions that led him into the mess he was crying about. He was raised by the rough hands of his father, beating the phrase "men don't cry" into his head and the Marine Corps boot camp of being tough or die.

Roy didn't benefit from the discipline or the school of hard knocks learning that Jake did. He was always indulged as a child, which quite honestly led to the path that his life took.

"You dumbass." Jake said, "You weren't even going to prison. The prosecutor decided not to prosecute you this morning. All you had to do was complete the treatment, and you'd be fine. Now, look at you. Stoned and fucked up in a crying crumpled heap in a part of the city that you can catch death like you can catch a cold."

Roy started crying harder, and Jake ordered him into the truck. They drove back to The Charter House, where Doctor Meaut was waiting.

"They have a Lockdown Wing at East Jefferson General Hospital in Metairie," Doctor Meaut said. "They can house him better than we can, although it is a temporary facility. They can hold him for three- or four days tops until he can sober up."

Jake agreed and asked if Doctor Meaut would accept him back.

"Yes, we will accept him, but he will be on 'Close Observation,' which means we will have an orderly with him every second of the day."

"You mean no privacy?" Roy exclaimed.

"Shut the fuck up, boy!" Jake said with his teeth and fist clenched.

"Yes," Doctor Meaut responded. "You now have no privileges. You are locked down. You will go nowhere until I say so, and I say no."

Just then, a white van with a cage appeared around the side of the building. The faded lettering on the van not quite scraped off and not painted over-read "Jefferson Parish Sheriff's Department." Roy asked, "Am I going to jail?"

"No. You are going in our transport van to East Jefferson, and then you will be transported in that van back here. One of my orderlies will be outside your room. We have a contract with East Jefferson, so don't even think about trying anything." Doctor Meaut said.

Two armed orderlies who looked like they could pass for Linebackers for the New Orleans Saints stepped out of the van.

"Your ride is here, Roy." Doctor Meaut said.

The two orderlies handcuffed, shackled, and restrained Roy in the cage in the back of the van. The van drove off and arrived about thirty-five minutes later at East Jefferson General Hospital in Metairie, or as it was known locally simply "E.J.." The hospital was slightly run down on the outside, as most of the infrastructure of Southeast Louisiana was, but on the inside, the hospital was state of the art. Roy was admitted for four days, declared sober, and the van was recalled returning him to The Charter House.

Once Roy arrived back at The Charter House, he was placed in a secure room with an orderly and watched around the clock. The only privacy Roy was afforded was when he used the restroom and showered. His condition and behavior was documented every fifteen minutes by an orderly. Roy was beginning to wish he were back in jail instead of in the rehab.

Chapter Nine

Judas gets caught

The day after Roy was released from East Jefferson General Hospital, Joe Holloway, the dishonorable campaign manager, met with Governor Creel in Jackson. "He had a secret meeting two days ago on the Air National Guard base in Gulfport," Joe reported.

"Yes, we know. Finch endorsed that son of a bitch." The Governor said. "He must have some powerful friends."

"Well, la de fuckin da," Walter added, "Should I kill him now?"

"No, no, no. don't do that; besides, if you go near him again, he'll probably shoot you, and lord knows he's always armed." The Governor replied.

"Just calm down, George," Joe said, "It's not worth it anyway."

"We got other leverage," Walter said. "His son escaped from a drug rehab facility in New Orleans the other day. I got a friend with the New Orleans Police Department that called me when the missing person's report came out."

"Oh really?!?" Asked the Governor, "Boy, that will surely play nicely with our plans to discredit him."

"He must suspect something with me. He hasn't said anything, and usually, he would have confided in me about little Junior Fuck-up." Joe said.

"See what you can find out. Just remember if he finds out you don't know me. If you squeal, I'll take care of you." Walter warned.

"Yeah yeah, I know…" Joe responded with a frown.

"Good. We have an understanding. Don't be stupid Joe." George threatened with a sneer.

The trio broke up, and Joe drove back to the Coast. When he arrived at the campaign office, he was met by Jake, a very pissed-off Coby Barhonovich, and Agent Ford.

"Welcome back, mother fucker," Coby said as he knocked him to the ground with a right cross. "How was your fucking drive home?"

"Jake, what the fuck is going on, bro?" Joe screamed in pain.

"Stay down, or I'll fuck you up some more, you son of a bitch!" Coby ordered.

"Did you give the Governor and his do-boy my warmest regards?" Jake asked

"What are you talking about, Jake? Have you lost your mind?" Joe cried

Just then, Agent Ford appeared. "Damn, looks like I missed the party." He said smugly.

"Who the fuck are you?" Joe demanded, and Coby reached down and slapped him. "Be nice, you son of a bitch!" Coby said.

"I am the man who sees nothing. I am not even here if you don't play ball. Should I give you three some alone time first?" Agent Ford asked almost with a grin

"Please just a few more minutes," Coby said eagerly

"NO, PLEASE, WHAT DO YOU WANT?!?!?!" Joe cried out

"Ok, Coby let him up," Agent Ford said as he took a seat. "You will tell us everything you know, or I'm going to let nature take its course. Do you understand?"

"Yes, sir, but who are you?" Joe asked again

"I'm the last person you want me to be right now." Agent Ford said

"I don't know anything," Joe said and hung his head low.

"Well, let's see what you do know. I want some water cooler-type stuff. Let's be simple. How long have you and the Governor been working together? Second, what was the plan? Third, what are your motives?" Agent Ford asked

"I started working for him about six weeks ago when Jake started showing great potential in the polls. The plan was for me to be his ears and to help George Walter with his tasks. I don't know the details of their discussion. My only motive was money. He paid me a measly $5,000 and promised more later if I continued to prove useful. My wife has some medical issues I need the money Jake I'm sorry" Joe said shamefully with blood dripping from his mouth and tears in his eyes.

"You son of a bitch." Jake said, "Get your shit and get your ass out of my office right now."

Joe Holloway packed his personal belongings. Before he left Agent Ford searched his personal belongings for anything incriminating. He found an MP3 recording device and asked what this was for.

"I use it for dictation so that I could accurately report what was going on throughout the day." Joe said shamefully.

"I'll be keeping this for a while. You don't mind do you?" Agent Ford asked.

"No, I guess not." Joe said. He knew that he would not have a choice as the device was taken from his possession anyway. Joe apologized again with tears in his eyes and quickly departed the office. "I'll be seeing you real soon." Agent Ford said as he left.

"Ok, so what do we do now?" Jake asked. "I need a campaign manager."

"I'll be your campaign manager." Agent Ford said. "Nobody but us knows who I am. It will give me a chance to see if the Governor approaches me, and I can use that as leverage to get what I need for a prosecution."

"You think that'll work?" Coby asked. "Mississippi voters are complacent, and they don't like outsiders."

Just then, the phone rang. "Jake, go check your email right now!" the voice belonging to Senator Kennard screamed, and the phone went dead.

Jake opened his laptop and checked his email. There was a YouTube link from the Senator saying, "Stacy Commercial" He clicked the link, and as soon as he did, he was hit with a big Mississippi State cut out on screen, with the logo on Stacy for Senate." It projected her on her plantation in Grenada, picking cotton, wearing overalls. Then it switched to her in what appeared to be a shipyard, wearing a welding hood and gloves, then standing in front of the Biloxi Lighthouse, the symbol of the coast since 1848, saying, "I am of you, I am Mississippi, I stand for Conservative Mississippi values. Vote for Christine Stacy on June sixth."

"Ok, boys," he said as he closed the laptop, "We got work to do. Ford, since the Department of Justice, has been so kind as to furnish me with a Campaign Manager your first order is commercials and to facilitate a debate."

"Done with a phone call." Agent Ford said.

"We also need to put pressure on Stacy to debate me. I want people around her talking." Jake said

"I can reach out to my social media gurus," Coby said.

"Have you considered a podcast?" Agent Ford asked

"Yes, genius idea. Let's keep people informed and give the public a way to respond." Jake said. "I have set up an interview with a local radio station not controlled by the Creel machine. It's a low-power FM Station in Waveland."

"Good, when do you go?" Agent Ford asked

"I have it set up tomorrow afternoon." Jake said, "I know him well as we are both ham radio operators."

"Good deal, you go do that, and I've got this." Agent Ford said, "Coby, you go back to Jackson as I'm sure you have things to do, and I'll work it from my end."

"I'm gone. I gotta go prepare a response to some lawsuits that your highness has caused." Coby responded.

Chapter Ten

Christine Stacy Debate.

The new friends broke up, and Jake made the thirty-three-mile drive west on US Highway 90 along the beachfront through Gulfport, Long Beach, Pass Christian, Bay Saint Louis, and Waveland. Hurricane Katrina destroyed the area and the empty lots where some of the most beautiful mansions were enough to depress any coast native.

While driving past the old houses, the empty lots, and the jet ski shacks on the beach, Jake wondered how his life would have been if he decided to be more of a family man instead of a career Marine. He pondered the sacrifices that he made.

Jake wondered, not for the first time if it was worth it. He lost his wife, his son's innocence, and aside from all of the benefits of being a Senator, it paled in comparison to those two things. Yes, he could be a part of history, and he could serve his country in a status that nobody else in his family had achieved, but the loss made him cringe.

Minutes after crossing the Bay of Saint Louis, Jake arrived at the small makeshift building on Indian Street in Waveland. The building had only been built to be a temporary shelter, but the owner, Joe Peterson, worked to gain funds. WHAN 106.3 FM-LP is a fully listener-supported low-power FM Radio Station covering Hancock County, Mississippi.

The radio station is owned and operated by a nonprofit organization called the Delta Amateur Radio Association, which assists the area in communications during natural disasters. Jake volunteered his time and stayed during Hurricane Isaac in 2012, which ironically happened on the seventh anniversary of Hurricane Katrina.

Joe was sitting on the porch drinking a beer and eating a shrimp po boy when Jake arrived. "Hey, Joe," Jake said with a grin. "You still owe me a pair of boots, you son of a bitch!" he joked. This was a running joke between the two when Jake volunteered during Hurricane Isaac on August 29, 2012 (the seventh anniversary of Hurricane Katrina) and made the mistake of wearing cowboy boots instead of proper footwear and ruined the boots.

"Well, you're the dumbass that wore 'em," Joe said with a grin as they shook hands.

Jake reached in the refrigerator that was sitting on the porch for a Barq's Root beer. "Yeah we had some fun times back then" Jake said as he reminisced.

"Well, it's your studio; you know how everything works." Joe said, "You have run it before."

When Jake stepped into the little studio, he remembered how it looked when he volunteered all those years ago. He remembered the carpet that used to be on the floor and all the equipment stacked on shelves. Twelve CD Changers still lined the wall, and there was an American Flag that was tacked to the wall with thirty-six signatures.

All thirty-six people stayed at the Hancock County Emergency Operations Center during Hurricane Katrina. When water threatened to flood the building, the EOC director said, "Ok y'all, everybody picks a number and remember your number. I want everybody's name and social security number written on a piece of paper with your corresponding number. Everybody took a sharpie marker and wrote their numbers on their hand, and the information was tacked to the ceiling. Thankfully, everybody survived, and Joe had the idea that all of them would sign the tattered American Flag with their corresponding number.

Jake took interviews from the public and answered questions concerning the corruption in Washington and the Governor's appointment. As soon as he would hang up on one call, the phone would ring again. Hancock County was extremely interested in the young candidate. A few callers asked about Jake's son, and he answered politely,

"He's doing fine; he is getting the help he needs." With a few people who were biased against him, he won the crowd over as he played music and took calls. It was the most enjoyment he had since starting the campaign.

Jake took note of the Icom 7000 that was sitting on the table. He recalled how he worked that radio to pass information using the ham radio frequencies. Jake was a licensed extra class ham radio operator, and he kept this from the public view.

Once he completed his hour of running the station, out of a feeling of nostalgia from the storm, he moved over toward the Icom. He clicked on the power supply, turned the frequency to 146.730 MHz, keyed the mic, and threw out a call. "W5BLX listening on the Biloxi Repeater." He said. A call came back from the radio saying, "This is K5MPD Mobile, name is Bill." Jake and Bill had a conversation that lasted about 10 minutes discussing general amateur radio topics and then Jake signed with him. "Good to talk to ya Bill, seventy-three, this is W5BLX going QRT." Jake then turned the radio off. Jake drank from a cup of sweet tea and thanked Joe for allowing him to run the radio, and the two decided to hang out for a while.

Jake went back to his home in Biloxi and retired for the evening very exhausted. He dreamed of his sweet Anna. He saw her long flowing blond hair, her ageless appearance, and her warm glow. She told him in his dream not to give up and that she was right there with him always.

It was a dream that comforted him through the night, and when he awoke the following day, he knew he could handle anything.

The following day, he awoke with a shock. Christine Stacy had left him a voicemail on his cell phone. "Alright, Mr. Fayard, I'll debate you." She said with her voice trailing off. It worked. She must have caught wind of the radio interview in Waveland.

The debate was to be held at the University of Mississippi Law School in Oxford in two days. Jake did all the research he could do on her tenure as Mayor of Grenada and the city's state before and after her election.

Jake's research found that the city was two million dollars in a deficit, one school had closed, the fire department had aging equipment that half of the time didn't work well, and some of the city's water infrastructure was crumbling.

"This is going to be a cakewalk," Jake thought.

Jake made the drive north on US Highway 49, bypassing Hattiesburg, and decided he would take the long way from there. He continued on US Highway 49 until he got to Jackson and then took the Interstate 55 north ramp toward Grenada and Memphis. He exited onto Lakeland Drive and followed it until it turned into Mississippi Highway 25. Jake hadn't taken this route in a long time and wanted to see parts of Mississippi he hadn't seen in a while.

Rural roads and small towns with the rolling hills of Mississippi comforted him as he made his way north. He turned left on US Highway 45 and drove into Tupelo. He visited Elvis Presley's childhood home and birthplace and then proceeded to US Highway 278 until he got to Oxford. Being a fan of Mississippi State University, he usually wouldn't have been welcome here, but he wanted to garner some votes from Oxford, so he figured he would keep his mouth shut about football. He checked into his hotel room and slept about half the day, exhausted from the long 8-hour drive.

The debate was held in the auditorium of the Ole Miss Law School. Three podiums were set up, one labeled Jake Fayard, one marked Christine Stacy, and one labeled Michael Holden, the debate moderator.

Michael Holden was a professor of Political Science at the University of Mississippi, an older man of about sixty-five, with white hair and horn-rim glasses. He stood about five feet nine inches and weighed about 185 pounds. He was a legend in the Mississippi political arena. He had made and destroyed more politicians by hosting debates than any man in the history of the State of Mississippi. He was nobody's man. He was as fair and impartial as they come for a man in his profession.

Mr. Holden took his place at his podium in the center of the stage. He introduced the candidate Christine Stacy, and she took her place at her podium on the right. Mr. Holden then introduced Jake Fayard, and he took his place at his podium on the left. Mr. Holden laid down the ground rules.

"Ok, folks, welcome to the University of Mississippi for the Republican Senatorial Debate between Christine Stacy of Grenada, Mississippi and Jake Fayard of Biloxi, Mississippi. I would also like to thank the various media outlets that are present to record this event. We are also being live streamed on Facebook and YouTube. Here are the ground rules. Number one, be respectful. Number two, I will ask a question and give each candidate two minutes to answer and thirty seconds to rebut—number three. At the end of the questions that I have asked, I will allow the candidates to ask each other some questions. I will also permit a one-minute introduction before the question-and-answer debate forum begins. I will start with you, Ms. Stacy," Mr. Holden said.

"Hey, y'all, my name is Christine Stacy. I am humbled to be your new Senator from the Great State of Mississippi. I have been mayor for two years in Grenada, Mississippi, and a city councilwoman before that. I have improved the lives of our citizens, and I stand on strong Conservative principles. I want to thank y'all for attending this event." She said.

"Thank you, Mrs. Stacy," Mr. Holden said, "Mr. Fayard, the floor is yours, sir."

Hey, y'all, I am Jake Fayard. I am a US Marine Corps veteran, a purple heart recipient, a father, an attorney, a policeman, and a Conservative. I served for twenty years in the Marine Corps, graduated from the US Naval Academy almost at the top of my class, and was a combat-wounded veteran before I attended because I believe in service to my country and my community. Thank you all for attending this event." Jake said.

"Thank you, Mr. Fayard." Mr. Holden said.

"Mrs. Stacy." Mr. Holden said, holding a card he was reading from "You were the Mayor of Grenada for two years. The term for Mayor is four years. When did you decide to accept the Governor's appointment, and why?"

"Well." She answered, "It took me by surprise being appointed as Senator by the Governor. I highly respect him, and we are old friends. He was an old friend of my father and had represented him on several occasions when he was an attorney. I accepted the appointment because I feel as though I have served the City of Grenada well, and I would serve the State of Mississippi well."

Mr. Holden frowned at her answer but kept going. "Alright, Mr. Fayard, why did you decide that you were going to run for Senator?"

Jake responded, "I am a man of service. I believe that the US Government has gotten too large and extremely powerful, and I would like to reign them in. To put it as my grandpa used to say they got too big for their britches. I believe in small government, freedom of choice, and personal responsibility. I also don't believe that the government should be required or should require itself to hold everybody's hand and infringe on the personal freedoms of common citizens like us."

The boldness of the statement shook the moderator and drew cheers and applause from the attendees. "Ok, Mr. Fayard," the moderator continued, "Next question is also for you. Mr. Fayard, you are a combat veteran. How do you feel about military spending, and do you support military contractors doing the job that military members previously did?"

"Yes, sir, I am a combat veteran. I don't care for military contractors as I think the military-industrial complex in this country isn't fiscally responsible. I want to reduce all government spending, including reducing the military contractor budget, and eventually eliminate the national debt, which is near twenty trillion dollars." Jake replied.

The answer shocked Mr. Holden as he assumed Mr. Fayard to be a significant military proponent being a Colonel in the Marine Corps.

"Mrs. Stacy," Mr. Holden asked. "How do you feel about the spending in Washington?"

"Well, as a mayor, with experience in fiscal duties to run a political entity, I can say that we need a military. We need roads, schools; police; fire, etc. so on and so forth. For this to occur, you must spend money. It would be great under the Libertarian philosophy if everything could fund itself, but that's not how it works." Christine said.

Jake raised his hand for a rebuttal.

"Yes, 30 seconds, Mr. Fayard." Mr. Holden said.

"Ms. Stacy has a city with failing infrastructure. You can fact-check this. The City of Grenada is also two million dollars in deficit. The Fire Department has a tanker truck that spends more time in the diesel mechanic shop than service ready. How in that can she say she is fiscally responsible?" Jake snapped back.

Christine Stacy lost her southern gentle lady charm. Her face turned from a blush pink to blood-red at the question. She didn't have an answer prepared for this.

"Mrs. Stacy?" Mr. Holden asked. "Would you care to respond?"

"Yes. Grenada is a poor town in the Mississippi Delta. I inherited this infrastructure, and I have asked for help in the way of bonds and grants. We are in the process of putting a plan in motion to fix the failing infrastructure." She said.

Both Mr. Holden and Jake Fayard looked at each other and frowned. The answer was confusing, and they knew she was lying. She raised taxes three times since being elected to the City Council, and once since being elected mayor, things still got worse.

"Mr. Fayard this question is to you. An allegation has been made about public funds being diverted to a famous football player in this state. This football player was paid essentially for services not rendered. How would you propose to stop this type of corruption in the future?" The moderator asked.

"I would say that the person who allocated the funds showed extremely poor judgement. I would ask what services were supposed to be rendered and if the services were not rendered then the person who received the money, regardless of who he is, should be prosecuted for fraud and the money immediately repaid." Jake responded.

The debate lasted for two hours and was immediately uploaded on YouTube. Online polls the next day showed Jake had a solid lead, 65 percent, to Christine Stacy's 35 percent. He hoped the polls would reflect that, but he also worried about what lay in wait for him.

Chapter Eleven

The Primary Election

The online polls showed Jake with a solid lead on Election Day, 55 percent for Fayard, 40 percent for Stacy, and 5 percent undecided.

The Polls in Mississippi opened at seven o'clock in the morning and closed at seven o'clock that evening. Jake stood outside of the Lee-Chin Fire Station on Veterans Avenue in Biloxi, holding a sign. Coby Barhonovich stood outside the Eudora Welty Library in Jackson, also holding a sign. Just to annoy the Governor, Agent Ford stood outside of the Governor's Mansion holding a sign as well.

The polls closed sharply at seven o'clock that night, and the entire Fayard Camp descended on Biloxi. They booked the Biloxi Welcome Center's convention room for the campaign party. By the time the eleven o'clock news came on the air, all precincts had reported in with 100 percent of the votes counted.

Five days later, all the absentee ballots were accounted for. A total of 315,208 votes were cast in the Primary Election. Jake won by sixteen votes. A total of 157,612 votes were cast for him, and 157,596 were cast for Christine Stacy.

"I want a recount," Christine said to the camera. "I want all of Mississippi to be counted in this election, and I don't think it was fairly done."

When Jake was asked for a comment, he said that he would support a recount only to ensure there were no errors and that every vote was counted accurately. Jake called another law school buddy of his, the Honorable Jodie Stamper, Esquire, who had a law firm in Brookhaven. Jake made his order clear that he would not tolerate anything that would dishonor the integrity of the election.

A representative of the Mississippi Republican Party, John Eubanks, would not certify the election. He was another "yes man" to the political machine that governed the Republican Party in Mississippi. He wanted every polling place in all of Mississippi's 82 counties rechecked and recounted. Robert Ross, the Secretary of State, who was no friend of the Governor, being one of the only Democrats to be elected to a Statewide office, refused to intervene.

"This is an internal problem with the Mississippi Republican Party, and it should be handled internally unless a Circuit Court Judge or a judge from the Mississippi Appellate Court gets involved," Ross was quoted as saying.

The other issue was that Mississippi didn't require voters to register their parties. This had been a point of contention in a previous Presidential Primary and had made its way to the Fifth Circuit in New Orleans, who promptly squashed the issue.

The votes were counted and counted again precinct by precinct, county by county, and finally certified by the

Circuit Clerk in every county until a new number was brought forth.

By the time all eighty-two counties were recounted, the new numbers were as follows. 157,606 votes were cast for Jake Fayard, and 157,602 voted for Christie Stacy. Jake was leading by a mere four votes in a Statewide election for a federal seat, which was almost unheard of.

Mississippi law requires a runoff election only if one candidate does not achieve fifty percent plus one vote. Jake had achieved this, but with the Mississippi Republican Party still refusing to certify the election and the local media in all the municipalities saying, "Election is too close to call," Jake was beside himself on what to do.

The Governor was planning some damage control in the Stacy camp and had put out a statement that said, "Christine Stacy is an honorable Senator. She represents the will of the citizens of Mississippi and will not rest until all the votes are properly counted.

Mr. Fayard is trying to ramrod this into certification by bully the Mississippi Republican Party and the Secretary of State into certifying an election that he has not won."

Minutes after the Governor put his statement out; Jake received a telephone call from a reporter in Jackson asking for a rebuttal.

"I have not bullied anybody. I haven't even contacted the Secretary of State nor the Chairman of the Mississippi Republican Party. Why would I do this when I have an advantage of polling numbers?" Jake replied, obviously annoyed at the question.

National media had turned its attention to the previously insignificant Senator's race in Mississippi. Reporters from the New York Times and USA Today had requested interviews from Jake Fayard and Christine Stacy.

Jake and Christine were becoming household names almost overnight. Several Right-Wing syndicated talk show hosts wanted to talk to Jake, and he granted every one of them. Most of the talk show hosts were well acquainted with the now-deceased senator.

One smartass radio host from Florida asked Jake why he was trying to destroy the Republican Party. Jake somehow managed to answer professionally. "Sir, I am not trying to destroy the Republican Party. I am simply trying to give everybody a voice, a vote, and to bring back integrity into Mississippi politics."

The Governor heard the radio show and decided to put out another statement. "Mr. Fayard doesn't have faith in the voters and the election process in the State of Mississippi. He thinks we are all a bunch of backward rednecks who have no integrity." Jake was forced to defend that statement repeatedly.

"The Governor has attacked me several times. I am not saying that the State of Mississippi is corrupt. I am saying that there is a system in Mississippi that threatens Democracy and threatens the principle of one man, one vote. The Governor and his political cronies spearhead this system." Jake said in a televised interview on Fox News.

Neither the Fayard camp nor the Stacy camp would concede the race. The Mississippi Republican Party refused to certify the election citing the race being too close to call and conduct unbecoming on Jake Fayard and his interviews. Jake asked his attorney to file a lawsuit for a Judge to decide.

A four-vote margin still separated the candidates in favor of Jake Fayard. Three weeks later, an impartial judiciary functioned as an arbitrator for the election. Both candidates signed an agreement that they would not contest the Judge's decision. The document was made public by both camps and the media outlets.

The Judge, a frail man of seventy-five, was Buford Daniels, a highly respected judiciary with forty years on the bench. He was known for quoting the bible in court and was known for his no-nonsense stance for grandstanding.

At the Lauderdale County Courthouse, the scene was high profile and heavily saturated with reporters. In his small but quaint courtroom in Meridian, Judge Daniels read the case's evidence and listened to the lawyers make their arguments in great courtroom theatrics that would make a great TV sitcom episode. The judge took a week to research case law and court precedence.

One week later, Judge Daniels came back with his verdict. "Jake Fayard has won his election by four certified votes." And the gavel banged on the bench. The Judge left his courtroom and retired to his chambers to write the order. He refused interviews from reporters, as was his custom. The Governor and his political cronies were furious.

At the Governor's Mansion in Jackson, Governor Creel was beside himself. "How the hell did this happen?" he screamed. He was upset that the young lawyer had tipped over the political machine, which was a first for Mississippi.

"What are you going to do now?" George Walter said, "Throw everything behind the Democrat?"

"The day I back Jim Bates is the day you can throw me in the nuthouse at Whitfield!" The Governor exclaimed.

"What about Dwight Skinner?" George asked. "I know he's an independent candidate, but he seems like he would love to play ball."

"Dwight Skinner would be a man that could take orders, and he would love some cash flow put into his campaign." The Governor said.

Dwight Skinner was a former Republican City Councilman from Jackson who served one term and was nearly a disaster. The Republican Party all but excommunicated him like the Catholic Church would a man who was full of abominable sin that refused to redeem himself. His political career had almost ended his professional life as a small business owner selling computer equipment. He was 63 years old. A loud, boastful man, usually known to be a vociferous vocal critic of the Republican Party ever since they ran somebody against him in the Primary all those years ago. He was known for his conspiracy theories of people who were out to destroy him, this country, and swore that the New World Order had sworn a personal vendetta against him using the Republican Party as it's vehicle of vengeance. Dwight Skinner was a complete nut.

"When would you like to meet with him?" George asked.

"I'll call him tomorrow." The Governor said. "It'll be a blast."

The two parted ways, and promptly at ten o'clock in the morning, the Governor called Dwight Skinner.

"What can I do for you?" Mr. Skinner asked the Governor.

"I think it's more of what I can do for you." The Governor replied. "Would you like to meet with me at the Governor's mansion this afternoon?"

"Sure… What do you have in mind?" Skinner replied, puzzled.

"Well, what I have in mind is money and a winning election." The Governor said. "Can I count on you to show up?"

"Sure, I would love to meet you this afternoon. I ain't got anything going on today." Skinner said.

"Ok, see you at two." The Governor said.

The two hung up, and the Governor prepared for his guest. Two members of the Mississippi Highway Patrol and George Walter were awaiting the guest at the end of a long mahogany conference table with the Governor on the other. A bottle of expensive Bourbon with five glasses was set aside. A check for $50,000 was printed as Pay to the Order of Dwight Skinner.

Mr. Skinner arrived on schedule in a grey suit that was wearing thin from overuse. His white shirt had a frayed collar. He looked almost like a 1930's hobo instead of a candidate for office. He didn't look like a man the Governor of the State of Mississippi would help gain a United States Senate Seat.

"I guess a tailor should have been employed as well," George Walter whispered to the Governor, who nodded his head in agreement.

Dwight Skinner stepped up with a confused look asked the Governor what he had in mind.

"Dwight, what I have in mind is making you a deal. Here's $50,000 to start, and more will be funneled in. If anybody asked you sold some computer parts or something. You should think about buying a new suit." The Governor said with a plastic smile.

"I'll be your campaign manager." George Walter said.

"I'll have to keep this quiet because I am a Republican Governor helping an Independent candidate, but when you get elected, you should switch back to the Republican Party." The Governor said. "I'll funnel every dime I can through backdoor channels to you if you accept my proposal. How does this sound?"

"Sounds too good to be true…." Skinner said. "What's the catch?"

"The catch is you take orders." The Governor said, frankly. "You will do as I say, but it won't be anything that will get you in any trouble."

"If you do get into any trouble…." George said, "I'll get you out."

"Do you accept?" The Governor asked.

"Yes, I accept with pleasure," Skinner replied with a grin.

"Ok, we'll have a drink with us to celebrate, and we will get started." The Governor said.

The five conspirators met for the better part of the afternoon and devised a smear campaign to discredit the Honorable Jake Fayard and his Democrat opponent.

Chapter Twelve

Jim Bates The Democrat

Jim Bates, a staunch liberal Democrat, was no friend of the Governor. He didn't particularly care for Jake Fayard or John Kennard and had plenty to say about both. He wasn't in the Democratic Primary as no other Democrat was running, so he was the de facto opposing candidate.

Jim Bates was a professor of History at Jackson State University. A Black man of about seventy years old, six feet one inch tall, 185 pounds, and was one hell of a basketball coach. He, too, was a veteran, having served in Vietnam as an Army Ranger. He, like Jake, had no vices, and for a man as old as he was, he stayed in excellent physical shape. He had no health issues. He remembered the struggle for Civil Rights in Mississippi very vividly. His father worked with both Medger Evers and Charles Evers when they fought for Civil Rights in Mississippi.

Jake was conflicted. He knew Jim Bates in passing and knew his background well. He highly respected the man for all his accomplishments and was once heard saying, "If I could do half of what that man has done, I might deserve this office."

Jake immediately called the campaign office of Jim Bates. He didn't know how his call would be received, but he had to talk with the great man off the record.

"Bates for Senate Campaign Office," a young female voice professionally answered.

"Yes, ma'am, this is Jake Fayard. I would like to speak with Mr. Bates. Is he about?" Jake asked very politely and professionally.

"Hold on just one minute, sir." The voice said.

"Hello?" a man's voice said on the phone with authority.

"Yes, sir, is this Mr. Bates?" Jake asked politely.

"Yes, sir, and with whom do I have the pleasure of speaking?" Jim Bates replied.

"This is Jake Fayard. May I buy you a cup of coffee and speak with you off the record?" Jake replied meekly.

"Of course, when do you want to do this?" Bates replied.

"This afternoon if you don't mind sir. I can drive up and meet you. It would be my great pleasure, sir." Jake responded.

"Fine with me, see you then," Bates said, and the phone went dead.

Jake told Agent Ford his plans to drive up to Jackson and converse with Mr. Bates. He started his truck and made the drive north to Jackson. His vehicle was racking up more miles this month than it had in the previous five years he owned it.

Jake arrived at the campaign office on Fortification Street in Jackson. He walked in, not quite knowing what to expect. A few of his campaign staff recognized him immediately and asked him what he was doing there as if he was a lost tourist. "I came to take Mr. Bates to lunch." He replied pleasantly.

Jim Bates walked into the main office from a back room. He was dressed in casual slacks, a polo shirt, and loafers. The two shook hands and introduced themselves. "I have a coffee pot over here," Jim said as he pointed toward an unoccupied conference room. "That would be fine, sir," Jake answered with a smile.

"I am going to start by saying that I will not run a smear campaign," Jake said. "I know all about you, and I respect you entirely too much. We're both grown men and veterans, so I refuse to do that."

"That's good, Mr. Fayard; I won't either." Jim Bates said.

"Call me Jake, please," Jake said

"Ok then, you call me Jim." Mr. Bates replied with a smile.

Jake was honored to be in Jim Bates's presence. Secretly he wanted to win but would be okay with either of the two gentlemen representing Mississippi in the Senate.

"I understand you are a member of the Sons of Confederate Veterans," Jim said.

"Yes, sir, that is true," Jake replied cautiously.

"My campaign will not be run on race." Jim Bates said, "Because that is the last thing Mississippi needs is a race war; however, I do have to ask. How do you expect Black people to trust a man like you?"

Jake hadn't anticipated the question. It was a very valid point the great man was making, and Jake understood it well, but it was completely unexpected. It set the tone of the conversation. Mr. Bates was used to asking his students challenging questions, and he knew he wouldn't be treated any differently.

"I would hope they would judge me on my merit. I am a historian, and I believe, though horrible things were done, and people were enslaved wrongfully, that history should be preserved." Jake responded weakly.

"I am a history professor, Jake, and I know about the atrocities that were done to my people. I also remember my father coming home from work with his boss, Medger Evers, when he was shot in his driveway in 1963. I also remember my father having a truckload of hooded thugs in white sheets drive by our home on Ellis Avenue making threats." Bates said with a tone of anger.

"I don't have any love for white supremacists. I'd shoot em just as quick, if not quicker than you would, Mr. Bates, I promise you." Jake replied.

"I also remember the day Emmett Till was found in the Tallahatchie. I remember the trial. I remember my mother begging my father to move to Chicago in the 1950s because she thought Jackson was too dangerous for Black people." Bates said. "His reply was one that he heard Medger Evers repeat time and time. I don't know if I am going to heaven or hell, but I am going from Jackson." Jim said.

"Jim, truthfully, sir, I am glad y'all stayed in Jackson. I believe Mississippi has moved forward from its racist history, although we still have some misguided fools that are among us." Jake replied.

"Jake, I got a phone call the other day. The caller sounded drunk and asked for the 'head nigger in charge. My granddaughter who answered the phone didn't know how to respond,"

Bates retorted. "I also had watermelon and a bucket of fried chicken delivered to my office. I once had a noose suspended above the front door of my house. Mississippi still has a long way to go." Jim said.

"I am sorry you are having these issues. Unfortunately, people can't behave like grown-ass men, and it pisses me off to no end." Jake replied, "I wish I could make this race shit go away and have people see each other like men and women, the way God intended." Jake replied.

"Do you see my point, though, Jake?" Jim asked. "It's a horrible thing to live in fear. My father knew it, my mother knew it, all of my brothers and sisters knew it, and I knew it all too well. People were killed by zealots and racists. Families were torn apart, and people were forced to move and leave their homes. We saw this every day and it's horrifying."

"Nobody should have to endure what you have endured, and sir, you have my utmost respect. Had I been alive back then, I would have fought the fight with you." Jake responded.

"I wish I could believe you. How do you feel about the Mississippi State Flag?" Bates asked.

"I don't have a problem with the flag. I voted for it in 2001, and I believe the 2001 vote was legitimate. I think it's a headline issue, and people are using it to create disorder dissention for no reason." Jake replied. "It has flown since 1894 and has not changed. Sixty-five percent of the state voted to keep it, so why would we worry about it now?" Jake replied.

"Would you push with me to ask for a new vote on the flag?" Bates asked.

"No sir, I'll tell you why too. Suppose y'all lose. Are we going to vote every fifteen to twenty years on the flag until those that want it changed to get their way? What if, by some stretch, y'all do change the flag. Can the ones who want it changed back have a vote in fifteen or twenty years? Where does it end?" Jake asked, almost annoyed.

"It's a very valid point, Jake. You have some points yourself. You can't please everybody, and I think we'll have to agree to disagree on this." Bates responded.

"How do you feel about ending the Federal Reserve?" Jake asked, pointing his questions to a more Senatorial job field.

"Why would you do that, Jake?" Bates asked.

"Well, sir, the Federal Reserve is an Unconstitutional entity. The Federal Government itself and only it has the power to mint coin and print currency." Jake responded.

"Makes sense, but I'll have to look into that," Bates said.

"What about the Patriot Act? Would you push to repeal that?" Jake asked.

"I am a little worried about that one. On the one hand, I can't stand the thought of another terrorist attack. On the other hand, I don't like spying on private citizens." Bates responded.

"What about 'Civil Asset Forfeiture? Would you be willing to stop having their money and property stolen by government officials simply because they may be in commission of a crime, without the benefit of Due Process?" Jake asked

"Yes, sir, I would be in favor of that," Bates responded.

"What about this unconstitutional gun control that is being pushed? Are you in favor or against that?" Jake asked.

"I am in favor of some gun control. We have entirely too many nuts out there with guns. Our children are being shot in schools and other places. I think we need a bit more of a background check on people before they can purchase a firearm." Bates responded.

"See, that's another point we disagree on. I believe the Second Amendment guarantees us the right to carry a gun anytime, anyplace, any kind of gun we want, without the need for permits and government intrusion." Jake replied.

"How would you protect the children in schools?" Bates asked.

"Well, you would call somebody with a gun when the shooting started, right? Why not have armed teachers who are trained by Law Enforcement and meet certain qualifications carry a concealed weapon." Jake responded.

"How would you know that the teachers would be willing to do the job?' Bates asked.

"Well, you're a vet. I'm a vet. How did you know the man next to you in the wars we fought would do the job? You train him and hope for the best." Jake responded.

"I heard you say you are against food stamps and other social entitlements," Bates asked. "What would you say to the families who are struggling and need the assistance?"

"I would say that while it's unfortunate that they are going through a tough time, everybody else shouldn't be forced to pay for their problems. Also, those struggling have to foot the bill for others struggling, which makes the first party's struggling almost as bad. Socialism doesn't work, my friend."

"Something else we have to disagree on, Jake," Bates said.

"Yes, sir, it appears we disagree on a lot, but we respect each other. I feel as if we are capable of running clean campaigns." Jake said.

"Yes, Sir Jake, I think so. When do you want to debate publicly?" Bates asked.

"I'm open anytime you are. Maybe we can mend this state just by being friends and bridging a gap." Jake said.

"I'm all for it. Let's try it." Bates said

"Well, I wanted to say congratulations on winning the Primary. I have to get a few things done, and you have a long drive, but at least we can be civil." Bates said as they shook hands.

"God bless you, sir, and please have a wonderful day," Jake said, and they parted like gentlemen.

Jake left and felt honored to have conversed with such a great man. He left Jackson with a smile on his face.

Chapter Thirteen

Governor and Agent Ford

At the same time Jake was driving back from Jackson, Agent Ford received a phone call from Governor Creel.

"Hello?" Agent Ford answered.

"Yes, is this Jake Fayard's campaign manager?" The Governor asked.

"Yes, sir, who is this?" Agent Ford asked, knowing full well who it was.

"This is Governor Creel." The Governor replied. "I would like to meet with you if I may."

"Uh... ok, sure." Agent Ford replied. "When?"

"Oh, let's do it in a couple of days." The Governor replied.

"Ok, sounds good." Agent Ford replied.

After they both hung up, Agent Ford called Jake.

"Hey, brother, you ain't gonna believe this. Guess who just called me?" Agent Ford said.

"Who called you?" Jake asked.

"The Governor. He wants to meet with me in a couple of days." Agent Ford said.

"Do it," Jake said.

"Oh, I'll be wired for sound too." Agent Ford said.

"Sounds good. Let's get this asshole on tape," Jake said as they hung up.

Two days later, Agent Ford was at a safe house in Jackson getting wired up. The safe house was seized in a narcotics raid by the DEA several months previous. It was a small, two-bedroom house with the windows boarded up. The owner of record was officially the US Court for the Central District of Mississippi, and the power was kept on for "investigative purposes." Agent Ford wore his best suit. A technician taped a microphone behind his suit shirt and placed a small, solid-state memory drive in his pocket.

Agent Ford arrived at the Governor's Mansion and was warmly greeted by the Governor and George Walter, the Governor's puppy dog Highway Patrolman as he was referred to in the Fayard Camp, and Joe Holloway, Jake's former campaign manager.

George Walter pulled his pistol, and Joe knocked Agent Ford across the face with a stiff right hook. "You mother fucker get up!" Joe demanded.

"We're not going to kill you, you son of a bitch, but you will quit!" George Walter ordered.

"Fuck you, sons of bitches!" Agent Ford shot back as he groped Joe's leg and brought him to the ground.

The highway patrolman struck Agent Ford on the back of the head, nearly knocking him out, but Agent Ford somehow managed to stay in the fight in desperation.

Agent Ford stood up and grabbed George Walter by his arm, snapping his elbow on the way down, using a standard police jujitsu move. George screamed out in pain. Joe grabbed George's gun, and Agent Ford slapped him hard in his jaw. The gun went flying across the room and discharged one shot, entering, and exiting through a window. Agent Ford then turned his rage and fury on Joe Holloway.

Agent Ford punched Joe Holloway so hard in his face that three teeth and a stream of blood flew out of his mouth. The next shot broke Joe's nose and blacked both eyes. The final blow to Joe Holloway included repeated knee strikes to his torso. Joe was out of the fight and in great pain.

The three fought like a cage match. For a two against one fight, Agent Ford could hold his own. He got the better of the two, but they kept coming. George Walter landed a crashing right foot to the midsection of Agent Ford and his recorder came flying out of his wardrobe, and the Governor retrieved it. "What the fuck is this?" The Governor shouted.

"I'm a fucking Federal Agent, you son of a bitch!" Agent Ford screamed.

The other two brawlers stopped. George Walter was mid-swing again when the words dropped his arm like a stone.

"Yeah, OH YEAH, you son of a bitch!" Agent Ford Screamed as he snatched the recorder and started to walk out. "You mother fuckers just fucked up!" he snapped as he left the building.

Agent Ford drove back to the safe house. He filed his report with his supervisors, and Jack Phillips, the US Attorney for the Central District of

Mississippi, was on standby to take the deposition.

Agent Ford relayed the events of the day. Attorney Phillips said, "Well looks like we got them on 18 US Code§ 241, which states, two or more persons are prohibited from conspiring to injure, oppress, threaten, or intimidate any person in any state, territory, commonwealth, possession, or district in the free exercise or enjoyment of any right or privilege secured to him or her by the Constitution or laws of the United States, or because of his or her having so exercised the same.

"Them bastards are done." Agent Ford said. "If they would have hit me one more time, I coulda got em on battery on a Federal Agent too."

"You might have been killed too, man," Phillips said plainly.

"Yeah the day a couple of old ass white men can whip my ass is the day hell will freeze over too." Agent Ford replied.

Agent Ford left the safe house and drove back to Biloxi. Jake had already received the call from Senator Kennard and was concerned. When Agent Ford pulled up to the campaign office, Jake leaped to his feet and almost dove out of the door to check on his friend.

"You ok, man?" Jake asked in a panic.

"Yeah, the mother fuckers jumped me. I blew my cover, but we may have something on them to indict." Agent Ford said.

"You better watch your ass from now on, dude. They know who you are, and they will come after you again. If you want, I have a spare bedroom at the house, and you're welcome to stay. I have several weapons that I keep hidden inside my house, and you will have access to them at all times." Jake offered.

"I thought I was supposed to watch your back?" Agent Ford said with a grin.

"We watch each other's back," Jake replied with a frown.

"I ain't worried about em." Agent Ford replied.

"You better. This is Mississippi, and things do happen here a bit differently than the rest of the country." Jake replied with a tone of caution.

"Jake, I grew up here, dude. I was born in Gulfport. I have lived here most of my life. I know how things happen." Agent Ford replied.

The two left the office. Jake checked every weapon he had at his house, expecting an unwelcomed visitor. When he was finished, he checked his door locks and fell into bed. He tossed and turned all night, not being able to sleep, very worried about his friend.

The following day Coby called from Jackson. "My sources are buzzing in the Capitol building." He said as Jake answered the phone in an exhausted voice.

"What do you mean?" Jake asked.

"Something about a fight at the Mansion. You wouldn't know anything about that, would you?" Coby asked.

"Yeah, man, they jumped Agent Ford, but he kicked their asses," Jake replied with a smile.

"I knew I liked him for some reason," Coby said.

"Yeah, I'd put him up against a team of girl scouts any day," Jake said and laughed while looking at Agent Ford.

Agent Ford flipped Jake the bird, laughed, and then said, "Yeah, well, next time, I won't be caught off guard."

It was the last time they laughed all day. Jim Bates showed up at Jake's campaign office, genuinely concerned, and wanted to know what Agent Ford was doing at the Governor's Mansion.

Jake introduced the two and explained the situation.

"I knew this would happen. It's unfortunate what somebody will do to hold power over people." Bates said.

"Just tell your people to be careful. Would you like Agency protection?" 'Agent Ford asked Mr. Bates.

"No." Jim Bates replied. "It wouldn't look good if I had a Federal Agent hanging around."

"I understand, sir." Agent Ford replied. "The offer is there should you need it."

"I'm campaigning on the coast today. Would you like to set up a debate anytime soon?" Mr. Bates asked.

"Anytime you want," Jake responded

"Ok, I'll set it up and get back to you. Y'all be safe. It looks like y'all kicked over a hornet's nest." Jim Bates warned.

Chapter Fourteen

First Debate

The debate was held on a Friday at the Forrest County Multi-Purpose Center in Hattiesburg.

Jake arrived two hours early to find Mr. Jim Bates already there. Jake had on a blue pinstriped suit with an American Flag tie. Mr. Bates had a grey suit with a blue tie. Both were polished and shined to perfection. The moderator was a Journalism student working on a minor in Political Science from the University of Southern Mississippi.

Each candidate thought it would be better for the young people of Mississippi to see one of their own on the stage. He was a young man named John Brooks, twenty years old, and was in his sophomore year. He was white, five feet ten inches tall, 165 pounds, and wore a rented tuxedo, which Jake paid for.

Each of the candidates stood perfectly erect at their respective podiums. The military bearing from both still shown as each stood at attention with their hands over their hearts as the National Anthem was played, something they both wanted. A local artist performed the song that Jake found through his contact at WHAN. He heard the young beautiful female artist perform on the radio station when they had local music Mondays and asked the owner, Joe Peterson, to arrange the meeting.

The debate was a near-standing room-only event. Questions from the audience would be limited to one minute and picked from a lottery by seat number assigned at the door for those interested. No more than twenty seats would be called, and they would be selected at random by the moderator from a giant fishbowl. Each candidate had a three-minute introduction, two minutes to answer a question, and one minute for a rebuttal. The debate was broadcast live on the internet and over statewide radio networks.

Jake offered to yield the first three-minute introduction to Mr. Bates as a sign of respect to the older gentleman.

The young Mr. Brooks called out for Mr. Bates to give his introduction.

"I am Jim Bates." He said as he took a step forward. "For far too long, the Establishment has held us as a whole in the Great State of Mississippi behind and kept us all in the bondage of corruption and racism. I would like to see us represented in Washington so that the nation would not look at us in the same light as we have been looked at for the last two hundred years. I would like to be your next Senator to ensure everybody gets a fair chance and has a chance to make a good life for themselves." Jim sad.

The young moderator pointed and called out for Mr. Jake Fayard.

"I am Jake Fayard. I, too, am tired of the corruption and racism that this state has been known for. It has been known as the land of the strong back and the weak mind for far too long. My platform will help middle-class families make a life on their merit. The American dream of working forty hours and buying a house, car, and whatever else you decide to work hard for is not dead. I want to see it live again like it did when I was a child." Jake said.

The first question was to Mr. Fayard. Some of the questions were picked by the candidates, and some were chosen by some of the Political Science students at the school. The questions would be asked at random and in no particular order.

"Mr. Fayard, what would you think about comprehensive gun control to prevent mass shootings such as the ones at Columbine in Colorado, Parkland in Florida, and Sandy Hook in New Jersey?" The moderator asked.

"My answer, sir, would be a simple one. When we have a mass shooting, we always call somebody with a gun to stop it. Why would we not want to be armed as a populace to prevent shootings and defend ourselves? Criminals don't follow the law, will refuse to buy guns legally, will refuse to get a conceal carry permit, etc. so why do we leave our citizens as sitting ducks?" Mr. Fayard responded.

"May I rebut that?" Mr. Bates asked politely.

"Of course, Mr. Bates. You have one minute, sir." The moderator replied.

"I live in Jackson. Jackson has become increasingly dangerous with the crime rate skyrocketing. I refuse to leave my South Jackson home, a home I have lived in for over thirty-five years. A criminal can get a gun very easily, and gun owners don't have a history of being very responsible for the security of their weapons. I would like to see mental health background checks as well as gun registration." Mr. Bates said.

"Mr. Fayard, I will allow you a one-minute rebuttal if you would like, sir." The Moderator said.

"Mr. Bates, I live on the Coast. My town is a lot safer than Jackson. I will grant you that. Still, Benjamin Franklin once said: 'Those who would give up essential Liberty, to purchase a little temporary Safety, deserve neither Liberty nor Safety,' and I believe those words wholeheartedly when it comes to anything in the Constitution." Jake replied.

The next question was for Mr. Bates. This question came from a seat in the very back of the audience near the exit doors.

Mr. Bates?" The Moderator asked. "Can you explain what you will do to better the future of the children in this country, specifically for college-age students?"

"Yes, sir, I can." Mr. Bates answered joyfully. "I am a professor at Jackson State University. I have seen my students have to get two and three jobs just to survive and live through a four-year degree and their grades suffer because of it. For far too long, the youth of this country has been plagued by high five and low six-figure student loan debt once they graduate, and they must work nearly until they are retired to get out of debt from their student loans. I think this is a travesty. I would like to see education become affordable and the cost of living factored into federal student loans."

Jake raised his hand for a rebuttal.

"Mr. Fayard?" The moderator said. "You may proceed, sir."

Jake took a sip of water and began. "I was fortunate to have my G.I. Bill pay for some of my education. I was also fortunate enough to attend the US Naval Academy to do my undergraduate studies. I didn't have much of a student loan when I graduated, but I, like everybody else, worked in my field of study until my debt was paid. I feel as though some people abuse college and become career students and some others do get degrees in subjects that you can't find a job in. If you want help from the Government, you should A have a subject that you can get a career in, B should perform some community service, and C should have to work hard for what you want. The American tradition of working for what you want is one of the greatest traditions that we have."

The debate lasted for about two and a half hours. Both candidates were respectful and friendly. At the conclusion, the young audience was fired up. Jake was so proud of them. He loved seeing young people get involved in local politics.

Chapter Fifteen

Assassination Plot

After the debate, Jake shook hands with Mr. Bates and the moderator. He answered a few questions off stage for curious spectators and greeted them warmly. Both of the candidates showed great respect and friendship toward each other after the debate. It was a success for both of them.

Once the congratulatory celebrations were concluded, Jake walked to his truck. Before he could step into his vehicle, he heard a shot ring out from somewhere and heard his back window shatter. Jake immediately grabbed his trusty .45 and ducked behind his open driver-side door. He heard another shot, followed by two more shots. After those shots glass shattered next to him from a nearby parked car. Another shot rang out followed by several screams. Two more shots rang out and Jake crawled under the bed of his truck. When the next shot rang out, it pierced the rear bumper of

Jake's truck and ricocheted into the tire of a Mercedes Benz parked next to him. People were in panic from the hail of rounds being discharged into the dark parking lot. The last shot almost made its mark, nearly hitting him.

The parking lot was filled with innocent bystanders, and somebody called 911. Moments later, the parking lot was filled with blue strobe lights, and Crown Victorias marked Forrest County Sheriff's Department. The shelling had stopped, but Jake's training had kicked in. He shouted from the safety of his cover, "IS ANYBODY HURT?" to which one person screamed, "YES, HELP ME." The young moderator was lying on the ground behind Jake's truck with a leg wound. Jake immediately made a tourniquet out of his necktie and rendered as much aid to the young man as he could. A deputy assisted him, and they got the young man to safety. An EMT stabilized the man and rushed him to Forrest General Hospital.

Witnesses described what they thought was a naked man carrying a rifle running into some nearby woods. Witnesses also stated that they thought they heard a pickup truck with no muffler crank up and drive away. Nobody got a good enough look at the man to identify him and the truck was on a back road behind the wooded area.

Jake gave his report in thorough detail to the deputy, who wrote down every word. Jake didn't see the shooter, but he heard where the report of the round had been fired from. A round was pulled from the tailgate of Jake's truck, and as he examined it, he said, "5.56mm NATO round. It looks like the sniper used an AR-15."

"How do you know that Jake?" The deputy asked, puzzled.

"Fire enough of these, and you can recognize one. Plus, I know what an AR sounds like. I own too many of them. From the looks of the damage to the round, I would say the sniper was within one hundred meters of my truck. Piss poor shot if you ask me." Jake growled.

The shot was fired from a ledge above the Forrest County Multi-Purpose Center. No trace of the gunman was found. Jake had his suspicions but couldn't prove anything. An investigation by the Mississippi Bureau of Investigation and a hushed investigation by the Department of Justice was conducted.

"Hey, brother, are you alright?" Coby said as he called his friend.

"Yeah, man, just pissed that the mother fuckers caught me off guard," Jake replied.

"Yeah, it takes a real coward to shoot a kid from a ledge. Nobody is talking up here. The media has everything covered, and the asshole in chief is ducking them." Coby said.

"He should be ducking me." Jake said, "I wanted that kid to see the good in civil service, not get his god damn knee shot out from under him. He's lucky if he'll walk again."

"You think Walter had a hand in this?" Coby asked.

"Yes, I do think he was trying to kill me. My only question is, what happens next?" Jake pondered.

The phone disconnected as Jake drove into a dead zone. He was so angry that he didn't even bother to pick it up when it started ringing again. He found himself on Interstate 59, headed north toward the direction of Meridian. His truck was aimlessly wandering across the state in an attempt to clear his head. He found the exit for Mississippi Highway 19 and started heading toward Philadelphia. He found himself suddenly lost on the back roads of Neshoba County, Mississippi, where he had acquired some land.

Jake turned left onto Highway 16 in Philadelphia. He passed through the downtown area and when he arrived at Highway 15 he turned north heading toward Noxapater. Shortly after the Neshoba County Coliseum, he turned off onto a dirt road and began driving west. After about five miles, Jake found his property, which included ten acres of land, a small cabin, and a shooting range.

Once on the property, he set up on the target range and began firing his Glock. It had been a long time since he had practiced at the range, and he knew he should hone in his skills as a marksman if the assassins made another attempt. He loaded thirteen rounds in the magazine and another in the chamber and started firing from the 7-yard line. Every shot made its mark dead center of the silhouette.

He moved back to the 15, 25, and ultimately the 50-yard line. His groupings became more considerable as he moved back, but every round struck its mark. He spent five boxes of 100 rounds of ammunition. He picked up his brass, deposited them in a sack in the bed of his truck, and started back toward Biloxi.

When Jake got back in his truck, he realized he had a missed call from a 202-area code. He returned the call and got a concerned "Where the hell have you been?" from a voice he recognized vividly.

"Mr. President?" Jake asked meekly.

"Yeah, where the hell are you. Are you alright? I heard about the shooting. How's the kid?" The President demanded.

"Yes, sir, I am fine. The kid is stable. He's still at the hospital, and I have been at my property shooting," Jake replied.

"Listen, Jake; I am asking the DOJ to put somebody on Bates. Somebody should watch out for him. Keep it quiet, but things are getting very messy down there." The President said.

"Mr. President, he'll never accept your help. He wants to be diplomatic." Jake replied.

"Well, I am not giving him a choice. I want this election as clean as y'all do. Please talk him into accepting my help." The President ordered.

"Yes, sir, will do. Thank you for calling me, sir." Jake replied.

"Yes, sir, and you be careful." The phone went dead.

Jake immediately called Jim Bates and relayed the President's message. He pleaded with him to accept the protection. Jim Bates finally conceded and accepted the help.

"Things are getting out of control, Jim," Jake said.

"Yeah, I know. I felt like I was in a war zone. I want to do something for that kid." Jim Bates said.

"You and me both, brother. Let's go visit him tomorrow." Jake said.

"Sounds good. Keep it a secret, and I'll see you around two o'clock tomorrow afternoon at the hospital." Jim replied.

They hung up, and Jake went back to his house. Upon his arrival, he found Agent Ford sitting on his couch with a weapon pointed at him.

"Woah, what the fuck, dude? I walk into my house and have a weapon pointed at me?" Jake shouted.

"Holy shit Jake I haven't heard from you in hours. You haven't been answering your cell, and you just pop in? You scared the shit out of me." Agent Ford said.

"Yeah, well, I needed some alone time, man. I took a drive up north for a bit. Needed some range time." Jake replied, a little calmer now.

"Alright. My bad about the weapon. Mind if I crash here tonight?" Agent Ford asked.

"Sure, Wyatt, just don't shoot me with that cannon, and we'll be fine." Jake joked.

"Sounds good. Goodnight, brother." Agent Ford said as he sunk back down on the couch.

The following day Jake awoke. He and Agent Ford drove to Hattiesburg and was met by Jim Bates. They went into the hospital room of John Brooks, the 20-year-old Political Science Major from the University of Southern Mississippi. He was not the same old joyful young adult, but he was a bitter and angry young man.

"I hope you find out who did this and make him eat his fucking liver!" John snapped.

"The police are looking into it, John." Mr. Bates said calmly.

"They better find something soon. I want an arrest. I am laying here shot up hurting, and that son of a bitch is out there having a fuckin party." John snapped back.

"I am sorry that you got shot, John," Jake said. "I hope you recover soon. Is there anything we can do for you?"

"No, just leave me alone," John said. "Close the door on your way out."

"Will do you take care, son, and we will come to see you again," Jake said.

"Take care, son, and God bless you." Mr. Bates said.

The two friends left and met up at a Starbucks on Hardy Street. They drank their coffee, but neither tasted it as they were too worried about the kid in the hospital.

"That kid took a bullet meant for me." Jake finally said.

"Yes, now you have a new lease on life. Go make the best of it and let's defeat these sons of bitches." Mr. Bates said.

The two left, and Jake headed back to Biloxi. He was more determined than ever to find out who the sniper was and what was going on.

Chapter Sixteen

The Investigation

The Governor had a meeting with George Walter. They met in his office in the Mississippi State Capitol building on High Street. "George, do we know who the sniper was?" The Governor asked bluntly.

"No, Billy. My men are working on it. So far from what we know is this man is a ghost. No fingerprints, no forensic evidence, and the shell casing that was found appeared to have been a reload. We think it's some random sniper, but we have no intelligence. We are pulling the camera feeds from all over the building and parking lot." George answered.

"George are you sure we didn't have a hand in this?" The Governor asked firmly.

"Billy I swear neither me nor my men had anything to do with this." George replied annoyed at the question.

"George, I need y'all to find out who did this. That son of a bitch will use this to bury us." The Governor said.

The meeting broke up, and George went to the Mississippi Crime Lab. They had footage from all over the premises and the spent shell casings. Attorney General Coby Barhonovich was there as well to personally oversee the investigation. He noticed George Walter walking in and stopped him at the door.

"Get the fuck out of here." Coby hissed.

"Excuse me?" George answered.

"Get your god damn ass the fuck out of here before I order one of these lawmen to take you into custody for obstructing justice right now. Do I need to speak slower, or do I just need a box of crayons to draw you a picture?" Coby snapped back a little louder this time.

"You won't do that, Coby," George said with a smile and brushed past him.

"LIEUTENANT LOCK HIS ASS UP IN THAT OFFICE! DO NOT LET HIM PASS BY YOU! THIS IS AN ORDER!" Coby shouted.

A Lieutenant named Mike Heckle tried to usher George into an office calmly when Coby yelled: "PLACE THAT SON OF A BITCH IN HAND RESTRAINTS AND DO NOT LET HIM OUT!"

The Lieutenant complied and offered an apology as George was detained in an office. "Stand at the fucking door and do not let him out until I can get some people here to transport that mother fucker," Coby ordered.

Coby reached for his cell phone and dialed the Rankin County Sheriff's Department. He demanded two senior deputies come and pick up George. Five minutes later, six deputies in dark blue uniforms arrived to take George Walter to the Rankin County Jail.

"Hold him for investigation. I want that son of a bitch held for 72 hours. Make sure you read him his Garrity Rights. He is being charged with Obstruction of Justice and being held on suspicion of Attempted Murder. I'll handle the judge." Coby ordered the Deputies.

"Yes, sir, we will. Will, there be anything else, sir?" a Deputy asked.

"Yes, just one more thing. He is currently Law Enforcement. Keep him out of the computer as an inmate. Also, request that he be placed in a single man confinement cell. Nobody talks to him. Nobody visits him. Nobody has any contact with him." Coby ordered.

"Yes, sir," The Deputy replied and escorted George out the door and into the back of a squad car.

When George Walter arrived at the jail, he was afforded a phone call contrary to the Attorney General's order. He called the Governor, who sent a team of lawyers and high-ranking Troopers from the Mississippi Highway Patrol. A call to the Sheriff was placed, and George Walter was released before his fingerprints were taken.

Coby received a phone call from the Rankin County District Attorney, who informed him that the Sheriff's orders released his prisoner. He decided he couldn't do much with the politics in play, so he decided to stay at the crime lab. He ordered the security detail made up of highway patrol officers and sheriff's deputies to deny entry to anybody not directly working the case or that he disapproved personally.

Jake Fayard spent that afternoon at the FBI field office in Gulfport giving his statement about the shooting to an investigator from the Department of Justice, some wiry dude with glasses that appeared to be bigger than his face by the name of Theodore Winningham.

Theodore Winningham had the attitude of a Yankee on the warpath. It was pretty evident that he didn't like being called "Ted" or "Teddy" and preferred his full first name being called. He was from New York, and he didn't enjoy the southern annunciation of words by the Mississippi lawyer.

"Why do you carry a gun like that in your car?" Agent Winningham asked Jake with a sneer.

"Which one?" Jake replied sarcastically.

"You have more than one?" Theodore asked annoyed.

"Yeah why?" Jake again replied sarcastically.

"Why would you need all that firepower in your car?" Theodore asked with a frown.

"Why wouldn't I?" Jake replied.

"What are you afraid of?" Winningham asked with a smartass laugh.

"Not a god damn thing, man." Jake snapped back.

Agent Winningham just shook his head in disbelief that people would freely carry weapons. This was a foreign concept to him. He had spent his entire career working the New York, New Jersey, Massachusetts, Connecticut, and Rhode Island, where it was nearly impossible for a private citizen to obtain a permit to carry a firearm. He was alarmed when he asked Jake if he had a permit to carry a firearm, and Jake answered in the negative. The northern agent seemed a little naïve, but he had a reputation of being one hell of an investigator.

"Has anybody made any threats against you, Mr. Fayard?" agent Winningham asked.

"Yes, sir," Jake said and told the story about Agent Ford being attacked and the illegal wiretaps in his campaign office.

Agent Winningham closed his eyes and rubbed his temples suffering from a headache as he listened to Jake tell about the fight, the Attorney General, and the corruption in the Mississippi mud that was amuck. Once Jake had finished the story, Agent Winningham finally said, "Ok, Mr. Fayard, I don't know why anybody would want to live here. This place has so much corruption that half of the State of Mississippi should be under indictment." He spoke with as much contempt for the south as possible and with a tone that pissed Jake off in ways he hadn't felt in years.

"Well, if you feel that way, Teddy boy, then go on back up north, and I'll handle it myself." Jake snapped back.

Agent Ford stepped in before the war between the states was restarted in the small room. "Look, ok, we know

Mississippi is corrupt. We live here. We're trying to improve it, and we need your help." Agent Ford offered meekly.

"Alright, I'm going to investigate this lovely melodrama that seems to be unfolding down here, but Mr. Fayard, if anybody needs to be doing any shooting, leave it to those of us with badges." Agent Winningham said.

Jake produced his wallet and flipped out his Biloxi Auxiliary Police badge. "Agreed," he said smugly.

The trio broke up, and Jake called Coby to see if he had any more information from the crime lab.

"The Feds seized everything," Coby said, and they hung up. Agent Winningham had the evidence sent to the FBI crime lab in Quantico, Virginia and removed the Mississippi authorities from the loop.

A nerdy-looking agent with the FBI with glasses containing the thickness of the bottom of a coke bottle was examining the bullet that was pulled out of Jake's truck. It indeed was a 5.56x45mm M855 green tip armor-piercing round. Had the round been fired from a closer distance, it could have pierced the truck bed and the gas tank. Had the sniper been a better shot, he could have killed Jake from inside his truck door. The FBI forensics agent decided that the shot was fired from about one hundred meters away, just as Jake suspected. The ATF was trying to ban such ammunition a few years ago, but the law never passed. The shell casing that was found left one partial thumbprint.

The computer was analyzing the print and, at a high rate of speed, was calculating and matching for a face to accompany the print. A similar M855 round was loaded into several AR-15's and M4 variants on the civilian market to attempt to duplicate the rifling pattern on the round. The brand was identified as a Colt M4 Carbine. The FBI had identified the make and model of the weapon, lifted a print, and identified the type of round used in under a day. The Mississippi Crime Lab would have taken about a week to do the same thing.

Agent Winningham ordered nobody associated with the Jake Fayard group or any Mississippi law enforcement to access any evidence, including Attorney General Coby Barhonovich. These orders were given to every agent who worked in the crime lab.

John Kennard called a friend at the Bureau and relayed that message to Jake.

"Winningham is a hard hitter. He doesn't like people butting into his investigation. He's an ass, but he's a very diligent investigator." Kennard told Jake and Coby. Agent Ford agreed.

"He is an ass." Coby hissed

"Well, somebody tried to fucking kill me, and I want to know who," Jake said, gritting his teeth. "I don't care if he thinks he's the love child of Sherlock Holmes and Dick fucking Tracy. I want to be kept in the loop."

Agent Winningham attempted to speak with Governor Creel but was rebuffed when five lawyers from his firm objected. He was able to get an interview with George Walter and discussed the contention between the two parties. George Walter was an excellent liar, but he was not used to going up against an investigator with such ability.

When the interview concluded, George Walter found himself on the suspect's list of having a hand in the shooting. The Governor also joined him on that same list.

Investigator Winningham retraced every step of anyone known to be in company with George Walter and had access to Jake Fayard but found himself running in circles. He found out how loyal friendships were down in Mississippi. He, as an insider, was also shunned, and interviews refused.

When Agent Winningham spoke to Joe Holloway, Joe told him that Jake himself was capable of shooting the kid or having someone shoot the kid to martyr the victim. This claim was investigated, and Agent Winningham decided to re-interview Jake.

When Agent Winningham interviewed Jake, he also brought a search warrant and test-fired all of Jake's weapons. This angered the candidate, and he swore that Agent Winningham was just "jerking off with the investigation." He wanted to slam the Agent publicly. He threatened to go to the media. Senator Kennard said this was unacceptable as it would shed light that Jake himself was under investigation for either actively participating in or indirectly hiring someone to shoot at the debate.

Jake, not used to being treated as a suspect, privately cursed the day the FBI brought that Yankee son of a bitch down here.

Chapter Seventeen

The Second Debate

Extra security was placed on the second debate. This time there would be three candidates that appeared on the stage. Jake Fayard, wearing a grey suit with a remarkable tie bearing pictures of the Mississippi Delta, it was a custom job that he ordered online for this occasion, Jim Bates wearing his blue designer suit and blazer, and Dwight Skinner, showing his wardrobe had a significant upgrade with the help of the Governor.

The stage was set in Long Beach at the University of Southern Mississippi Gulf Park campus, Jake's turf. The majestic oaks that lined the campus, complete with Spanish Moss falling over the branches and the added smell of the Gulf of Mexico, was a pretty nice touch. The debate was recorded by several local and statewide news outlets and was live streamed on social media. Seating capacity was limited because the high-security risk and armed police officers on loan from the Harrison County Sheriff's Department and the Long Beach Police Department as well as Biloxi Police Bomb Squad were on high alert. An ambulance was stationed close by but far enough from campus as not to cause alarm.

Jake and Jim had agreed early on that this clown running as an independent candidate would not be welcome to their events, but a sudden influx of money into his campaign had made him hard to ignore. They had learned some of his folly with public speaking on the floor of the Jackson City Council and knew he would make a fool of himself once baited. They knew of his failed policies to reduce crime in Jackson, which had become one of the most dangerous cities in the South. They also knew he was a conspiracy nut and decided that it would be fun to play with this.

The moderator was another student, this time a young 21-year-old female named Casey O'Brien. Casey O'Brien was a law student at Mississippi College and had a very keen interest in politics. She also tried to hide the crush that she had developed for Jake.

Jake opened the debate and made his introduction, followed by Mr. Bates and finally Dwight Skinner. Dwight Skinner seemed a bit uneasy being watched live on the internet by several thousand of his possible constituents.

Jake opened first with a question for Dwight Skinner. "Mr. Skinner, may I ask you to explain your sudden influx of cash?"

Jake already had a suspicion about his source, but he wanted to draw first blood. "I have a lot of loyal and charitable contributors." Mr. Skinner answered coolly.

Jim Bates tried not to laugh and somehow managed to retain his bearing. Jake, the lawyer, knew when someone was deceitful, somehow managed not to cross-examine this liar and impeach his integrity like a lousy witness in court. He knew how much money was in his last campaign finance report, and the one before, and the math didn't add up for a mere independent candidate. He had $500 in one quarter and $300,000 the very next. Coby was already thinking about getting a forensic accountant to investigate his finances and search for campaign fraud.

Jake asked Dwight about his theories of people who were "out to get him" as he often said. Dwight rambled on about certain people in power in Jackson who were trying to destroy him and even mentioned some of the richest people in Mississippi. Dwight showed his lack of credibility and his borderline psychosis to everybody in attendance.

The debate railed on, and about 20 minutes into being questioned by the audience and the other two candidates, Dwight Skinner, appeared to fall apart at the seams like a cheap Chinese ragdoll in the mouth of a pit bull. He seemed to stammer when he spoke and began his sentences with the words "uh" and "well" with exceedingly long pauses before making his weak points. It was a disaster, which is precisely what Jake wanted.

After the hour-long debate, Dwight Skinner appeared to be unable to stand without shaking behind the podium. He felt weak in the knees and very heavy on his feet. His health seemed to deteriorate with every crushing verbal blow he received from both candidates and spectators alike. After the debate while Jake Fayard and Jim Bates entertained the crowd of reporters with interviews and answers to their questions, Dwight Skinner quickly and quietly escaped to his 1986 Cadillac Sedan Deville and hurried back to Jackson.

The debate was a disaster for the Governor. When Dwight returned to Jackson, George Walter was waiting on him. "Get in the fucking car!" George snapped with authority, and Dwight obeyed the command.

Dwight was driven to the Governor's Mansion by George Walter and one of the Governor's aides. The aid opened the doors and let the other two out. Upon exiting, they were directed to a side entrance and led into the Governor's study.

The Governor was sitting behind a black cherry desk with a rage of fury that could have set the building on fire.

"What the hell happened at the debate Dwight?" The Governor hissed.

"They hit me with so many questions it was unnerving," Dwight said, shaking.

"It's called a fucking debate for a reason, stupid!" The Governor shot back. "Weren't you involved in one when you were elected on the City Council here in Jackson?"

"No, sir, I was not," Dwight replied faintly.

"The point of a debate is to show why you are smarter than the other bastard. It is not to get your ass handed to you like a child getting called to the blackboard which hadn't studied for the quiz." The Governor yelled.

"Ok, so what do you want me to do?" Dwight asked.

"Stay the fuck out of the limelight. We still have time, and maybe we can discredit Fayard and Bates to where you will be the only viable option." The Governor Said.

"Yes, sir," Dwight said.

"Just don't do a god damned thing, Dwight." George snapped.

"Y'all get the fuck out of here. I have to do some damage control." The Governor said, and with that, Dwight was ordered back into George's car.

The Governor called his media gurus to start a slam campaign against Jake. Radio Actors were hired from all over the state, and infomercials were cut. Television ads were placed and paid for under ghost political action committees that had vague registrants. The Governor and his political machine knew this was futile, though, as the independent candidate in Mississippi rarely carried double digits at the polls.

The Governor employed his statewide radio network to interview his political experts to pick apart the Fayard camp. The bias sickened most Mississippians, and the ratings of the radio stations soured. All of this was in the name of anonymous contributors, though. Nothing could be traced to The Governor, or anybody connected to him.

Chapter Eighteen

The Shooter

At the same time the debate was wrapping up, the FBI agents who worked at the Crime Lab got a hit on the thumbprint from the spent shell casing. It was only a 9-point match, far from being admissible in court, but it gave the FBI a place to start looking. The FBI was only an investigatory agency and wasn't responsible for prosecuting an attempted murder case because it was a state charge. That would fall to the Forrest County District Attorney.

The thumbprint belonged to a disgraced Marine that received a Bad Conduct Discharge in a case that Jake had prosecuted years earlier. This gave the FBI and the local police enough probable cause to obtain a search warrant for the home of Lance Corporal Lawrence Mathews. He had been a disaster in the Corps, and his life was a total mess as a civilian. He was 30 years old, five years since he was kicked out of the Marine Corps and had spent two years as a guest of the Mississippi State Penitentiary in Parchman for stealing a car. He lived in a small trailer with his mother, an alcoholic with several diagnosed mental disabilities, and was unemployed. He held a massive grudge against the man responsible for having him relieved of his duties as a United States Marine.

As the team was preparing to strategize their raid a 911 call came in from the Shady Pines Trailer Park on Highway 42 reporting a naked man running around with a semi-automatic rifle slung over his shoulder. The caller alleged that this individual was peeping into windows and shaking his privates at people. Two police officers responded and took the deranged man into custody. The man was obviously high on illegal drugs and was found to not be in control of his faculties.

The Hattiesburg Police Department SWAT Team assisted by the Forrest County Sheriff's Department staged at a gas station near the Shady Pines Trailer Park. The officers suited up in black tactical gear, loaded their semi-automatic rifles and descended on the trailer precisely as scheduled at two o'clock that morning. The house was dark with only a small television on in his mother's bedroom. With the assistance of a battering ram, the SWAT Team entered the house armed with a no-knock warrant. The subject they were looking for was already getting booked into the Forrest County Jail.

Upon entering the house, several firearms were located with the serial numbers scratched off, several boxes of M855 rounds, and newspaper clippings about Jake. The house also contained a stash of drugs, including a methamphetamine laboratory in the shed behind the house.

The disgraced Marine was transported from the Forrest County Jail in a sheriff's department van to the Hattiesburg Police Department. When he arrived, he was read his Miranda warning, and upon his waiver of counsel four Department of Justice agents and Agent Winningham interviewed him.

Agent Winningham was convinced that the disgraced marine was a part of some militia group, which was self-evident, according to the investigator, by the sheer number of weapons located in the home. The deputies tried to dismiss this as unproven, stating that most Mississippians had a cache of arms.

Lawrence was arraigned the next day, and a Circuit Court Judge set a bond of two million dollars. After the arraignment, he was afforded one phone call in an attempt to call a bail bond agent. He called Jake's campaign office instead.

"Hey, remember me?" was the voice belonging to Lawrence on the line when a campaign worker answered the telephone.

"No? Should I?" The worker replied, puzzled.

"You should. I will kill you when I get out. You robbed me of everything." Lawrence said before a Deputy grabbed the phone. Lawrence snatched the telephone receiver away from the Deputy, which initiated a fight in the holding cell. Seven officers and deputies entered the holding cell and attempted to subdue the deranged man.

Once they got the young man under control, they placed him in a single man confinement cell, and he was housed there until he was able to regain control of himself.

The Governor was briefed about the arrest. He was pleased that George Walter didn't have a hand in trying to kill Jake. He had feared that his partner in crime had finally snapped and decided to act on his own.

Agent Winningham proudly and glibly relayed the news to Jake and mentioned that civilians carrying guns without a permit is a bad idea. "If we had more gun control and background checks, maybe that kid wouldn't be trying to learn how to walk again." Agent Winningham said in a condescending tone.

Jake vaguely remembered the case. He had been out of the Marine Corps for two years, and the Corporal Matthews case was about three years before Jake retired. He had called his old boss, Rear Admiral C.J. Drinkwater, to pull the court transcripts of the case. Admiral Drinkwater had the transcripts delivered to the Law Office of Jake Fayard by overnight courier.

The Court Martial was a straightforward proceeding. The Article 32 hearing took minutes, and the case never made it to trial. Corporal Matthews was charged with being drunk on duty for the fifth time, stealing a tank, and driving it into the motor pool building in Germany. Thankfully, nobody was injured so that he could plead out. He pled to two years at hard labor, suspended sentence, a bad conduct discharge, and forfeiture of all pay and allowances. The case took five minutes from open to close. He heard that Jake was coming to Hattiesburg and desired retribution.

Lawrence was charged with attempted murder and booked into the Forrest

County Jail. He was designated a public defender due to his indigent status, such a sad case for this man who threw his life away at a very young age. He was bound over for a Grand Jury and found to be competent to stand trial. The prosecutor offered him 25 years in prison for his actions in exchange for a guilty plea, which he accepted.

After the conviction, Lawrence was transported to the Mississippi State Hospital at Whitfield, where he was placed in a confinement wing for being criminally insane. His therapist was convinced that he would not rejoin society successfully and his hate for Jake and all authority was readily apparent. Whitfield was meant to house criminals with mental illness and proved to be the final home for Lawrence.

Chapter Nineteen

Snatched

The weather was turning a bit cooler. The campaign had been in progress for seven months now. It was one of those false fall days that was famous in the south. Mid-September and the morning temperature was 59 degrees. It was a beautiful cool day in New Orleans, and Roy Fayard had regained the trust of Doctor Meaut.

Since the incident in early June, Roy had been clean when he snuck out to Central City and found some dope to score. He spent four days at East Jefferson General Hospital and was declared sober. He returned to The Charter House and, so far, had no incidents. Doctor Meaut allowed him to have a pass to exit the facility and go to the Baskin Robbins on South Carrolton Street.

Roy boarded the Streetcar at Saint Charles Avenue and rode it passed the monumental Universities of Tulane and Loyola, passed Audubon Park, passed all of the lovely and impressive architectural structures in the Garden District, Around the bend where Saint Charles Avenue became South Carrolton Street and stopped to get some ice cream.

Long since had passed the withdrawal symptoms from the lack of drugs. He could have used this time to sneak a smoke or a snort but decided against it. This was the longest he had been clean and sober since his 15th birthday. He proudly took the green Andrew Jackson that Doctor Meaut had given him and bought two scoops of Neapolitan with three cherries on top.

He decided not to wait for the Streetcar and walked toward the River on South Carrolton Avenue. It was a gorgeous day under the Spanish Moss and the majestic oaks that lined the neutral ground near the Streetcar tracks.

He rounded the bend at Saint Charles Avenue and began walking back toward Audubon Park. Tourists with their cameras took pictures of the mansions, and college kids walked about with their backpacks. He even heard live, very loud, Jazz and decided to walk in the direction of the music.

All at once, a black work van with a Louisiana license plate partially obstructed by a broken Lamarque Ford license plate cover pulled beside him. The van had no windows behind the driver's door, and the back windows were heavily dark-tinted. A fat man with a full beard and dark sunglasses displayed a small pistol and said, "Get in the van Roy or I'll blow your fuckin head off right here right now." Roy immediately complied, and the van sped away and headed toward New Orleans East.

"What the hell is this all about?!?" Roy shouted as the van sped toward Interstate 10. Roy felt a slap on his face that knocked two teeth loose and another punch to the stomach. "You don't get to ask questions." The man responded angrily.

A New Orleans Police Officer noticed the license plate and pulled the van over on the Pontchartrain Expressway. The driver displayed a phony smile and asked, "Officer, what seems to be the problem?" Roy was bound and gagged before the van stopped.

"You have an obstructed license plate, and you were going 70 in a 60." The Officer replied. "May I see your driver's license and proof of insurance?"

The man complied and gave the officer his license. The other man in the back yelled: "Dude, what the fuck did you give him your license for?"

"Dude, I ain't going to give a high-speed chase here. NOPD will kill everybody in this van, and I don't want to die." The driver said.

All at once, the officer returned with the man's license and insurance. "I'm going to give you a warning for the speeding and a fix-it ticket for the license plate."

Just then, Roy began to struggle. He kicked the side of the van hard, and the other man in the back tried to restrain him. Roy managed to use his legs to throw the man off him and kicked the side of the van hard again. The officer instinctively drew his weapon and ordered everybody to exit the van.

"108 108 108 OFFICER NEEDS ASSISTANCE I-10 AND DOWNMAN I-10 AND DOWNMAN EASTBOUND!!!!!!" The officer yelled into his radio, and sirens from all over the city could be heard. In seconds, the High Rise was full of New Orleans Police cars, and traffic was shut down.

Roy was ungagged, and the restraints were removed. An officer wanted his statement, but he was very shaken up. Officer Guidry arrived on the scene upon getting a call that Roy had a card in his wallet belonging to The Charter House. He took Roy into his car and returned him to the facility. Doctor Meaut physically examined Roy for any injuries and called Jake, who was campaigning in Greenwood, Mississippi.

"I am on my way, Doctor Meaut," Jake said firmly and in a very concerned, almost scared tone. Agent Ford accompanied him on the 280-mile ride down.

Roy was transported via ambulance to Touro Infirmary on Fourcher Street, where they X-rayed his mid-section. He had three bruised ribs from the punch and a fractured jaw from the hard slap. Doctor Meaut reported this to Jake.

By the time Jake got as far as McComb, Mississippi, on Interstate 55, he had heard the news on talk radio. "Mississippi Senatorial candidate's son kidnapped from a drug rehab facility in New Orleans." Jake was driving at over one hundred miles per hour when he heard the news.

The New Orleans Police Department had detained the two thugs at the Orleans Parish Prison. The hawking structure located at Tulane and Broad was known to be a very rough place. Louisiana didn't have 'County Jails' like most of the country, mainly because

Louisiana doesn't have any counties; they have Parish Prisons. Orleans Parish Prison was one of the most dangerous in the country. Inmates were known to have several contraband items such as alcohol, drugs, shanks, and even firearms.

The two detectives who were questioning the two thugs dove right in. A heavy detective named Mark Thornburg and a smaller, more fit man named Detective Sergeant James Hood. "Look, fellas, in about an hour, a Federal Agent with the Department of Justice will be sitting where I am sitting. You would much rather deal with us than deal with him." Detective Hood said.

"What are your names?" Detective Thornburg asked.

The driver of the van answered coolly, "Marcus Breaux." The man that was in the back of the van with Roy kept silent. "I assert my Fifth Amendment rights to remain silent." He said finally.

"That's cool." Detective Hood said as he motioned for a Corrections Deputy to remove the man from the room. "We'll respect that."

"So, Mr. Breaux…" Detective Hood said when the other man left the room. "Do you mind telling us what happened?"

"Yes. I don't want to go to jail. I want witness protection. I am in deep fear of my life." Breaux said.

"It's a little late for that, but we'll see what we can do to accommodate you with a protective management cell." Hood sneered.

"Let me know when the Fed gets here, and I'll spill all of the dirty little secrets. There's a lot at play, and I don't wish to tell a lowly New Orleans cop shit." Breaux said almost shaking.

"Ok," Hood responded professionally. "He'll be here in a little while."

The Detectives ran a background check on Marcus Breaux. They found that he was formerly employed with the Mississippi Highway Patrol as a Trooper, but he had been terminated due to a bad use of force that landed one suspect in the hospital and killed three more. Marcus Breaux only narrowly escaped prison for his actions. A civil suit from the families was still pending in Federal Court but the docket was slow.

Jake and Agent Ford arrived at The Charter House in record time. Jake was allowed a private visit with Roy, who was visibly shaken to the core. "What happened? Why did you leave the facility?" Jake demanded from Roy.

Roy told the story with vivid detail and, in a shaky voice, begged: "Get me the fuck out of here, Dad, please!."

"Ok, let me find out what the fuck is going on first," Jake said.

Jake discussed the day's events with Doctor Meaut. Doctor Meaut was apologetic when he was confronted by

Jake, who informed the good Doctor that he had nothing to apologize for. "You have been wonderful to both my son and me," Jake replied. "It's not your fault what some son of a bitch does."

Jake left Roy in the rehab place and went to the Orleans Parish Prison with Agent Ford. Jake knew he wouldn't be allowed to help with the interrogation, but he insisted he go along anyway.

Agent Ford walked into the interview room and met with the two detectives. The detectives told Agent Ford about the connection to Mississippi, and Agent Ford quickly pieced the puzzle together. Agent Ford requested to interview the suspects one at a time, starting with Breaux.

Agent Ford identified himself to Marcus Breaux and asked about the details of the plot to kidnap Roy.

"George Walter used to be my supervisor with the Mississippi

Highway Patrol. Do you know who that is?" Breaux said meekly.

"Yeah, I know him. What about him?" Ford replied.

"He called me at my house in Brandon, Mississippi, about a job. He wanted me to snatch this dope head that nobody cared about. He paid me $5000 cash and said there would be another $5000 upon completion." Breaux said almost shaking.

"How will I corroborate this?" Ford asked.

Breaux informed Agent Ford of the location of the currency. "There is about $2300 left. I had to pay some bills, and I used some of the money."

After the interview, a Federal Bureau of Prisons transport team showed up and took Breaux to the airport. The team boarded a flight from New Orleans to Miami and Mr. Breaux was to be housed in a holding facility in San Juan. He was flown by a small government Leer jet to Miami and then transported by prison plane to Puerto Rico. Upon his arrival, he was placed in a single man protective management cell, where he would only contact the Correctional Officers.

Agent Ford called a field agent of the FBI in Jackson and gave him the address and location of Breaux's house. The currency was found, inventoried, and dusted for fingerprints. One fingerprint matched the MHP service jacket of George Walter.

A federal warrant was issued for Interstate Conspiracy to commit kidnapping and five FBI agents arrested George Walter from the Jackson field office. He was transported to New Orleans and placed in a federal detention facility.

Agent Ford smiled as he entered the interview room and sat comfortably across from George Walter. George smiled and said, "You know I should have killed you in Jackson."

Agent Ford laughed at this. Usually, threatening a Federal Agent could have carried extra charges, but Agent Ford was more amused than anything. "Tell me more." Agent Ford said as he laughed.

"Fuck you, asshole! I want my attorney." George demanded.

"You'll need him. Write down his number, and I'll call him, or would you rather me call the Governor?" Agent Ford laughed.

"Lawyer ASSHOLE!" George demanded as Agent Ford left the room.

George was arraigned in Federal court on the charges of Interstate Commerce to commit Kidnapping. His bail was set at $500,000, and he was returned to his cell. The hearing was held via videophone conference due to security concerns.

Chapter Twenty

Closing In

Governor Bill Creel sent an errand boy to bail Mr. Walter out of Federal custody. The errand boy was an ex-con that was promised a pardon and a clean record if he would perform this favor for the Governor. He had orders from the Governor to deliver him directly before him at the Governor's private residence in Madison, Mississippi.

Ben Walker, a parolee who was freshly released from Central Mississippi Correctional Facility in Rankin County, was the errand boy. He was a petty thief and low-level drug dealer, but he had done other things for Governor Creel in the past. It was unclear how the two met each other, but the fact that they were there together was something unlike what anyone would ever expect.

Ben picked George up in a ragged-out 1980's Ford LTD Crown Victoria. The car was on its last leg, and George wondered if he would ever make it back to Jackson. He didn't know the con, but he did notice that he had an old Ruger P-95 9mm under the seat. George wondered if the man driving the old car wasn't ordered to shoot him instead of taking him to Jackson.

When the old car arrived at the Governor's house in Madison, smoke came from under the hood. The vehicle died in the driveway and was ignored by all except George and one security guard. The pair walked up to the front door of the house.

When George Walter arrived inside the residence, he was ushered in and seated poolside to wait on the Governor, who was shooting skeet with an old double-barrel 12-gauge shotgun, handed down from his grandfather, a magnificent weapon.

A glass of sweet tea was offered to Mr. Walter, and he accepted. He heard a loud shot from the ancient weapon; he froze and dropped his glass, shattering it all over the ground.

"PULL" shouted the Governor, and then BANG! The second barrel was cleared.

The hearing protection was removed, and the Governor joined his old partner in crime at a table by the pool. "I'm very disappointed with you, George." The Governor said plainly, "You just cost me a lot of money and a huge headache."

"Well, how the fuck was I supposed to know they would fuck up so bad and get stopped by a nosey cop?" George snapped.

"Who gave the order to go ahead with the kidnapping? I sure as hell didn't." The Governor hissed.

"I thought we needed leverage. I thought if we grabbed the dope head, stick a needle in his arm with a hot dose, and drop him in the 9th Ward, they would think he escaped as he did before." George said stammering.

"You have made a fool out of me, George. I give the fuckin orders!" The Governor cracked. "You have fucked me royally. They know we are close. They know you take orders from me. What does that mean? It means I gave the orders as far as they are concerned, and we're both going to get fucked up."

"No, I'll handle it," George said.

"You couldn't handle your dick to take a piss." The Governor snapped.

"I will fix this shit, Billy!" George shot back in distress.

"Oh yeah, I'd love to know how especially with the fucking Department of Justice so far up your ass, they can taste your wife's cookin." The Governor said.

"It's really simple, Billy; we can still take the kid. We're looking for him as we speak. If we take the kid, it should give them enough to do. Priority number one will be finding the anointed dope head while we distance ourselves and cut all loose ends." George said in a panic.

"George, you are a genius. Cut all loose ends. Sounds like an excellent idea." The Governor replied as he reloaded both barrels. The sight of the three-inch shells being placed into the old barrels of the weapon and the breech being closed unnerved George. He knew what this could mean.

"George, get out of here. Go home. Don't do a god damn thing. This has already fucked us like a football bat, and had I known you would get this sloppy, I wouldn't have ever involved you in this shit."

Chapter Twenty-One

Explosive situation

George left the Governor's house in a taxi and headed toward his own house. The house was a red brick home located in an old subdivision built in the 1970s and was remarkably well kept.

The house across the street, which was for sale, looked as though it was now off the market. A car was in the driveway, and after two years of being listed on the real estate market, George barely noticed the new residents.

The new residents noticed George, though. They saw when he stepped out of the taxi, they heard when his key entered the deadbolt lock, they heard him in the bathroom relieving himself, they watched him in his den, and even when he made a quick sandwich, which he threw half of it away.

Agents were watching. The house was rented as a short-term lease by the

Federal Bureau of Investigation to figure out George's next move. Half of the agents had a pool on whether George would kill himself, turn state's evidence, or try to flee the country.

When George got there, he had a voicemail message on his home phone from Jack Phillips, the US Attorney for the Central District of Mississippi. "Mr. Walter, please give me a call when you get this. My office would be interested in discussing a deal with you." The voice said.

George thought long and hard about this. "Why would the US Attorney be calling me?" he thought to himself loudly. He pondered the reasons in his head. It could be a deal, or it could be immunity. It could also be a trap. He was almost afraid to pick up the phone and call him back when suddenly the phone rang again.

"Hello?" George said nervously.

"George Walter?" the voice asked.

"Yes, who is this?" he demanded.

"Please hold for Mr. Phillips." The female caller said in a very professional tone, and the call was placed on a brief hold.

"Hello, George." The voice calmly and smoothly said on the other end of the phone. "How is life in the free world?" He asked.

George thought to himself, "you have got to be fucking kidding me." He replied to the caller, "Things are great. What are you taking a fucking survey or something?"

"Yes, George, that's exactly what I am doing. I am using taxpayer resources on a recorded line to take a survey of random Americans who are freshly released from Federal lockups." The voice said with a hint of a laugh.

"What the fuck do you want anyway?" George hissed in anger.

"Oh, what do I want? Um... I want to retire tomorrow and have my own private island in the Bahamas, I want the Saints to win another Super Bowl before I die, I want a few million dollars in my bank account, oh and I want you to tell me all the dirty little secrets that you and the Governor have, in exchange for oh say, ten years in prison." Phillips said.

"Sounds like you want a lot," George said half-amused at the boldness of the lawyer.

"I'm offering a lot." Jack replied, "You assaulted a Federal Agent remember? That carries 20 years by itself. Not to mention kidnapping, transporting a controlled substance across state lines, racketeering, conspiracy, wiretapping, and I could go on. You've been a busy boy George. I could leave you locked up for the next century or two."

George pondered this and said, "Ok, I'll arrive at your office in two hours."

"Don't be late, George. I am not a man that likes to be kept waiting." Jack said with a grin.

The phone was replaced on the cradle. George suddenly felt sick to his stomach. Another call came in about the time George came out of the bathroom from the return of his breakfast. He didn't answer, but the voicemail recorder took the message. "Sergeant Major Walter? This is Colonel James Fink of the Mississippi Highway Patrol. I am informing you that you are now on an unpaid suspension, pending the outcome of your charges. If you have any questions, you may call the Mississippi….." George unplugged the recorder. He knew what that message meant. He was about to get fired, no retirement, no benefits, and some time in Federal prison.

Agent Mark Hardy, an agent from the FBI field office in Jackson, was stationed outside of the home of George Walter. He was ordered to place the soon-to-be-former Highway Patrol investigator under surveillance for his protection and see what moves he would make. His boss smelled a nuclear bomb brewing in the Governor's mansion.

Agent Hardy was a mediocre agent. He was just passing the time with the bureau until he could move on to bigger and better things. He had no interest in the case that was looming and could care less about his job. He hated Jackson but had been stationed here for three years. He hated the hot, muggy summers and the cold winters. He longed for the day he could return to Seattle and sit on the Puget Sound. He missed the snow. He missed the hustle and bustle of a real Northwest city. He missed the Pacific. He sat in his old Chevy Cavalier and fell asleep.

About 20 minutes into Agent Hardy's slumber, a man approached George Walter's Lincoln Towncar. He set a device under the gas tank and wired it to the ignition. He then picked up his tools and left in a hurry.

An hour and a half after Jack Phillips made the phone call, George Walter put on his best suit, stepped outside his front door, looked around the manicured yard of his quiet Ridgeland neighborhood, and sat in his car. He thought to himself for several moments while deciding to start the car. He knew that he was betraying a friendship of over twenty years. He had ten years looking at him square in the face one way and the rest of his life looking at him the other way. He knew he wouldn't make it in prison. He thought about asking for immunity and witness protection, but he knew they wouldn't grant his request.

"Fuck it!" George said aloud as he stuck the key in his ignition. He heard the click of the ignition lock engage. He said a prayer as he turned the lock cylinder to start the car when he took his last breath. His face rested against the horn. His hand fell from the lock cylinder. The horn was loud and annoying. Agent Hardy woke up to the unpleasant sound of the honk. He ran over and checked for a pulse. There was none. He pulled George out of his car and attempted to administer CPR. This, too, was a failure. George Walter had suffered a massive heart attack just a mere moment before he would have been blown into the stratosphere.

A dozen agents and deputies with the Madison County Sheriff's Department and the Coroner, Ridgeland Police Department, and the Jackson Police Department Crime Scene Unit all showed up. It was a zoo of blue uniforms. The vehicle was searched, the house was searched, and the device under the vehicle was located. A tow truck was dispatched for the Lincoln, transported it to the Mississippi Crime Lab, and it was processed for prints.

The bomb was a simple device made from bits of plastique. The blasting cap and coiled wire were sent to the FBI crime lab in Virginia. The fingerprints matched the same man who picked George up from the Federal detention facility in New Orleans. He was arrested for the attempted murder of a police officer and tampering with a federal witness.

Agent Hardy was placed on suspension for dereliction of his duty and sent home. The next day he was fired, and his certifications were revoked. He would never again work in Law Enforcement.

Chapter Twenty-Two

Governor's Folly

Jake heard the news about George Walter's passing. He found out what funeral home would handle the arrangements and sent flowers with a generic card. Agent Ford was puzzled at this, but he understood playing politics.

Jake hated being fake. He would rather piss on his grave, but he knew George had many friends, and he also knew that he had run afoul of the Governor. Coby sent a bouquet himself. Thirty years in Law Enforcement, most of it was full of corruption, and he was receiving flowers from two people who hated his guts.

The Governor did not attend. He was in his second term and being a termed-out Governor; he knew he wasn't going to lose any constituents. His errand boy was in custody, and he wondered what was being said.

He didn't have many friends in the FBI field office in Jackson, and intelligence was scarce. The Governor was falling apart. In control for years, the man had suddenly found himself locked in his office in the Mississippi State Capitol building, praying for refuge.

The two Federal Bureau of Investigations and four Department of Justice agents arrived at the Mississippi State Capitol building armed with two indictments for the Governor to testify before a Federal Grand Jury. The Sergeant at Arms fetched the Governor out of a meeting with the Speaker of the House, and he was presented with the indictment.

The Grand Jury summons wasn't until January, but the fact that it was presented to the Governor in a public fashion just to annoy him hit home. The fat, pompous ass that ran the state was suddenly shaken to the core. Privately he cried in his office. Agent Ford reported the news to Jake with a smile on his face.

"We think the Governor will hit his errand boy." Agent Ford proclaimed proudly. "When he does, we'll be waiting."

"Aww shucks… It couldn't happen to a nicer guy." Coby blurted sarcastically.

"It's about time that son of a bitch gets what he has coming to him," Jake said almost involuntarily. "The sooner he goes down the better off Mississippi will be."

The friends broke up and continued to work on the campaign, which included stops in Jackson, Vicksburg, and Yazoo City.

The campaign went on as scheduled. Agent Ford proved to possess great skill at organizing and planning a campaign. The press releases were all top-notch, never a filing deadline missed nor a typographical error on any publications. The stops in the Delta were also a nice touch, and people came out to greet Jake, one of the few white Republicans to set foot in the Delta for a campaign rally, with the hospitality that was second to none.

When Jake arrived in Greenwood, he met an old friend at a roadside blues and barbeque joint. Word got out in the small town, and people stopped to say hello and ask Jake questions. The unscheduled stop turned out to boost his strength in Leflore County.

Wherever Jake went, people followed him and asked to meet with him. His social media page showed a zig-zagging pattern across the state with events large and small, on open venues, in parking lots, high school auditoriums, city halls, wherever Jake could meet and talk to people. He established himself as a grassroots people's candidate. He never shied away from a question. Occasionally he would run into Jim Bates, and they would coordinate their efforts to answer questions jointly and give people a real sense of feeling like their voice actually mattered. To both candidates, their voices did matter.

Chapter Twenty-Three

October Surprise.

Jake and Agent Ford knew the Governor would try to retaliate against them for the indictment. They knew that he might try to hit Roy again. They didn't want to take any chances.

Roy was moved from The Charter House and placed in a lockdown rehab facility in Boston. The move was a prudent one because of the New Orleans incident. Roy knew nobody up north, and he was sure to be out of danger.

Roy boarded the plane in New Orleans at Louis Armstrong International Airport and flew first class with Jake. The two landed at Logan International Airport in Boston, and Jake rented a car. Roy was driven from the airport, around Interstate 90, and back to Interstate 495 around Boston's busy epicenter. The drug rehabilitation center, known as Providence, was located in Lowell, Massachusetts, on School Street.

Jake saw no street characters hanging around, no psych patients on the grounds; it looked almost like The Charter House in New Orleans, except for the armed security guard.

Jake went through the three-hour-long intake with Roy and the file from The Charter House and Doctor Meaut's recommendation. After saying his farewell to his son, Jake flew back to New Orleans and drove back to Biloxi.

A week after the Boston trip, Jim Bates called Jake to debate again, the final debate before the election. The two had advanced further than they thought they would have and had become good friends through the ordeal and proved that two opposing candidates could remain gentlemen.

The act of being gentlemen and friends in both the public and private eyes of any campaign by two opposite candidates, two different agendas, two diverse backgrounds, and two different parties was almost unheard of in Mississippi. Mudslinging was the way to go. They kept true to their word that they would run their campaigns on merit, and that's precisely what they did.

The final debate was set in Jackson on the site of the debate between Jake Fayard and the last Senator Robert Wallace. Security was tight, and people were made to pass through a large metal detector. The temperature on this beautiful fall day was 78 degrees, and the air was filled with the smell of barbeque.

Jake crossed the parking lot with his friend Jim Bates on their way to the door of the Mississippi Coliseum. They were discussing the governor's state and about to enjoy a debate and a good plate of barbeque ribs. A moment later, they heard an engine rev up. They didn't pay it any attention, being they were on High Street in Jackson, a busy thoroughfare. Suddenly, out of nowhere, a Chevy Impala raced its engine, was placed into drive, and sped toward the two.

Jake instinctively pushed Jim into a parked car away from the speeding

Impala, but Jake was clipped in the leg by the bumper. Jim was dazed by the violent shove that quite possibly saved his life, but as soon as he regained his composure, he went to his friend's aid where a crowd had formed.

When the ambulance arrived, they quickly loaded Jake into the rear and transported him to the University of Mississippi Medical Center. His knee was shattered. His leg was broken in four places, with a bone protruding from the skin. He was treated for shock, placed under anesthesia, and surgery began on his leg.

Jim ordered his staff, granddaughter, and campaign manager to cancel the event while he rushed behind the ambulance to the hospital with Agent Ford in tow. When they arrived, they were ordered to remain in the waiting room while Jake underwent treatment. The surgery lasted four hours. An hour after they arrived, five Department of Justice agents arrived as well.

Agent Smith, an Agent with the Department of Justice for six years, almost immediately ordered the cameras in the parking lot to be played back from all angles. The driver had done an excellent job of covering the license plate, and the camera screen was unable to zoom far enough to capture the image and read it accurately. Moments later, another agent with a laptop computer walked in and downloaded the footage.

The footage was emailed to Washington and analyzed by the FBI Crime Lab, and the license plate was identified. The car was stolen out of a repair shop three days prior in Greenwood, Mississippi, and the shop was not equipped with a video camera system. The vehicle was found abandoned on County Line Road near the Interstate 55 interchange in Jackson.

Two FBI agents questioned the Governor and being a lawyer; he refused to answer any questions without his counsel present.

"Awful suspicious having a Governor take the fifth." An agent said rudely. "Should I call the media?"

"You do what you feel you must." The Governor said with a smirk.

Jake recovered from his surgery and would be wheelchair-bound for the next several weeks. He couldn't put any weight on the knee, but this didn't slow him down.

Roy heard the news from his rehab center in Boston, and he paid three of his friends to drive up from Biloxi and break him out. He arrived in Jackson, three days later, at the hospital and at first, was turned away by armed officers.

Being dressed in jeans and a T-shirt with several holes in it, the same T-shirt he was wearing when he was at the rehab center in Boston, the guards thought he was one of the would-be assassins trying to finish the job.

He then went to the office of his Godfather, the Attorney General, where Coby was sitting behind his desk fuming and cleaning his .40 caliber pistol.

"What the fuck are you doing in my office, boy?" Coby snapped as he shot up from his chair in a rage of fury. "Don't you know how fucking dangerous shit is around here, son?"

"Yes, Uncle Coby, but I have to check on my dad," Roy said meekly, almost in a panic.

"Ok, I'll make some calls, but you ain't going anywhere until I get you some security." Coby said, "Just park your ass in that chair and don't move. I want you under guard to take a piss at this point. Your dad was almost killed by some son of a bitch the other day, and the last thing we need is some asshole taking another shot at you."

"Yes, sir, I'll move not one inch," Roy said as he slipped into a leather chair.

Just then, a secretary and an agent from the FBI ran into Coby's office. Coby summoned an armed security guard to watch Roy, and he was whisked away. The door was closed, and the stone-faced look on the faces of the intruders let Coby know he was in for a long night.

"Alright, what the fuck happened?" Coby demanded.

"We lost the two kidnappers in San Juan." The agent said. "They were hit while in Detention."

"How the fuck did that happen?" Coby demanded as he reached for a pack of Rolaids.

"Somebody fucked up the paperwork and moved them to an open bay dormitory. We are still investigating that. We think it was a lazy officer and a paperwork SNAFU. They were eating lunch, and a fight broke out. One of the inmates took a homemade knife and stabbed both men before Officers could subdue the brawlers." The Agent said.

"Well, that closes the book on whatever they knew," Coby snarled.

"We'll get his ass. We think it was random. We don't know of any connection to Mississippi in the detention facility in San Juan." The agent assured Coby, who knew he was lying about the prospect of 'getting his ass.'

The corruption in Jackson was so rampant that it seemed unfazed. Coby was sick of it all.

Roy was allowed to visit his father and then immediately returned to the rehab facility in Boston. Coby began working on what would seem to be a futile endeavor to piece together a case against the Governor and company.

The media sensationalized Jake getting hit by a car in Jackson. It was on all of the in-state and syndicated networks. What made it more sensational was the part about Jake saving the life of his opposing candidate.

Jake modestly admitted that it was pure instinct and proudly admitted that he and Jim Bates were friends, good friends, regardless of the difference of opinion as far as politics went.

Jim proudly checked on his friend every day until he was released from the hospital a week after the incident. Agent Ford and Jim Bates gave Jake a ride back to Biloxi and spent the night in his home.

Coby kept the heat turned up on the investigation. He pressed the FBI to investigate this as a continuation of harassment and worse from the Governor. The FBI determined that there was nothing to tie Governor Creel to what would amount to a drunk driver in a parking lot. Coby was furious.

Chapter Twenty-Four

An Honest Senator

The day was among us. The Governor was facing an indictment for his crimes, Senator Kennard was preparing for a speech about the Governor, The President was getting ready to make a trip on Air Force One the day after the election, officially to give an address about the growth of the economy, but unofficially to congratulate Jake.

The polls open at seven o'clock in the morning. Jake walked into the Lee-Chin Fire Station in Biloxi and cast his vote for himself. This being a mid-term election, a high turnout wasn't expected; however, Mississippians love to vote.

By noon there were three hundred voters at the Lee-Chin Fire Station, and this was nearly a record for the mid-term election. By seven o'clock that evening, when the polls closed, the party was kicked off in the Biloxi White House Hotel. The growing reporting precincts slowly reached 100%, short a few absentee ballots, by midnight.

Jake won the election beating Jim Bates by 20%. 55% went to Jake, 35% went to Jim Bates, and 10% went to Dwight Skinner.

The following day Jim Bates called Jake to say he would concede to the election results. "Jake, I have to hand it to you, my friend. We have pulled off the first honest election in Mississippi's history in my life." Jim said.

"Thank you, my friend. It was a pleasure to have met you and to call you my friend and a trusted brother."

The two hung up, and Jake proudly sat back in his chair to relax before his ultimate relocation to Washington.

Jake Fayard was the newest elected Senator from Mississippi. He had beaten the political machine that plagued the state for generations. He put on his best suit, shined his boots, which he did himself, and got a haircut.

Jake looked his best when he walked into the Senate Chamber on his crutches. He was still injured from the attempted assassination in Jackson at his last debate against Jim Bates, the Democrat he was running against.

Though Jim Bates and Jake Fayard were political opposites, they became and remained incredibly good friends. Jim Bates accompanied him to Washington, helped him move into his apartment, set up his new office in the Dirksen Senate Office Building, and furnished it.

Jim Bates was in the Senate Gallery watching his friend take the oath. "Jake Fayard, please take your place in the center of the floor," The Vice President said as he administered the oath. "Please Raise your right hand." Jake did as he was told. "I do solemnly swear that I will support and defend the Constitution of the United States against all enemies, foreign and domestic; that I will bear true faith and allegiance to the same; that I take this obligation freely, without any mental reservation or purpose of evasion; and that I will well and faithfully discharge the duties of the office on which I am about to enter: So help me God."

Jake Fayard became the newest Senator from Mississippi on January 3rd. After a relatively uneventful morning of swearing in new mid-term Senators, he decided to take his friends Jim Bates and Senator Kennard to lunch. Jake saw a seafood restaurant that boasted Chesapeake Crab Legs on the sign and wanted to treat his friends.

"Now that you're here, Jake," Kennard said, "You do realize that you have a target on your back. Just as a precaution, I am going to see about getting you Agent Ford to be your security." Jake nodded and took another bite of a shrimp. Just then, a man appeared, and a friendly voice boasted out, "What you sons of bitches can't invite a lowly civil servant?" It was Agent Ford in a new $500 suit.

"Hey, brother, glad to see ya. Pull up a chair." Jake said with a smile. The four friends enjoyed a peaceful lunch while looking at the Potomac below.

On the way back to Jake's office, the tone was a bit more serious. "Jake, a lot of people have questions about what happened back in Mississippi. I have heard that there will be a Congressional Inquiry. You will be asked to testify. All of us will." Senator Kennard said.

"Good," Jake said. "I want this out because the sooner this gets out, the sooner Mississippians can heal and recover from this mess."

Chapter Twenty-Five

The Hearing

Jake left his friends and headed back to his office. He began preparing for the hearing that he would be required to testify for. He would be faced off with members of the United States House of Representatives on both sides. He prepared his documents furnished for him by Senator Kennard and DOJ Director Trenton Scott.

Some of the House Subcommittee members on Corruption knew the Governor, Bill Creel, of Mississippi, who had been a staunch opponent of Jake's. John Fitzgerald, the Republican Representative of the 8th Congressional District of Texas, was the House Chairman of the House Select Committee on Mississippi Corruption.

Jake had heard how deep the corruption of Mississippi had reached the House Chamber in Washington, but he didn't realize exactly how real it was until he researched every committee member.

Jake sat down in his chair at his laptop the day before the hearing. He researched one by one all twelve Congressmen and women. Jorge Peterson was a Democrat from the 26th Congressional District of Florida in Miami and was no friend of Jake's or the esteemed Governor of Mississippi. Jake almost decided he would either be a friend or would remain mute.

There was Jim Greer, who was a Republican Congressman from the 9th District of Georgia. He could go either way because he seemed to be a bit preoccupied with Football from his Alma-Mater, the University of Georgia recently winning a BCS Bowl Championship, the first since 1980,

Benjamin Harrison, from the 4th Congressional District of Mississippi, known well to Jake as a snake who helped the Governor, He was known to have extreme feelings against Jake for daring to fight the Mississippi Political Machine that had funneled so much money into his campaign and got him re-elected eight times.

Kathy Yates was a hard-left Democrat from the 20th Congressional District of New York. She represented the district around Albany and was known to have little patience with Southern Republicans and anything Conservative. She openly hated the Gentleman from the 4th District of Mississippi and cared little for Jake. She was there as a ranking member only because she wanted to see the Republican Party tear itself to pieces.

Andy Young was a Republican when he got elected. Still, he switched parties in a daring political move to the Libertarian Party while representing the Second Congressional District of New Hampshire. Jake knew the man and his hardcore stances on Corruption. He knew Andy would be a friend on the Committee and would give him a fair chance.

Jim Woodhull a Republican from the 1st Congressional district of California, Jake knew little about him.

The others were a Representative from Oregon, Nebraska, Michigan, Illinois, Alaska, and Maine. In all, Jake was faced with four Democrats, Seven Republicans, and one Libertarian. Six women and six men. It was almost like a trial jury.

Jake awoke from his sleep promptly at 4:30 in the morning. He walked a lap around the Washington Monument in 25-degree weather with sleet in the air. He was still recovering from his injury in Jackson that he sustained when a car almost ran him down, so he couldn't run his usual three miles every morning, but he decided he could walk.

When he reached the fence of the White House, he rested. He hadn't had to run in freezing weather in years. Once, he was stationed at Reykjavik, Iceland, for a few months during his hitch in the Marine Corps and swore he would do whatever he had not to feel that cold again. The wind bit like an alligator. "Oh, how I wish I was back in Mississippi," Jake thought to himself.

Just about the time, he turned to walk back to his truck; he saw a large man in a dark grey hoodie approaching him. Jake grabbed, instinctively, for his pistol that he was used to carrying but then remembered he left it at home. "Fucking Washington D.C. gun laws suck ass," he thought as the jogger was pulling something from his pocket.

Jake immediately assumed he would be jumped by the man who was running toward him at an incredible speed, but the man stopped about ten feet from him and said, "What the hell are you doing out here, man?"

"Who are you?" Jake demanded, not recognizing the man or the voice in the dark.

Just then, the man reached into his pocket and produced a badge saying Department of Justice. "Ford said you were fuckin nuts, but I didn't believe him. We've been watching your house, and when I got the call that you left your house on foot at five o'clock in the morning, they got concerned."

"Tell Ford if the DOJ can't keep up with a one-legged man, y'all need more PT. I'll gladly offer my services as a Drill Instructor." Jake laughed.

The man introduced himself as Agent Manning and said, "Oorah Devil Dog. Now let's get your crazy ass back in some heat."

"Gladly," Jake said with a smile.

Just then, Jake's cell phone rang. It was Agent Ford calling in a panic. "Jake, what the hell are you doing running around the National Mall at 5 am? Don't you know this ain't Biloxi, and you had better be unarmed. You have people trying to kill you, man. Get in the fuckin car and go back to your apartment. We'll pick your stubborn ass up at seven o'clock." And he rudely hung up. Jake smiled and said, "Man, I guess he was pissed at me."

"We're installing a treadmill today at your apartment. Try not to wake the neighbors." Agent Manning responded. The agent drove him back to his truck and followed him home.

At precisely 6:30 that morning, Jake exited his apartment on Third Street. He walked to his old trusty Ford F-150 and slid in. His leg still hurt, but he wasn't about to show any pain. When he backed out of his parking spot, he heard a "thunk thunk thunk" hitting the fenders of his truck. He pulled back in and parked. Jake realized his truck had two flat tires on the passenger side, and his spare was also slashed.

"MOTHER FUCKER!!" He screamed as he surveyed the damage. Just then, three agents rushed him and his truck. "What's wrong, Mr. Fayard" one of the men asked.

"What y'all can't watch a man's fuckin truck?" Jake asked very sarcastically and with extreme rage and emotion.

"No, Mr. Fayard, we were being debriefed on last night's events when it happened. The truck was fine fifteen minutes ago." One agent nervously answered.

"I'm calling D.C. Metro Police and filing a report." Another agent responded.

"Yeah, I'll fuckin wait. I want the camera footage from this parking lot." Jake demanded.

Just then, a security guard appeared and said, "Sir, those cameras were disabled somehow during the night."

"Are you fuckin kidding me?" Jake snapped at the security guard.

"No, sir, they were working until about 4 am, and then the cameras covering this part of the parking lot went out." The guard said.

"Just this part?" Jake asked.

"Yes, sir, just this part." The guard frowned.

"Well, that's fuckin lovely," Jake replied.

The police showed up and began their investigation. Jake called a taxi, refusing the ride from his protection from the DOJ, and took off for Capitol Hill. When he arrived, a court of press was waiting for him.

Jake stormed by the press, red-faced and getting angrier with every step. He walked into his office with his suit in a wreck. He changed clothes into a spare grey suit he kept hanging in the closet.

Jake walked out of his office to a herd of reporters asking him about his role in the Mississippi Political Machine. Jake almost grabbed one for trying to get between him and an exit door to get to the House Chamber. The news reporters were live commenting on how rude and imposing the young Senator was. The reporters declared him hostile to questions and violently aggressive. By the time Jake arrived in the House Chamber, he had heard some Representatives discussing what had just occurred.

Jake found his seat. He was scowled at by the members of the House Select Committee. John Fitzgerald, the Chairman from Texas, looked down over his glasses at Jake and said, "Welcome, Mr. Fayard. Can you please rise and be sworn in to testify?"

"Yes, Mr. Chairman," Jake said as he rose.

"Please repeat after me," The Chairman said.

"I do solemnly and sincerely and truly declare and affirm that the evidence I shall give shall be the truth, the whole truth and nothing but the truth. I promise before Almighty God that the evidence which I shall give shall be the truth, the whole truth and nothing but the truth."

Jake complied and repeated the oath.

The Chairman opened with his usual speech about the rules of conduct and etiquette. He also gave a brief lecture on why he was investigating a Federal Election in Mississippi. He praised the integrity of the Governor, Bill Creel, of Mississippi, and his late friend Senator Robert Wallace.

Jake grimaced as he listened to the speech on how wonderful these people were. He thought about the car that almost killed him in Jackson. He thought about the attack on Agent Ford at the Governor's mansion. He thought about the bomb under the Governor's old friend and confidant, Highway Patrolman George Walter's car. He almost wished his best friend, Attorney General Coby Barhonovich, would have shot the little piss ant that this pompous ass with a Texas drawl was praising when he had the chance.

The minority ranking member of the House Select Committee, Kathy Yates of New York, opened with her speech on why small southern states were so corrupt. After the first five minutes, Jake wanted to yell, "Shut the hell up," but he restrained himself. Finally, after about 20 minutes, she stopped.

Jake got his turn. He opened with a thank you to the House of Representatives for allowing him the liberty of speaking. He informed the Speaker of his friend, referred to as the Gentlemen from Texas's "BFF," of his attempt on several lives, including his son. He told about his son being kidnapped in New Orleans. He told about the bum rap in Florida. He told about the assassination attempt in Jackson. He also told about what happened to his truck here in Washington this morning and vowed that it would not happen to his truck again. Every sentence that Jake spoke made him angrier while looking at the smirk from the pompous ass who called himself the chairman.

Jake looked over his shoulder and noticed Jim Bates, Coby Barhonovich, Agent Albert Ford, DOJ Director Trenton Scott, and Senator Kennard. He knew that they would probably be called to testify and could be excellent witnesses in favor of cleaning up his image.

Jim Bates was dressed in a black suit with a black tie as if he were attending a funeral. Director Scott was wearing his best blue suit with a grey tie, a man of 65 years old he was a giant in the room, and Agent Ford was wearing one of his $500 suits, no doubt paid for out of the budget of the DOJ, and thoroughly enjoying his new makeover.

"Ok, Mr. Fayard." The Chairman said with a frown, "Just what happened in the Mississippi Senatorial Election that led us to investigate a kidnapping, racketeering, and public corruption?"

"Well, sir," Jake started with a massive attitude of a man on the edge of snapping, still thinking of his truck and the security cameras. "Your BFF, Governor Bill Creel of Mississippi, first had his Highway Patrolman plant illegal narcotics on my son. Then he made the mistake of bribing my campaign manager to flip on me; then he made the biggest mistake he could ever make by trying to kill me ……."

"Hold on right there, Mr. Fayard." The Chairman interrupted.

"Oh no, you hold on, Mr. Lawmaker. I am talking, and you will sit down, shut up, and listen to me answer your question before you interrupt me. I'm going to tell you now. I've had a pretty bad morning. My tires on my truck have been slashed, my leg is killing me from when your friend tried to have me killed a second time, and all before my morning cup of coffee. I don't give a damn about a contempt charge because you, sir, have earned my contempt." Jake shouted like a Marine Corps Drill Instructor.

Representative Kathy Yates spoke up and said meekly, "Mr. Fayard, do you realize where you are?"

"I understand clearly where I am, and I respectfully ask that the Chairman recuse himself from this hearing because of his friendship with a possible felon who is at the root of all of this." Jake snapped back.

"Alright, we'll break for one hour, let everybody cool down, and address the motion of Mr. Fayard to recuse the Gentleman from Texas." Ms. Yates said.

The friends left the Chamber, and, in the hallway, Jake got some nods from most of the committee members in admiration and a scowl from Congressman Fitzgerald.

The committee members deliberated in a private room not accessible to Jake or his comrades, but the heated tone and high volume may as well have been broadcast on the nightly news. The shouting match between Yates and Fitzgerald sounded like a boxing match instead of a serious congressional meeting among professionals. She accused the Gentleman of attempting to whitewash the investigation, and this was agreed to by about eight others on the committee.

The committee broke from the private room, and the eleven remaining members summoned the Master at Arms to have the rest of the gallery rejoin them. When Jake arrived at his podium, he was pleased to see that the Gentlewoman from New York, Kathy Yates, had assumed the role of the Chairman.

Ms. Yates loudly proclaimed that this hearing would come to order and reminded Jake that there would be no more outbursts. Jake agreed and apologized for his remarks.

"Let's be professional and clear." Ms. Yates ordered.

"Yes, ma'am," Jake replied.

"Mr. Fayard, you started your campaign in February of last year. Can you tell us what happened in your own words?" Ms. Yates asked.

"Yes, ma'am," Jake replied, and he told about the slow start of the campaign before the article. He told about Joe Holloway; the campaign manager turned Judas. He told about the visit from Senator Kennard and Agent Ford. He told about the Governor and his Highway Patrolman. He only spoke of what he had personally witnessed, and he would leave the details to the rest of the entourage.

When he got to the part of the moderator being shot in Hattiesburg, there were more questions than answers. "This man tracked you down to kill you, years after you had him booted from the Military?" Ms. Yates asked in a surprised tone.

"Yes, ma'am," Jake replied.

"What about you holding a State Trooper hostage in your garage and threatening him?" Benjamin Harrison, the Gentleman from Mississippi, asked.

"George Walter was a snake with a badge," Jake replied with a tone of contempt. "Yes, he was at my house, armed, in a state vehicle, and not on official police business. I have reason to believe that I cannot articulate here because it is just my gut feeling that he has killed people."

"But did it happen?" Congresswoman Yates asked.

"Yeah, we held him and asked him a few questions. We didn't torture him, but we gained certain intelligence about his plans, including eliminating me from the race and possibly from this life. He also admitted to both myself and Mississippi Attorney General Coby Barhonovich that he participated in trying to frame my son for a felony in Florida." Jake replied.

Coby Barhonovich was next on the witness list. He was sworn in and asked about his role in the Mississippi Corruption Scandal. For once Coby kept his temper in check and answered all questions accurately. He informed the committee about his meeting at the Governor's Mansion after Senator Wallace died. He told of the threats he received from the Governor and Highway Patrolman George Walter. He told of Agent Winningham stonewalling the Mississippi authorities after the shooting in Hattiesburg. He let it be known that there were few alive with the character that could match Jake Fayard of Biloxi. He told of Jake's heroism during the Gulf War and his long and distinguished career in the United States Marine Corps.

Once Coby was finished, Agent Albert Ford was next on the witness stand.

"How did you come to know Jake Fayard?" Congresswoman Yates asked.

"I came to know Jake as a direct result of a meeting with Senator Kennard." Agent Ford responded.

"Who assigned you to the case?" Congresswoman Yates asked.

"Senator Kennard requested me for this assignment. We worked together some years back when he was an FBI agent. We have been well acquainted for almost twenty years." Agent Ford answered.

"So, we have Senators assigning Federal Agents to cases now. That's great. What was the first thing you noticed about this case?" Congresswoman Yates asked.

"I have lived in Mississippi most of my life. I witnessed the corruption in my state from the time I was a child. I knew how corrupt the Governor was and when Senator Kennard gave me the chance to step in and do something about it I was honored for the task. The first thing I noticed about Senator Jake Fayard was his passion for the truth and his temper when the truth wouldn't show itself." Agent Ford replied.

Congressman Harrison of the 4th Congressional District of Mississippi, the District that Jake and Agent Ford resided in, asked to be recognized by the Chairperson.

"The Chair recognizes the gentleman from Mississippi for five minutes." Congresswoman Yates announced.

"Agent Ford, you said you are from Gulfport correct?" Congressman Harrison asked.

"Yes sir I am. I have lived there for about fifty of my 56 years on this earth and I am proud to call it home." Agent Ford said.

"Me too. I also live in Gulfport. Do you remember the 1980s?" Congressman Harrison asked.

"Yes I do. What about it?" Agent Ford responded. Agent Ford didn't particularly care for the gentleman from Mississippi, but he showed due respect.

"Do you remember the corruption that ran the coast back then?" Congressman Harrison asked.

"Yes sir I do." Agent Ford responded.

"There was a lawyer on the coast who was well acquainted with some of the corruption named Cal Fayard. Do you remember him?" Congressman Harrison asked.

"I think I remember him vaguely. What about him?" Agent Ford replied cautiously.

Jake could feel his blood boiling. He knew they were about to ask about his uncle's connection to certain figures in the Biloxi underground, who were his clients at the time. He started to get a headache from the slander that he knew was forthcoming.

"Cal Fayard, who is Jake's uncle, was a hired gun for the Dixie Mafia. He was their main go to lawyer when things needed to be fixed. Isn't that right Agent Ford?" The Congressman asked smugly.

"I'm not sure about that. I know Jake has an Uncle Cal in California and they barely speak. Exactly what are you implying Mr. Harrison"? Agent Ford responded.

"I'm simply saying that if a man has that kind of pedigree, do you really want to defend him?" The Congressman asked and smiled.

"Jake Fayard is nothing like his uncle. Jake is an honorable man and would never defend such criminals as the Dixie Mafia. His uncle's clients have nothing to do with him." Agent Ford shot back.

"I yield back the balance of my time Madam Chairperson." Congressman Harrison said. The intent was to personally attack Jake and it was effective, but it didn't have the desired effect. Congressman Harrison wanted Jake to blurt out something rash but somehow Jake held his temper.

The committee wrapped up the first day and informed Jim Bates that he would be called to testify the next day. In the corridor to the meeting room, Jake saw Congressman Harrison and the two exchanged words.

"That was a cheap shot bringing up my uncle." Jake said with a snarl.

"Why? Does the apple not fall very far from the tree?" Congressman Harrison asked.

"I am not my uncle. I am not responsible for who he represented in the 1980s when I was still in middle school. Only a genuine son of a bitch would even bring up my uncle. You sir are a genuine son of a bitch and are a disgrace to the people of the State of Mississippi." Jake shouted in the direction of Congressman Harrison, who was already walking away.

The friends retired to Jake's office. Agent Ford asked Jake if he thought the Congressman was a part of the problem. Jake responded in the negative. "He's just a little piss ant who thinks he's living in a man's world." Jake retorted.

The next morning, Jim Bates was called to testify, sworn in, and sat in the center of the room.

The questions to Mr. Bates were of Jake's character and how the two had become friends even though they were on opposing sides of the ballot. Mr. Bates testified that he was proud to call Jake a friend and told of the way he selflessly put himself in harm's way to save the older man in Jackson. He told his side of the assassination attempt in Hattiesburg. He told of the moderator who was still learning how to walk after taking a bullet meant for Jake.

The committee wrapped up the first week of hearings and went to deliberate. Jake sat in his office when he got the call from Senator Kennard telling him to get back to the House chamber and address the committee one more time.

Jake walked into the Chamber with his entourage. He was sworn in again and reminded of the rules of etiquette.

"Mr. Fayard?" Ms. Yates said. "I don't know what the hell is going through people's minds down there, but you guys have a twisted way of living. We talked to everybody involved that is still alive and did an investigation that uncovered one of two things.

Either you are a victim of a very corrupt political system, and the entire state needs to be indicted, or you had it coming."

"Yes, ma'am," Jake replied. "I am not a victim, though. I am a survivor. None of these things that happened will ever have any effect on the way I serve the citizens of the State of Mississippi."

"That's good to hear. I believe we are adjourned." Ms. Yates said, and the committee broke.

Chapter Twenty-Six

Senate Debate

Jake Fayard returned to his office to catch up on legislation being debated in the Senate Chamber. It felt good to finally be at his real job, the one that he was elected to do.

The Senate was debating stricter gun control. A wave of mass shootings has plagued the country as of late, and the Senate was under pressure to do something. Very few people knew where the young Senator from Mississippi actually stood. A skinny, frail, bald man from Florida that Jake recognized as Dick Schwartz was on the floor of the Senate rambling on about something he called "Red Flag Laws." Red Flag Laws are a piece of legislation designed to take guns from otherwise law-abiding citizens without due process simply because somebody thinks they may be a danger to society. Jake listened for a few minutes before asking to be recognized.

Jake was recognized by the Senate Majority Leader, a man of about sixty-five from Michigan, named Bill Pete. Bill Pete was an establishment Republican who had been in the Senate for 24 years. He only vaguely knew of Jake and had never met him until now.

Jake stood up and said, "Ok, I have several questions about so-called "Red Flag Laws." First off, are we going to suspend the Second, Fourth, Fifth, and Fourteenth Amendments to the United States Constitution? Second, are we going to just snatch private property from our citizens for no reason? Third, when we all swore an oath to uphold and defend the Constitution, was that just a statement to get elected, or did we actually take that seriously here? Benjamin Franklin once said those that would give up essential liberty for temporary security deserve neither liberty nor security. Each and every one of you have armed bodyguards who would kill to protect you. Our banks have armed guards to protect your money. Property owners have armed guards to protect their premises. Athletes, singers, and actors have armed guards that have the job of protecting them. The President is protected by a complete armed agency of the Federal Government to protect him. Why is it that we don't allow armed guards to protect our children in schools and why is it that we can't trust our employers to protect themselves with their own firearms? Do you think your lives are more important than the lives of the average John Q. Public? These are not rhetorical questions; these are earnest questions that I have been wanting to ask for a long time. I was a Marine Officer; I served this country in war where, at 19 years old, I was issued an M-16 and ordered to kill people by the actions of those in this room. If y'all had your own way this population would be nothing more than a sheep barbeque for the wolves howling in the next pasture. This is unacceptable and I am against it. I yield back."

Jake knew he made a power play, and his statements would draw blood. He also knew he would not make many friends, but he didn't care. He stood on the side of the Constitution, and that is what he cared about. He was a Constitutional Scholar and would stand squarely on the side of that sacred document for better or worse.

The Senate Majority Leader recognized the Gentleman from Florida again for a rebuttal. Jake was almost blinded by the light reflecting on his perfectly bald head as he stood and glared at Jake.

"Obviously, what we have here is a man who wants to push for the gun lobby and push against the interest of Public Safety. He cares about his little guns and his little Second Amendment over the protection of little children in a school." Schwartz snapped. "I yield back."

Jake asked to be recognized again to respond to Senator Schwartz's comments. Recognition was granted and Jake began with a history of the Second Amendment. "The Founding Fathers just got finished fighting a war against the most powerful Army and Navy in the world when they wrote the Constitution. Any law that is pertaining to firearms is a direct contradiction to what the Founding

Fathers wanted. It wasn't about hunting or shooting varmints off the front porch, it was about survival against a tyrannical government. Looking back historically at gun control laws, most of them were passed during the Jim Crow era and designed to keep armed Black men from protecting themselves. Therefore, by my calculation they are racist laws. A woman in New Jersey was murdered by a deranged ex-boyfriend, whom she had an order of protection against, and couldn't defend herself, because the State of New Jersey refused to process her application to own a firearm in a timely manner. This is sickening that we would want to stop private citizens from protecting themselves when almost every police department is shorthanded, Judges are suspending sentences and allowing felons back out on the street in record numbers, simply because they can't find enough people to staff a jail, and more and more people are turning to a life of crime as a survival method, preying on good law abiding citizens who are wanting to feel safe and secure in their own homes. This is a disgrace. I yield back the balance of my time." Jake said with authority.

The other Senators in the room were shocked. Jake Fayard had made his first statement in the Chamber, and it was piercing. Lawmakers have historically shown that they don't trust an armed populace and have often looked for ways to restrict firearms and self-defense laws.

A protest was scheduled on the grounds of the Capitol. Several thousand citizens had driven in from various areas across the country. The sound of Harley-Davidson motorcycles filled the air, and the rumble made the ground shake. Various cars and trucks with license plates as far away as Idaho were seen. Capitol Police was on high alert from the protest and checking everybody for weapons. Senators and members of the US House of Representatives were on edge.

Jake was furious. How could a group of people disregard the very document that made our country a free country? How could people who were elected to represent us not care about those same people having a way to defend themselves? How could people like them, with their armed entourage, deny people the right to personal property they bought and paid for? Jake was so disillusioned with what he had just witnessed he felt sick to his stomach.

Jake decided to address the crowd with a television interview. A news anchor from a local Washington television station was summoned and Jake made a statement supporting the protestors.

Once in front of the camera he urged people to act respectfully and cordially. He assured the general public that he shared their sentiments. The reporter wasn't friendly to the idea of people owning guns and this was apparent to Jake. He didn't care. He urged people to follow the law as written and to keep the protest peaceful and within the law.

When the Senate returned from lunch, Jake walked into the hallway where Dick Schwartz met him.

"Hey man, what the hell was that?" Schwartz yelled to Jake.

"Yeah, exactly what the hell was that? Do you believe people should give up their guns simply because you say so?" Jake snapped back and wanted to belt this pompous ass standing two feet from him.

"Let me tell you something, Mr. Fayard. When you have seen the damage done by people who possess these weapons, then you can talk. I am tired of seeing kids get shot by cowards with semi-automatic weapons." Schwartz snapped.

"Then do the right thing and arm the teachers. You don't travel anywhere without an armed bodyguard, so why should I, as a private citizen, be forced to give up my gun? I hate living in Washington where I can't even carry my own god damn gun just because assholes like you say I can't, and I bet I can outshoot half the police force." Jake replied. "Oh, wait, you'd rather protect banks with armed guards and your own sorry ass as opposed to allowing people to defend themselves. You're pathetic." Jake said as he rudely walked away. After the encounter, Jake decided to return to his office instead of going to the Senate Chamber.

Chapter Twenty-Seven

The Reporter

A reporter was nearby and heard the exchange. She tracked Jake back to his office, where she walked in and saw him drinking some heartburn medication and rubbing his temples.

"Mr. Fayard, may I speak to you off the record?" She asked.

"Who are you, ma'am?" Jake replied.

"My name is Pam Sledge. I am a reporter for the Washington Post. I would like to talk to you about the exchange in the hallway." She responded pleasantly.

She was a beautiful woman of thirty-eight, and she had aged very gracefully. Her Shirt was just big enough for her to wear without popping a button, and her blonde hair was flowing. Her accent was that of someone from Maryland. Not quite southern but not quite the whiny cadence of the north. Jake also took note of the absence of a wedding ring on her left hand. He took a minute to admire her as he prepared for an answer.

"Sure," Jake responded. "What would you like to know?"

"How long have you been in the Senate?" Pam asked.

"Oh, about a week and a half," Jake replied with a pleasant smile.

"I see. Please forgive me as I know almost nothing about you. I just saw the argument and heard the passion in your voice, and I figured you were somebody I could talk to." Pam replied.

"Well, fire away. Ask me whatever you want." Jake said as he sat back in his executive chair.

"Well, tell me about your personal life. What brought you here? What are you trying to accomplish?" Pam asked.

Jake told about his family history and his goals in Washington. He told about his campaign and the corruption he had to fight. He told about his friendship with Jim Bates. He told about his son being a drug addict. He told about his stint in the Marine Corps. She wrote down every word and seemed a bit impressed.

"Have you ever been to Mississippi?" Jake asked her.

"No, I don't believe I have." She responded with curiosity.

"I am going to take a trip home next week. I am going to drive down and see some old friends. If you are available, you are welcome to tag along." Jake said.

"I accept with pleasure." She said.

The two parted, and Jake called Coby, who was dealing with the aftermath of the House investigations.

"Hey Brother, I'll be home next week," Jake said.

"Oh, they finally ran you out of there, huh?" Coby replied.

"No, I just need a po boy and a bowl of gumbo," Jake replied.

Jake told about the reporter and said he would be glad to introduce him to her.

"Sounds like we need some good press," Coby agreed.

The two hung up, and Jake got to work on his itinerary.

The protestors on Capitol Hill were getting increasingly hostile toward lawmakers and several vague threats were made. Senators began spending more money on security and bodyguards.

Jake didn't spend any extra money on such things, probably because he had a DOJ agent at his side, but primarily because he felt that it would make him look weak. He felt that his own security was his responsibility and lived by that principle.

Jake was greeted coldly by his colleagues as he arrived in the Senate Chamber. Every one of his Democratic colleagues and most of the Republicans treated Jake as if he was a carrier of some communicable disease. His fellow Senators largely ignored him as he took his seat.

Dick Schwartz, the pipsqueak from Florida, addressed the Senate floor and openly accused Jake of putting their lives directly in danger. He accused Jake of conspiring to incite a riot on Capitol Hill. He demanded Jake be censured for his television interview.

Jake requested recognition and was granted the floor. When he stood up he shot a look of absolute contempt to the Gentleman from Florida. He described the interview as a call to peace, not a call to arms. He told that though he was thoroughly disgusted and completely disagreed with his colleagues on this issue, he was equally opposed to an insurrection or any riots. He told that he was probably the only person on the Senate floor that has taken human life, or seen a human life taken under violent conditions. He stated that he wished no harm to anybody.

The Senate Chamber was in an uproar. Half of the Chamber wanted Jake's head on a platter and the other half didn't know what to think. Censure was voted on and the resolution failed. When the Senate broke for lunch, Jake returned to his office for some much-needed aspirin.

The rest of the week proved to be a repeat of the last couple of days and Jake was already sick to his stomach. He knew that he would have to fight like hell to earn the respect of the noble office he fought so hard to gain. His thoughts were on the upcoming trip home, a break he desperately needed.

On the appointed day, Pam Sledge arrived at Jake's office right on time at six o'clock in the morning. She was wearing a T-shirt that was almost too revealing, blue jeans, and cowgirl boots. Jake laughed at her get-up and said, "Well, I guess if you're going to go on a road trip with a redneck, why not be comfortable."

Jake fired up the old truck and headed toward the Interstate 495 Capital Beltway. The two talked about what would be a lovely vacation for the both of them. Jake told her that she could stay in a spare bedroom of his house if she desired. She accepted the invitation and asked if she could interview him on the way down. Jake agreed and said she could also record the interview for the record if she desired.

About the time they were on Interstate 64 headed through the mountains of Virginia, she produced an MP3 recorder and affixed a microphone to Jake's shirt and hers. "I guess we're connected, huh." Jake laughed. Pam laughed and said, "Yup, we're connected."

The drive was pleasant. The sun was shining, and the show-covered mountains gave the perfect backdrop. The temperature was 35 degrees, and Jake thanked God for the heater in his truck working well. "It'll be almost 60 when we get home," Jake said with a smile.

"Why don't you buy a new truck?" Pam asked Jake.

"Why should I? This old girl does the job well. She was new when I bought her and almost 20 years later she still runs like a top." Jake replied.

"What's with all the gadgets?" Pam asked.

Jake pointed to his radio collection. "This one is a Yaesu FT-857. I use this for talking to people around the world. The other one is a Yaesu FT 300. I use it for short range local communications. These are called ham radios and are beneficial when we have natural disasters or manmade disasters such as what happened on September 11th, 2001.

Would you like a demonstration"? Jake replied pleasantly.

"Sure, I think I would." Pam replied.

Jake grabbed the microphone of his FT-857 and tuned it to the 20-meter band. The screwdriver antenna began automatically raising until it reached the proper resonance and he checked into the YL Systems net on 14.332 MHz and immediately began talking with someone in Colorado. The conversation lasted several minutes, and Pam was intrigued.

After the ham radio conversation Pam got personal again with her questions. She asked about Jim Bates and Coby Barhonovich. She also revealed a bit about herself.

As it turns out, Jake learned that Pam was divorced from an abusive husband and had no children. She grew up in

Baltimore but had lived in Columbia, Maryland, for the last six years. She, like Jake, had not been in a meaningful relationship since she left her husband. Jake told about his wife, Anna. Her picture was stuck in the instrument cluster part of his dashboard.

Jake told her of his love of history. She also shared a similar interest on the subject. Pam told about her research on Fort McHenry during the War of 1812. She said she grew up with the history and was intrigued at a young age.

The trip rolled on, and they discussed politics and what her beliefs were. She disagreed with some of his stances on social entitlements but mostly agreed with him.

Around the time they arrived in Sevierville, Tennessee, on Interstate 40, Jake suggested they stop for the night. His leg was still hurting him, and though he hadn't needed the crutches for a few days, it was taking a toll.

They checked into a hotel on the Parkway in Pigeon Forge, and Jake promised to take her to Cades Cove. They rented two separate hotel rooms, which Jake paid for, and they enjoyed dinner at Dixie Stampede.

When they woke up the following day, Jake took her to Gatlinburg, and though it was in the offseason, he was still able to show her some of the sights. When they arrived at Cades Cove, the view was breathtaking. They passed by houses long turned over to the National Park Service and drove at a top speed of almost five miles per hour on the one-lane road.

When they arrived at the old one-room church, the two noticed Pamela's hand was in Jakes. Neither said anything as they kept driving, but the hands were removed. When they exited Cades Cove, Pam said she had never seen anything so beautiful.

The pair decided to continue the trip to Mississippi, and when they got back on Interstate 75, she saw signs for

Ruby Falls and Rock City. She made a note to visit these places in Chattanooga.

They continued passed Lookout Mountain, passing through Georgia and Alabama before entering Mississippi at Meridian. Jake told her of the land he owned in Philadelphia and called it God's Country. They drove down Interstate 59 and on to US 49 in Hattiesburg. Jake showed her the place of the first attempted assassination. Her heart was in her throat as she could almost hear the shots ring out as Jake told the story of the kid that was shot.

Once in Biloxi, she smelled the salt in the air as they drove west along US 90. She rolled down her window and was amazed at the beauty of a Mississippi Gulf Coast sunset over the Mississippi Sound. The color of the sun accented nicely with the reflection on the water.

"I had no idea all this was down here." She finally said in amazement.

"Yeah, it's beautiful," Jake said with a smile.

When they arrived at Jake's house, they were greeted by Coby Barhonovich and Jim Bates. Coby had two gallons of fresh gumbo and a bag of shrimp and oyster po boys.

The two introduced themselves to the beautiful lady that accompanied Jake.

"You two fought against each other in a campaign?" She asked Jim with the recorder rolling.

"Yes, ma'am. We may have been on opposite sides then, but today we stand as great friends now." Jim said with a smile.

"I would like to interview all of you." She said with a smile. She knew this would boost her status, and she knew there was a remarkable story here. She also had grown fond of Jake.

They ate their supper and enjoyed a lovely quiet evening in Jake's house. Coby found his place on the couch, and Jim took the spare bedroom. Jake offered to put Pam up in a hotel room for the night, to which she declined. Jake had a three-bedroom house, but one room was Jakes, one room was Roy's, and the other was for guests. Jake knew Roy's room was probably a mess as nobody had been in there since he was sent to rehab.

"I guess I'm bunking with your big boy." Pamela laughed.

"I guess so," Jake said with a laugh.

The two travelling companions slept in the same bed without touching, and Jake was comforted, although he felt awkward, being the first time, he hadn't slept alone in quite a few years.

When they awoke, Jake gave her a tour of the city. He showed her the lighthouse, which had stood since 1848, Beauvoir, the last home of Confederate President Jefferson Davis,

City Hall, a marble building that was built in 1908 and was originally a Federal Building before being deeded to the city in the 1960s, he took her for a walk down Water Street, a walking mall behind the hospital full of old buildings reminiscent of old New Orleans architecture, and Old Brick House, which was built in 1790 that faced the Back Bay of Biloxi. He promised to take her to New Orleans later that night to show her, as he said, "how to pass a good time." She took all of this in with great amazement.

After the tour of Biloxi, Jake and Pamela made the hour and a half long drive down US Highway 90 through Gulfport, Long Beach, Pass Christian, Bay Saint Louis, Waveland finally made a left on Mississippi Highway 607, where they later crossed into Louisiana. Jake took the back way because it was more scenic and beautiful. He stopped at a roadside park at the intersection of US 190 and US 90 just outside of Slidell, Louisiana.

The pair walked hand in hand down a pier that looked over into a bayou where he saw two Bald Eagles flying freely. They watched the birds play, and all at once, she leaned in to kiss Jake. His heart raced as the last woman he was involved with was over eight years ago. He accepted the gesture, and the two shared a long kiss that seemed to last for ten minutes.

They entered New Orleans East and proceeded to the French Quarter. Jake made the reservations at one of the premier steakhouses in New Orleans. They enjoyed steak and white wine before a night walking down Bourbon Street. The brass bands of the Quarter could be heard everywhere they went.

"Let's stay here the night," Pamela said, and Jake agreed.

They stayed at the Hotel Monteleone on Royal Street and slept in the same bed. Jake, who was guarded with his feelings, allowed himself to start falling for the blonde bombshell laying in the bed with him. Sex would eventually happen but not on this night. Jake wasn't sure if he wanted to pursue it and Pam was unsure of the thoughts in Jake's mind. They wanted each other but they couldn't get passed the initial steps of romance.

The two spent a week touring the backwoods and the old plantations of Mississippi. When she arrived at Natchez on the third day, she knew she would one day live here in Mississippi, and she knew why Jake called it God's Country.

Jake showed her the beauty of the Mississippi Delta, and when she tasted her first bite of Mississippi barbeque, she could feel herself gaining weight with every bite. Jake showed her the Delta Blues Museum in Clarksdale and introduced her to the sounds of renowned artists like Robert Johnson, Muddy Waters, Leadbelly, BB King, and other assorted artists.

On the way back to Washington at the end of the week, Pam asked when they would make a return trip. Jake promised to take her back soon.

When Jake read the Washington Post, he saw a big headline about the Senator from Mississippi fighting corruption. A picture of Jake Fayard, Jim Bates, and Coby Barhonovich standing in front of the Biloxi Lighthouse was on the front. The writer was none other than Pam Sledge.

She covered the trials of Jake's campaign and the friendship with Jim Bates. She talked about the investigations by Coby Barhonovich and his crusade to stomp out corruption in Mississippi. She mentioned the trip but didn't say that Jake asked her to accompany him. Jake decided she did a fair job of being as impartial as she could.

Jake heard a knock at the door and some commotion outside. When he opened the front door to his house, he was greeted with two Department of Justice agents holding Pam's arms. "Do you know this woman, Mr. Fayard?" an agent asked.

"Yes, that's my girlfriend, and I strongly advise you remove your hands from her," Jake said with a hint of anger in his voice.

Pam shot from the grasp of the agents and ran behind Jake. "I guess you boys didn't realize she had a key, huh?" Jake said as he closed the door.

"Girlfriend, huh?" Pam said with a smile. "I didn't know we had put a label on it yet."

"I know but it was the only thing I could think of at the time." Jake said embarrassed.

Pam turned red from blushing. She liked the idea of being Jake's girlfriend but still was unsure on how to proceed. Her last relationship ended in a disaster that would have made a Jerry Springer episode and she was a bit shy, which Jake was very shy about it as well.

"Well let's try it and see what happens." Pam said confidently. Jake readily agreed, smiling from ear to ear.

Jake placed an angry phone call to Agent Ford and said, "What are the DOJ agents doing back at my house?"

"Yeah, brother, sorry to tell you, but your detail is back on. We've had some threats stemming from your article already. Not even two hours off the press, and people are already talking about killing you." Agent Ford said.

"Mother fucker," Jake said. Who made the threats? Do we have any solid leads?"

"We have a tap on the Governor's cell phone. He's been talking about getting you to shut up." Agent Ford said. "Your girlfriend may be in danger too."

Jake hung up the phone and told Pam about the threat. "I think you should stay here. That way, I can make sure you're safe," he said as he grabbed his Glock 21 and put it in a holster.

"Oh God, you're serious," Pam said with shock and horror.

Jake retrieved a Ruger P89, 9mm pistol and handed it to her. "Do you know how to use this?" he asked.

"No, I have never fired a gun in my life," Pam said.

"Well, you might want to start," Jake said with a voice of concern. "These bastards play dirty."

"Alright, I'll learn how to shoot," Pam said, a bit concerned.

Jake took Pam through the fundamentals of firearm safety, weapons retention, and shooting. He found a range just outside of Alexandria, Virginia and started to teach her how to shoot accurately.

"Whenever you go to Mississippi always carry this pistol with you." Jake instructed. "If they find out we're together they may come after you."

Pam just nodded. Never in her life would she have thought about carrying a gun. She was just a small-time reporter at a big newspaper. Capitol Hill wasn't even her usual turf, but she was covering a story for someone else, a colleague who was on maternity leave. It was because of this fateful assignment that she met Jake and her life changed as she knew it. She didn't mind the change for the most part but some of it she could do without. The carrying a gun to report on things would definitely be one of them.

Chapter Twenty-Eight

Business as usual

After a cup of coffee and a breakfast of bacon and eggs, Jake was back in his truck and on his way to Capitol Hill. When he arrived, reporters swarmed him asking about the article. He said he would take questions in his office later today and promised to make himself available.

Upon entering the Senate Chamber, he was greeted with a warm handshake from his friend Senator Kennard and a few friendly greetings from Republicans on his side. He was greeted with a scowl from the Gentleman from Florida whom he earlier destroyed.

A Senator from Louisiana named Will Casey introduced himself to Jake and offered to explain the rules on how they do business here.

"We all try to go along to get along. We sometimes vote NO on legislation that we would normally vote YES on, and vice versa as our colleagues need us to. One hand washes the other. We are occasionally forced to trade our votes for the spirit of cooperation." Casey said.

"I don't care if that's how you do business. My representation is for the People of the State of Mississippi, and my vote is not for sale to anybody for any favors to be paid at a later date. I gave my word, and by God, I will stand tall on my word!" Jake replied. "Everybody will know me as the man that is not for sale in this Chamber. If y'all wanna sell out, then that's your problem."

Jake took his seat in the aisle. Senator Kennard was not impressed with what the Senator from Louisiana told Jake and commended Jake for standing on his principles.

"It's about time we had a politician with some balls, brother," Kennard said.

"Well, you know me, I ain't taking shit from anybody. I came here to do a job, and God damn it I'm going to do that job." Jake replied.

The next few hours were filled with the typical mundane housekeeping legislation bills that kept the Senators looking like they were doing a job, and Jake was immediately bored. He voted no on most of them due to their enormous spending legislation and yes on some that he thought would be good for the country. He was generally in the minority, and he did not vote along party lines as most of his Republican colleagues did.

After the morning in the Chamber, a Democratic Senator from Colorado approached Jake and asked if he could speak with him.

"Mr. Fayard, I am Senator Craig Dawes from Denver, Colorado. I don't think we have been formally introduced." Senator Dawes said.

"No sir I don't think so Mr. Dawes what can I do for you sir?" Jake replied puzzled. He had never been approached by a Democratic Senator before and was curious. Almost every other time he was approached in the corridor, it was a Republican trying to tell him what he was doing wrong.

"You claim to be a Libertarian and you seem to vote that way. I think maybe you can help me work on something near and dear to the hearts and minds of my constituents." Dawes said, "May we step in your office and chat about it?"

Jake was refreshed that the politeness of Mr. Dawes and the professionalism he showed. Jake pondered on the type of legislation he could help on, but he was definitely open to the idea.

"Yes sir let's step in my office." Jake replied pleasantly.

The two stepped in and Jake removed his jacket, laid it across his large brown chair, and engaged his visitor with curiosity.

"My Fayard, I can see that you are having trouble here and I think I know why. You follow your heart and unfortunately that's something a lot of us have forgotten how to do. You claim to represent the people and I honestly think you try your best. I have something that is personal to me and a lot of people across the country. How do you feel about marijuana?" Senator Dawes asked.

"Well, I don't smoke it. I have never smoked it and I can't stand the small of it, but who are we to tell somebody what they can or cannot do with their own bodies?" Jake replied with a smile.

"Am I to understand that you agree with what I am trying to do?" Dawes asked excitedly.

"Yes sir I am. Let me know how I can help. My questions are, though, are we talking about blanket legalization, taxing recreational uses, or simply medical marijuana?" Jake asked.

"Medical would be the start of it and then once medical was passed we could talk about recreational and then blanket legalization." Dawes said.

"I think that's an excellent idea, but we are going to get a lot of push back. Two junior Senators who don't have many friends and are not part of the good ole boy system don't get much done around here." Jake said with a frown.

Senator Dawes was elected at the same time Jake was. He was a civil rights lawyer from Denver before throwing his hat into the ring of politics. His donors pumped thousands of dollars into his campaign and his seat was being vacated by a fellow Democrat who was retiring. At 50 years old, he had practiced law for 25 years and bared a youthful appearance compared to the antiques in the Senate Chamber.

Senator Dawes was about 5'8, 175 pounds, and had a quiet presence in the Chamber. He never spoke on any issue. Jake saw something in his new friend that most ignored. He saw his friend was always listening to the other candidates but looking to find the person that would listen to his ideas. He found that in Jake.

The two friends worked on the legislation until about 10 o'clock that night. The next day they entered the Senate Chamber with a fresh idea and knew that very few would approve of what they wanted. They cared not.

Jake remembered how Mississippi's ballot initiative process was robbed from the people due to political pressure over a medical marijuana bill. He remembered a Republican Governor and Mayor from Central Mississippi who sued to stop the ballot initiative. Seventy-four percent of the State of Mississippi voted to legalize medical marijuana using the ballot initiative process, but legislators who thought they knew better than their employers killed the bill and with it the ballot initiative process. It was a mess.

Jake and Craig Dawes worked on this legislation for about two weeks before letting any of their colleagues know what they were doing. The first one to be told was Senator Kennard, who was not exactly thrilled with the idea but was supportive of his friend. He warned that this could become a political mine field, but he also knew that Jake could really care less. He was gonna do whatever he thought was right and there was nothing Kennard could say to stop him.

Senator Dawes entered the Chamber three weeks after meeting Jake. They had drafted the legislation as much as they could and sought more help from other colleagues. Dawes thought it would be more productive to pass it around his side of the aisle.

The senior Senators were not impressed when they saw Jake Fayard as the co-author of the bill but took it out of politeness anyway. They vowed that they would read it and decide which committee they would assign it to. Dawes sensed their attitude and wasn't hopeful. Jake had other plans.

Jake called his girlfriend Pam and leaked the story to her. She promised that she would publish the story and did two days later. The headline read "SENATE BILL TO LEGALIZE MEDICAL MARIJUANA BEING DISCUSSED," and Jake's heart swelled with pride. He called Senator Dawes to provide more comments and Pam interviewed both of them. Pam was becoming an asset to the Washington Post when it came to issues on the Senate Floor and when she broke this story her readers were in awe.

Only Pam's bosses knew of her relationship with Jake, and she intended to keep it that way.

After Jake and Senator Dawes were interviewed by Pam Sledge and the live video went on Facebook, the other Senators were incensed. How dare two junior Senators who were on opposite sides of the aisle blindside the entire Chamber with this issue. They were unimpressed.

Phone calls came into every Senator in support of or against the impending bill. A pompous ass from Arkansas who was elected by the Religious Right decided to confront Jake. His name was Darren Preston, a preacher from a mega church in Hot Springs, and he had plenty to say about the devils lettuce.

Jake ignored him and the Chamber broke for lunch. When Jake took lunch in his office, he had no less than 50 missed calls from constituents. They demanded he vote yes or no on specific legislation, including the medical marijuana bill, and he listened to all of them. Jake decided he would set up an online poll for his constituents to give him their input on legislation and called his webmaster, a friend he knew from college named Chris Williamson, to set it up.

He would abstain from voting on any legislation until his website was updated and the poll was active for 24 hours. He decided to be a true representative of the people of Mississippi, and to do that would require their input. He also decided he would make his office as transparent as possible.

When he got home, Pam had supper cooked. It was a dinner of meatloaf with mashed potatoes and corn. He realized that she was a lovely cook and admired her in every way. He told her of his plans to make a website for his constituents to tell him how he should vote on the critical issues, and she nodded.

"I'll give that some press coverage, and maybe we can get others on board with that." She said. "My editor has learned of our relationship and now I am covering things on Capitol Hill."

"That's wonderful, congrats baby. I'm proud of you." Jake said with a smile.

"This is what I have been waiting for. How would you like to proceed with your story on the website?" Pam asked.

"I work for the citizens of the Great State of Mississippi, and I cannot think of any other way to represent her interests than to listen to her people directly," Jake said.

A week later, the website was online, and a poll was created. Pam broke the news in the Washington Post and passed it on to newspapers and other media outlets in Mississippi. The website had 500,000 hits the first day, with about 20,000 from Mississippi alone. It was full of different bills being debated in the senate and was cataloged by the type of issues that would be voted on. An application for smart phones was also built to coincide with the website.

This was the first of its kind, and when Jake got to the Senate Chamber, he was met with some handshakes and some scowls. Will Casey, the Senator from Louisiana, was not impressed.

"What the hell do you think you are doing, Mr. Fayard?" he snarled.

"I am representing my employers to the fullest extent of my abilities," Jake replied.

"You didn't listen to a word I said about to go along to get along, did you?" Will said.

"Hell, no, and I refuse to do business that way. I am nobody's 'yes man.'" Jake snapped.

"Mr. Fayard, we are elected to do this job. Some of the legislation we will pass here is too complicated for the commoner to understand. It's too important to leave up to the voters, most of which are stupid and don't care unless it interrupts their football game on TV." Will snapped back.

Jake just ignored him. He almost wished Pam was around to inform the good people of Louisiana what their elected official thought of them. Other than the verbal fight, the day went on as usual. Jake checked his cell phone for updates from his website on specific issues and voted the way his constituents told him. It worked beautifully. His votes annoyed his colleagues on both sides of the aisle, and he cared none.

The argument with Will Casey saw the marijuana bill passed to a committee where it died on the floor. Jake wasn't surprised at this, but he was annoyed. It was politics as usual and with the Republican Majority in the Senate, he knew he could do nothing about it.

Chapter Twenty-Nine

The Indictments

Six months had come and gone since Jake was first sworn in as a Senator. He had so far managed to upset his colleagues and tip the balance of power back to the people from the Washington elite. So far, three other Senators had copied his idea of the website. They didn't always vote with the online polls, but they did take them into account.

Governor Creel was on his way out. So far, the Department of Justice had been able to indict half a dozen co-conspirators. Three had copped a plea for a lesser sentence in exchange for information on the Governor. The investigation was heating up, and a Grand Jury was being prepped for Racketeering and Corruption charges against the Governor and other key players in Mississippi's political machine. Congressman Harrison was also indicted for his role in the Mississippi Corruption scandal.

Pam was on the story. She had traveled to Mississippi several times in the last several weeks to give her reports. She stayed in a hotel on Capitol Street where she drafted her reports and emailed them daily back to Washington.

Thus far, she had no incidents, and people mostly left her alone. This trip started no different. Pam entered her rented Toyota Corolla and began driving down Fortification Street. Jake and Coby both had warned her to keep a sharp eye out on her rearview mirror.

She noticed a green Dodge Neon and just had a strange feeling about the driver. She went to Coby's office and met with him for her daily report. It was a routine both enjoyed. Coby gave her information and files that he would otherwise have withheld from others. She stayed in his office for about an hour before leaving and going to another source that she had met.

When Pam turned right onto High Street heading toward Interstate 55, she spotted the green Dodge Neon again. She felt a bit uneasy. She jotted down the license plate number just in case she was right. She also retrieved the Ruger from her purse and laid it on the seat next to her. She didn't tell Coby about the Neon because she felt a bit silly to be paranoid and it was a popular car, but when she saw the man's face, she vaguely recognized him as someone she'd seen before.

Pam kept driving, turned onto the ramp marked for Interstate 55 South McComb, and raced down the highway. She looked down and noticed she was traveling at 95 miles per hour. She was weaving in and out of the traffic of South Jackson like a NASCAR driver when she saw a Dodge Charger with blue lights on top speeding behind her. She slowed down and pulled over. A six-foot-tall 180-pound Highway Patrolman named Trooper Musk walked up to her car. He snatched on the door handle and ordered her out of the vehicle. His hand was resting on his Glock, and she immediately complied with his order.

"Where's the fire?" He rudely demanded.

Pam was placed in handcuffs and placed in the rear of the patrol car. Another trooper showed up, and they searched her car. They ran her driver's license for warrants and came up with nothing.

"Why the gun?" The State Trooper demanded.

"It's for protection sir." Pam said meekly, wishing she would have left it in her purse.

The trooper returned to the weapon, ran the serial number on the weapon to make sure it was legal, and returned it to the seat. Pam, being from Maryland, thought she was going to jail, not realizing that in Mississippi it's legal to carry a weapon in your vehicle.

Pam had never been arrested before, so she didn't know what to expect. When Trooper Musk opened the rear of the squad car and removed the handcuffs, she was relieved.

"Ma'am, you cannot drive nearly 100 miles per hour on the highways of the State of Mississippi." He said as he gave her a ticket. "Also keep that weapon safe. We don't want any accidental shootings."

"Yes sir, thank you." Pam replied meekly to the trooper.

She was back on the road and on her way to her meeting, and when she neared the exit for Wesson, Mississippi, she saw the green Dodge Neon again. She hurried until she got to her exit in Brookhaven, and when she got to US 84, she quickly left the interstate.

Minutes later, she found herself in rural Lincoln County, Mississippi, on her way to Silver Creek. Her source was a former aide for Governor Creel, who contacted her and said he had some "good dirt" on the Governor. When she neared the small community of Monticello, she spotted the green Dodge Neon again and felt sick to her stomach. She heard how people who asked the wrong questions would disappear in the Mississippi backwoods and being in the backwoods of Lawrence County was no comfort.

Pam arrived at her source's home. Jason Bragg, a sixty-year-old man who was dressed in coveralls, was sitting on his porch. She introduced herself, and they walked inside the small single-wide trailer. Jason offered her a glass of sweet tea poured in a mason jar, and she accepted.

Jason produced a cardboard box containing files on dirty business deals, state contracts that were granted without proper bids, and other evidence of corruption from the Governor's mansion, all containing the eloquent signature of W.M. Creel.

Pam asked why Jason didn't turn the files over to the FBI or the Department of Justice, and he answered simply, "I have no clue who I can trust. You're not from Mississippi, and that's why I trust you. Be careful, Miss, it's a hot potato."

She thanked him for his hospitality and asked if there was another way back to Jackson. He sensed that she felt she was in some type of danger, and he offered her a less direct route that took her deeper in the Mississippi backwoods. She thanked him again and left.

Once back on US Highway 84, she decided to take Jason's advice. She traversed the road to Prentiss, Mississippi, and took Highway 13 north. When she saw the road for Mississippi Highway 28, she saw the green Dodge Neon again. It was parked with the driver's window next to another vehicle's driver's window. The car appeared to be a blue Dodge Charger, but she couldn't be sure. She quickly turned right on Highway 28 and made her way to Magee, Mississippi, where she noticed the green Dodge Neon and the blue Dodge Charger closing in fast.

Pam retrieved the Ruger P89 from her seat and dialed 911 on her cell phone. She chambered one round and placed the weapon on her lap. She was directed to the Simpson County Sheriff's Office by the 911 operator. The sheriff's office dispatched a squad car to meet her at the Dairy Queen on Highway 49 in Magee. Pam thanked them and was happy to see the squad cars when she arrived. The green Dodge Neon and the blue Charger were pulled over, and the drivers questioned.

The driver of the blue Charger produced a badge of a detective with the Jackson Police Department and was promptly let go. The driver of the green Dodge Neon identified himself as a private investigator but could provide no credentials stating that fact. He was arrested for stalking and immediately bonded out. Pam returned to Jackson and called Coby. She told him about the green Dodge Neon and the Jackson Detective, whom she didn't get his name. Coby told her to meet him in her hotel room.

"Go straight there. Do not stop. I'll meet you there in 45 minutes." Coby said.

Coby arrived at her hotel and took possession of the files. He promised that they would go over the contents the next day.

Coby called Pam, and both met at his office. When she got to his office, she noticed a black semi-automatic pistol lying on his desk.

"What's that for?" She asked.

"You really don't know what you have here, do you?" Coby asked.

"No, I don't. What is it?" She asked, concerned.

"Sweetheart, what you have here is the whole Governor's mansion and half of the cabinet by the balls," Coby responded. "People would kill to keep this quiet. I want you on a plane right now and go back to Washington. You are in danger, and you could be killed. I will have these files scanned and emailed to you within the hour."

"Jesus Christ, you're not joking." She said.

"No, I am not. That's why I am driving you to the airport myself and putting you on a plane," Coby said as he handed her a ticket. "You are booked on the next flight out. Don't even pack; just leave. I don't want you back in Jackson for a while. I'll get your stuff back to Washington, don't worry."

Coby drove Pam to the airport. He waited with her and watched her as she entered the tube to board the airplane. He didn't leave until they were airborne.

When Coby returned to his office, he saw a green Dodge Neon parked in the front of his building. He reached for his pistol and checked the car. The vehicle was empty, but the engine bay was warm. When he walked into his office, he saw a face he vaguely recognized but couldn't place.

"Hello, Mr. Barhonovich." The voice said.

"Yes, and who might you be?" Coby responded.

"Oh, my name isn't important." The man said with a smartass grin.

"I guess the green Dodge parked outside isn't important either," Coby said equally as sarcastic.

"You have something that belongs to me." The man said.

"Yeah, it's about four-tenths of an inch round, weighs 180 grains, travels about 1100 feet per second, and I have eight of em," Coby replied.

The man reached for his gun, but Coby beat him to the draw. A second later, the man was staring down the business end of a 40 caliber Smith and Wesson M&P Shield.

"WHO THE FUCK ARE YOU, MAN!?!?!?" Coby demanded.

"Fuck you." The man replied.

A minute later, six security guards who heard the struggle pinned the man down on the ground and placed him in handcuffs. Five Capitol Police Officers and three Mississippi Bureau of Investigation agents took the man into custody.

"Put this man in a segregated cell. Nobody talks to him. Nobody sees him. He does not get a phone call or anything until I find out what the fuck is going on." Coby instructed. And the man was carried away.

Coby immediately called Agent Ford and, an hour later, was greeted by four agents. Agent Ford would not be in Jackson for another three hours, but he personally vouched for every man there.

The mysterious visitor to the Attorney General's office was whisked away into Federal custody and held incommunicado. They threatened him with everything from Leavenworth to Gitmo if he didn't talk.

The man didn't identify himself to the Agents or police. He refused to be fingerprinted, and his license plate was phony. The license plate came back to an address in Clinton, Mississippi, that had been vacant for years. He never made a sound. He didn't even ask for a lawyer.

When Agent Ford landed in Jackson, he immediately ordered the man in custody to be transferred to a federal holding facility in Brownsville, Texas. The facility was poorly kept and was without air conditioning. He was fed a management meal otherwise known as "the loaf" three times a day and was held in a segregated housing unit. Officially he was charged with accessory to attempted kidnapping, and his arraignment was pending. Oh, the power of the Federal Government.

A week later, a Correctional Officer at the facility called Agent Ford with some news. Somebody smuggled a razor blade to the mysterious man, and he slit his throat. When they did a 15-minute security check, they found him in a pool of his own blood. Agent Ford relayed the news to Coby, who was furious.

The files started slowly leaking out in the Washington Post. Pam did her best to report the facts accurately, and she checked everything she posted with her sources in Jackson and other places. The papers were spot on every time.

She revealed her source to Coby, who had him placed under protective custody as a federal witness. He wasn't thrilled at all about leaving his home in Mississippi, but after hearing what happened to the man in the green Dodge Neon, he was all too quick to accept the help of the Government.

After a few days of stories leaking out in the Post, Pam started getting phone calls on her cell and office phone. People would breathe in the phone, and one person kept hitting the cylinder of a revolver on the phone. By the fifth day of the phone calls, she started noticing strange things around her car. She saw a rat screwed to her hood on one particular day.

She reported the events to Jake, who was terribly upset. He wanted to expose these people but not at the expense of a woman he had come to fall in love with. Jake realized he had to balance his love of the truth and justice against his love of his girlfriend.

Chapter Thirty

Last Days in Jackson

The Governor was in retreat in the Mansion. Six months left before he had to vacate the office, and already, he was feeling the pressure. He was grooming his replacement, his Public Service Commissioner, Daryl Grossman.

Grossman was a yes man to the Political Machine that kept the status quo in power in Mississippi and would be a shoo-in for Governor. He was 59 years old, five feet eleven inches tall and about 210 pounds, and was just down-home enough to connect with most Mississippians. He also had name recognition as the man that enacted strict voter ID laws in Mississippi. He had been sued years earlier by the ACLU for voter suppression during his tenure as Secretary of State that his second home was the Fifth Circuit Courthouse in New Orleans. He was defeated by the current Secretary of State in a race that upset the balance of power. He ran for Public Service Commissioner in a special election when his predecessor was indicted on conspiracy and corruption charges.

Grossman was well on his way to winning the Primary, and Jake decided to abstain from any Statewide elections in Mississippi as he saw no honest candidates running. He sat quietly in Washington and watched from a distance. The only race he would comment on was the Attorney General's race which was being unchallenged from the Republican side. The Democrat who announced he would run against Coby was an egotist who wanted his name on the ballot but made no serious effort to run.

Mississippi liked to vote a lot. They have an election in some fashion every year. Every two years is the House of Representatives. Every four years, the Presidential elections. The Statewide races were conducted the year before Presidential races, and the County and Municipal races were run the year after Presidential races.

Unfortunately for a state that liked to vote a lot, Mississippi voters mostly stuck to party lines. The Delta and Jackson voted Democrat and the rest of the state voted Republican. It was something that had kept Mississippi in a vicious loop since the 1990s. Everybody took for granted that the person who won the Republican primary would be the man who would win most of the Statewide offices, including the Governor's race, and 90% of the time, they would be correct.

Mississippi voters cared little about the issues, judging by how they voted, so much as they did the party. Name recognition and headlines would capture the day as opposed to real problems that actually mattered. If a candidate took a stand on a hot button issue, he or she would garner votes based solely on that. The candidate wasn't necessarily qualified to have an opinion on whatever topic they talked about; all they were required to do was take a position.

It was a trick that was deployed before the War of Northern Aggression. Back then, the hot-button issues were slavery and secession. Later became the days of Jim Crow and Segregation.

Today it was gay marriage and illegal immigration mixed with local problems such as the Mississippi State Flag.

Jake refused to partake in such reality television politics. He knew where he stood and on the issues that mattered, so did everybody else. He wasn't about to prostitute himself for the media, and even if he wanted to, he was already in office, so it was pointless. Local and State issues meant little to a United States Senator, and Jake knew he had almost no control over them.

Chapter Thirty-One

Roy's Redemption

It had almost been a year since Roy was sent to rehab in New Orleans. He emerged from his designer drug rehab facility in Boston, a clean man, and sober man. This was the first time he could say that he was clean in a long time.

Roy returned to Biloxi, a changed man. He was happy to be back on the coast and to have a shrimp po-boy sitting on his plate. The food wasn't that good up north, and they didn't have Barq's Root beer in a glass bottle, sweet tea, po-boys, gumbo, or jambalaya. Roy ate like it was his last supper.

While he was eating, a man approached him. The man flashed a badge and introduced himself as Investigator Joe Breland of the Biloxi Police Department.

"What can I do for you?" Roy said, usually hesitant to talk to the police.

"You can come with me once you finish your lunch," Breland said.

"Am I in trouble?" Roy asked.

"No, sir, Mr. Fayard, I just have someone that wants to talk to you," Breland replied with a smile.

"Uh, okay," Roy said, a little nervous.

Roy finished his meal and was escorted pleasantly to the back seat of an unmarked police car. Once inside, he was traveling east on Pass Road toward Keesler Air Force Base. The car turned right on Veterans Avenue and then left onto Irish Hill Drive. They stopped at the Police Department, and Roy was greeted by a narcotics officer that he had met many times.

"Hello, Roy." The investigator said.

"Officer Marks," Roy said almost silently.

"Roy, you're not in trouble, and I am retired, so there is no need for formalities. I am your guardian angel. Some threats have been made against your father, and he has hired me to look after you. I had you brought here to let you know that you do have friends on the police force. Your dad says you are to stay at his place, and I will be looking in on you from time to time. If you see anything suspicious or receive any threats, please do not hesitate to call me." Marks said.

"Yes, sir, will do. Can I go back to my car now?" Roy asked politely.

"Absolutely. We have equipped your car with a GPS tracker so that we can make sure what happened in Florida doesn't repeat itself." Marks said.

"I'm never going back to that fuckin place!" Roy said quickly.

"I wouldn't blame you." Marks said. "Have a good day, Roy. Take him back to his car Breland." Marks said.

The two rode silently back to where Roy had parked his car, and Roy went to his father's house.

Chapter Thirty-Two

The Governor on trial

Six weeks after the Grand Jury received all the evidence, the Honorable Governor, Bill Creel, received a True Bill. A True Bill is a Grand Jury Indictment in which case a prosecutor may move forward with a trial.

The trial was to take place on October 8th at the Federal Courthouse in Gulfport, Mississippi. A special prosecutor, Jarrod Davis, was brought in to prosecute.

Jarrod Davis was a 58-year-old man who had been the US Attorney from the Southern District of Florida for eight years. He researched every document that Pam received and placed every witness under protective custody whether they wanted it or not. He petitioned the judge to sequester the jury throughout the trial for fear of jury tampering. He took every security precaution that he could think of and was confident that he would secure a conviction on the Federal charges of Corruption, Interstate trafficking of narcotics, Kidnapping, and Racketeering.

The 110-page indictment included witness statements from Roy Fayard, Jake Fayard, Miguel Suarez, Albert Ford, Coby Barhonovich, and countless others associated with the governor as several underlings of his staff.

The Governor hired his own law firm to defend him and decided, unwisely, to sit second chair. The adage of "A man that represents himself in court has a fool for a client" was apparently missed on him. The Governor also put out several press releases despite gag orders from the judge from all parties to avoid jury tampering and possibly influence the outcome of the case. He knew the judge could not stop him from talking about his case because of the Sixth Amendment to a speedy and public trial, but it could provoke the judge and bias him against the defense.

The potential jurors were led into a large foyer. They were handed questionnaires and instructed to answer them honestly. The jury pool included seventy-five potential jurors who were selected at random. All the jurors complied with the request.

The voir dire took three days. One juror stated that he could never convict the Governor no matter what the evidence was. At the end of the fiasco, seven men and five women were on the jury, with two women and one man as jury alternates.

The State charges of murder and attempted murder were not included in the indictment since this was a federal trial. They would be argued later in a Mississippi Circuit Court. The indictment of the Federal charges was enough to put him away for the next century or so.

Agent Ford insisted on acting in his official capacity as an Agent of the US Department of Justice. Still, his supervisor made him sit in a safe house with Jake Fayard and Coby Barhonovich. The trio was housed in a safe house in Saucier, Mississippi, about twenty miles north of the Courthouse in Gulfport. The three hated the isolation. Jake felt that he was better serving the citizens of Mississippi in Washington D.C., and Coby was beside himself.

On the first day of the trial, the trio was transported to the Federal courthouse in Gulfport in a blacked-out van. They were dressed in tactical gear, complete with a bulletproof vest, and were accompanied by no less than 12 agents. They made the 20-mile drive without incident.

When they arrived, they were met by six US Marshalls and escorted to a secure room near the courtroom. The vests were removed, and they could change clothes to something more appropriate for their courtroom appearance. When they arrived outside of the courtroom, they noticed three armed US Marshalls and a large body scanner. Security was very tight for the trial.

The Governor, Honorable William Creel, Governor of the Great State of Mississippi, charged with the attempted kidnapping, conspiracy, racketeering, corruption, and on a state charge attempted murder, was about to finally face his justice.

The Prosecutor stood perfectly erect in his confident pose and began his opening statement to the jury.

"Ladies and Gentlemen of the jury, what I am about to open for you is a one hundred plus page indictment of one man, William Creel, Governor of the State of Mississippi, and a crook. I intend to show that while this man, William Creel, was supposed to be serving the State of Mississippi, he was, in fact, serving himself and his cronies. You will see documents that show various transactions that start with state contracts that never received one bid, you will see evidence that Governor Creel hid these documents from public view, and you will also see evidence that when Governor Creel was supposed to be serving the citizens of Mississippi, he was busy doing so many other illegal activities that it was a free for all. You will hear eyewitnesses to the Governor's corruption. You will at the end of this lengthy process see how he has hurt any credibility of the

State Government of Mississippi." The Prosecutor said with authority.

The defense attorney, a wiry man in a blue suit that hung from his slight frame, stepped forward to address the court. He was about forty and had been practicing law for almost ten years. Most of his career was in civil tort litigation, but he was rumored to be one of the best litigators in the firm of Taylor, Creel, and Simpson. Being the junior partner, Austin Simpson was a bit nervous when he addressed the jury and made his opening argument.

"Good morning y'all." He drawled. "I am Austin Simpson, and I represent our Governor, William Creel. Bill Creel is an honorable man who has an unimpeachable character. He has served the Citizens of Mississippi for almost eight years and would never commit the crimes he has been accused of here today. I personally know Bill as an honest and fair man with more integrity than most."

It was a weak opening argument, but it was direct and to the point. The Governor sat at the defense table and exposed a mammoth chip and boasted of the confidence that he would be acquitted. The young lawyer sat down and was visibly skeptical. He appeared to be worried about something a little more important than his reputation as an attorney.

"Mr. Davis?" The judge called out from the bench, "Are you prepared to call your first witness?"

"Yes, Your Honor." Mr. Davis replied. "The Government calls Mr. Jake Fayard."

"The witness will now be sworn in." The Judge ordered. "Mr. Fayard, please raise your right hand. Do you swear that the evidence you give shall be the truth, the whole truth, and nothing but the truth, so help you, God"?

"I do," Jake replied and took his seat in the witness chair.

"Good morning Senator Fayard." The Prosecutor started. "Are you acquainted with the defendant?"

"Yes, sir," Jake replied.

"How are you acquainted with the defendant?" The Prosecutor asked.

Jake went into detail about the campaign, much as he did in the House Subcommittee Hearing that went nowhere. Jake explained about the campaign manager, Joe Holloway, who was set to testify later in the trial. Jake told of his son arrested in Florida; he told about George Walter and the conversation in his garage; Jake recalled every encounter he had with the Governor, including the funeral of the former Senator Wallace.

Once Jake was finished testifying for the Prosecution, which took about two hours, a recess was called. Jake felt like a couple of million tons of grief was lifted from his shoulders when he finished testifying for the prosecution, but he knew a cross-examining was coming. He wondered what tricks Bill Creel had up his sleeve. He pondered what possible questions would be asked. His wait seemed like a week, but the recess was only thirty minutes long.

Once back in the courtroom, all eyes found the defense table. The young attorney, Mr. Simpson, started to rise, but a hand shot out in front of him. The Governor stood to his feet with a smirk and very arrogantly said, "Mr. Fayard, you have previously testified that your son was arrested for narcotics possession. Was he arrested before the charge in Florida?" The Governor was baiting him.

"Objection!" The word came from the prosecutor's table.

"Sustained," Came from the bench. "Stick to the topic at hand, Mr. Creel."

"Your honor, Mr. Fayard has attempted to assassinate my character here in this courtroom. Am I not allowed to impeach his?" The Governor asked.

"Mr. Creel, you are an experienced litigator. You have argued before this court before. Having researched you, your license, and your firm thoroughly, I would expect you to have more regard for my court's courtroom procedures and etiquette. The Prosecution's objection is sustained." The Judge replied.

The Governor sat down in his chair and pouted. He knew from this instant that he would not get any breaks from this Judge and that this courtroom might actually end up sending him to prison for a good bit, if not the rest of his natural life. He was visibly shaken.

"No further questions for this witness, Your Honor." It came from Mr. Simpson, who was beginning to wonder if he had bitten off more than he could chew.

The next witness was Captain Miguel Suarez, formerly Lieutenant of the Narcotics Interdiction Team, Pensacola Police Department, in Pensacola, Florida. Captain Suarez was not thrilled about appearing in court 140 miles away from home and was not thrilled to discuss this particular case. He just got promoted to Captain, and he was now on an inter-jurisdictional task force that on occasion required Federal resources. Knowing how crucial these resources were to his team, he didn't want to cause any strain with the Federal Bureau of Investigation or the Department of Justice.

Mr. Suarez was sworn in much the same fashion as Jake was and instructed to take his seat. Captain Suarez was asked about the arrest of Roy Fayard, the tip he received with as much detail as possible, and a recording of the call was played for the jury. The recording shocked the Governor as he didn't realize that the tip line was recorded for clarity.

The captain could not identify the voice on the phone; however, he did recall listening to it; the recording described in grave detail a 2012 Ford Fusion with a Mississippi License Plate HAN 101, Harrison County, and the location of five kilograms of cocaine. The tip also offered information that a pistol may be found under the driver's seat.

The captain confirmed the tip and the discovery of the contraband in the car. The captain confirmed the reports from the crime lab that mentioned no fingerprints were on either the drugs or the weapon. The captain could not answer as to how this could have happened.

When the Prosecution was finished with Captain Suarez, the Defense had their turn to cross-examine.

"Captain Suarez, in your years as a police officer, how many times have you seen a Federal Agent sweep up evidence and tell you not to prosecute a felon?" Mr. Simpson asked.

"Not very many, but there were a lot of firsts in this case for me." Captain Suarez replied.

"Such as what?" Mr. Simpson asked.

"Such as my dealing with a politically charged case, my having to turn over evidence to the feds, my having to be deposed by a soon-to-be Senator, for arresting his son, a lot of things." Captain Suarez answered, annoyed.

"Did they leave you any ability to complete your investigation?" Mr. Simpson asked.

"No, sir. I had no control or evidence to conduct my investigation." Captain Suarez replied.

"Did they give you a reason?" Mr. Simpson asked.

"Yes, they said that because a federal crime had been committed by transporting the narcotics across state lines, they were asserting jurisdiction." Captain Suarez replied.

"Who physically transported the drugs?" Mr. Simpson asked, a bit more confident now.

"Roy Fayard transported the narcotics." Captain Suarez replied.

"So, Roy Fayard transported illegal narcotics in his car from out of state, which subsequently means that it was he, not Governor Creel, who broke Federal law?" Mr. Simpson said.

"Objection." The Prosecutor said, and the judge sustained it.

"Alright, we're going to take a recess in my chambers right now." The Judge said.

When the lawyers were in chambers, his honor articulately informed the defense that he would not stand for character assassination in his courtroom.

"You pull another stunt like that again, Mr. Simpson, and I will hold you and your client in contempt." The Judge warned.

"I motion for his honor to recuse himself." The Governor blurted out.

"Mr. Creel, you sir are in contempt. You will spend the next two nights in jail. Would you like to continue?" The Judge said.

When the Judge re-entered the courtroom, he adjourned the court until the next day. Two Deputy US Marshalls took the Governor to the Harrison County Jail, where he spent his first night in jail.

The Governor was strip searched in a holding cell by a correctional officer who showed him no favoritism. He was divested of all personal property and issued an orange jump suit. He was placed in a crowded holding tank with ten other defendants.

Three hours later, the Governor was pulled out of the cell and escorted to the pod. He was placed on the floor of the pod and given one blanket, two sheets, one pillow, and a plastic boat laid in the middle of the floor.

The overcrowded jail was not very welcoming to the Gentleman of means, and he spent the night sleeping on a rubber boat in the middle of the pod floor. He would remain there until six thirty the next morning when a corrections deputy retrieved him and prepared him for transport back to the Federal Courthouse.

The following day, while Jake enjoyed a breakfast of steak and eggs, the governor enjoyed a breakfast of pre-frozen coffee cake and instant coffee. The Governor, who was used to sleeping on 8000 thread count sheets, was hurting from his back being subjected to a thin mat placed on a rubber boat, on a hard concrete floor. He was given no preferential treatment. News media outlets were outside of the courthouse when the Governor emerged from a Harrison County Sheriff Transport Van, handcuffed, shackled, and adorned with a waist chain and black box. Three Harrison County Deputies and six US Marshalls surrounded the Governor, who had lost all of his charm, and looked like a hardened criminal.

Jake and Coby both remarked that those chains looked so good on him. "That orange jumpsuit fits him pretty good," Coby said as they both shared a laugh. Roy Fayard yelled at the Governor, "Hey Billy Boy, what kinda bird don't fly? JAILBIRD!" and a few of the Marshalls almost lost their professional bearing in laughter.

Jake and his entourage returned to the courtroom. The Governor and his lawyer were meeting with the Judge in Chambers.

"Your Honor, my client is under terrible stress. We are petitioning his honor to forgive the infraction and commute the rest of Mr. Creel's sentence." Mr. Simpson said, pleading.

"Absolutely not. Your client has gotten away with far too much already. He will not openly disrespect me in my own Chambers and expect to get away with that too. I absolutely refuse, and when we adjourn today, Mr. Creel can return to jail in the custody of the Harrison County Sheriff's Department. Thank you." The Judge replied.

"Yes, Your Honor, I certainly understand, and I hope that you do accept our sincere apologies." Mr. Simpson said in regret.

Everybody returned to their respective places in the courtroom. "ALL RISE." The call came from the bailiff, and his honor entered the courtroom.

"The defendant was placed in contempt of court yesterday evening. The defense has requested that I commute the two days in jail that I have ordered the defendant to serve. I am going on public record to say that my decision to allow the defendant the liberty to spend a mere two nights in jail will stand. I will not tolerate blatant disrespect and or contempt for this court. I hope I have made my point clear." The Judge thundered from the bench. Jake and Coby couldn't help but smile.

Agent Ford was next to be called as a witness. He was sworn in and took his seat.

The Prosecutor asked him how he was involved, and he told his story. It was a similar one of Jake, and after about an hour of questioning, the defense attorney was allowed to cross-examine.

"So, my tax dollars are paying for someone else's election campaign?" Mr. Simpson asked.

"I have gone undercover in a lot of different job descriptions." Agent Ford answered.

"Name some of those." The lawyer demanded.

"I can't name them all as some of those investigations are open." Agent Ford replied.

"Your honor the witness is refusing to answer questions that are germane to the case." The lawyer stated plainly.

"The witness is an agent of the United States Department of Justice. His undercover work in previous investigations are not relevant to this case. Move on, Mr. Simpson." The Judge ordered.

The questions continued, and Agent Ford was allowed to step down. The rest of the witnesses and the box of evidence were placed on full display for the media and the jury to examine. At the end of the twelfth day of testimony, the case was handed to the jury.

The jury deliberated for six hours. The Judge ordered the jury to return to the courtroom and questioned the foreman about the decision.

"Your Honor, we are currently deadlocked," Was the response from the Foreman.

The judge ordered another round of deliberation and allowed for another day.

The next day the jury was recalled into the courtroom. When the jury returned, they had the verdict.

"The defense will rise and face the jury." The judge ordered, and The Governor and his defense team stood.

"I'll now ask the jury to stand and face the defendant." The Judge ordered. The jury complied.

"The jury foreman will now read the verdict." The Judge said.

The jury foreman stood perfectly erect. He parted his lips and said as eloquently as possible, "We, the jury, find the defendant, William Creel, guilty on the charge of Corruption. We, the jury, find the defendant, William Creel, guilty on the charge of Conspiracy. We, the jury, find the defendant, William Creel, guilty on the charge of Racketeering. We, the jury, find the defendant, William Creel, guilty on the charge of Attempted Kidnapping."

The Governor was beside himself. His lawyer was shaking. Jake and Coby were ecstatic. The jury of twelve just gave the final crushing blow to one of the largest corruption machines in the history of the State of Mississippi.

"We will adjourn until next Monday for the sentencing phase of the trial. The court is adjourned." The Judge said with no emotion.

The Governor was led away in handcuffs and escorted to a van. He was transported to the Harrison County Jail and dressed in a red and white horizontally striped jumpsuit.

He spent the weekend in the special housing unit, being a high-profile inmate, and was kept away from the general jail population. His segregated cell was dubbed "The Mansion" by the deputies, and they made it a point to offer him "room service" three times a day. Room service came in the form of powdered eggs and grits for breakfast, baked beans, and hot dogs for lunch, and some sort of chicken and rice substance for supper with red punch, made without the benefit of sugar.

The sentencing phase of the trial was a routine event. The Judge ordered his sentence to be stiff. He received 20 years for the Racketeering charge, Five years for Corruption, Five years for Conspiracy, and Thirty years for the Attempted Kidnapping. He was ordered to serve the sentences concurrently and would be eligible for parole in twenty years.

Jake Fayard was glad to put the trial behind him. He and Pam were married six months after the trial, and he served with distinction for 12 years in the Senate. He made a name for himself as one who would listen to his constituents and prided himself on his open-door policy. He left the public sector and returned to his small law office on the Mississippi Gulf Coast. Jake is still committed to helping his fellow Mississippians stomp out the culture of corruption that Mississippi is known for.

Coby Barhonovich served another four years as the Attorney General for Mississippi before running for Governor. He was defeated in the Primary Election and returned to private practice, where he and Jake ultimately created Fayard and Barhonovich.

Agent Ford served another four years with the Department of Justice before deciding on a career as a private investigator. He now works exclusively for Jake and Coby.

Governor Creel was sent to a Federal Correctional Facility in Oklahoma. He was caught trying to bribe a guard and received an additional five-year sentence. He will not be released until he is 81 years old.

Senator Kennard is still serving in the Senate. He is still committed to serving Mississippi and has a reputation for being a Pitbull when it comes to stomping out corruption.

Jim Bates stayed close friends with Jake Fayard and his friends until he died at the age of eighty-five. Jake was asked by his daughter to give the eulogy at his funeral, and he did this with honor. The great man was and would forever be memorialized in Jake's words. Jim didn't retire as he loved to teach his students and pushed for bettering race relations in Mississippi and healing the wounds left from the old days. The City of Jackson is planning a statue in his honor.

Made in the USA
Columbia, SC
13 April 2025